I0636956

BLINDED BY DECEIT

BLINDED BY DECEIT

LEVI JOHNSON MOUNTAIN MAN SCOUT

BOOK THIRTY

ASH LINGAM

WOLFPACK
PUBLISHING

EST 2013

Wolfpack Publishing
1707 E. Diana Street
Tampa, Florida 33610

www.wolfpackpublishing.com

Paperback ISBN 979-8-89567-242-6
Ebook ISBN 979-8-89567-241-9
LCCN 2025946436

*This book is dedicated to my old
Tennessee Walker, Sugar.*

Contents

There will come a time when you believe everything is finished. That will be the beginning.

— LOUIS L'AMOUR

BLINDED BY DECEIT

TRACKS IN THE SNOW

AT FIRST, THEY ONLY SAW THE ODD TRACK IN THE LIGHT snow that had fallen the previous evening. It was so slight and hard to see that Money walked right by. Every hundred feet, they found footprints, and then suddenly, they were none. Whoever it was wore Indian moccasins, so they probably weren't White. Little Money looked where Levi pointed, but he saw nothing out of the ordinary or strange.

"How is it you can see things that I can't? Why are they invisible to me and not to you, Levi?"

"Look from the side at an angle. Move over here, use the edge of the sunlight, and you'll notice the slightest shadow. See it? It's a footprint. You're looking for something visible to anybody, and I'm looking for traces of someone passing, trying to hide their tracks. Some clever Indians hardly leave anything to follow."

"I see it now, but it's barely visible." Money shaded his eyes with his flattened hand. He looked at the ground from the edge and saw it, too. "Well, I'll be. It's right there in front of my eyes. I can see the outline of a shadow now. This must be a clever Indian to leave so little sign of his passing." The boy shot a glance over his shoulder to ensure nobody was sneaking up on them from behind. If the Indians were so clever, he felt they might be watching them now.

"That means this track is from an expert. I saw a broken branch first, making me feel like somebody did it on purpose. So, why would he hide his footprints? There's something going on here that I don't understand."

They continued on foot like they had done all day. They had to leave their mounts in the compound corral since they planned a short journey into the mountains, where the country was too difficult for a horse or even a mule to climb. A long loop of stout rope hung from Levi's shoulders. Money didn't know quite what he had planned, but he followed faithfully. When he was with Levi, he didn't feel so scared.

As they peered into the distance, they saw the mountainside covered in ponderosa pines alongside plateaus of green grass covered in white. Above them towered snow-covered peaks. They occasionally saw the odd buffalo but weren't hunting bison today. They were after something special. Yet they put all their plans on hold until they discovered if the man they were following was a threat. Few people traveled these dangerously steep trails, and even fewer came to climb some of the barely reachable peaks. In the wilderness, when you encounter something out of the ordinary, you must approach with caution.

"Scouting is thirsty work, Money. Sometimes you end up hot, hungry, freezing, and tired all at the same time. I reckon I've rattled on long enough and maybe more than I should have. I know you've had hard times. You follow me and do as I say, and you'll be all right."

At those altitudes, the trees became dwarfed, and rock faces replaced vegetation. Yet great bald eagles lived there in their massive nests, perched on impossible ledges where they could spy for prey below. White flashed off their backs as they glided on thermal currents through the air so far above that they appeared to be tiny specks on a field of clear blue sky. The sun wavered mercilessly overhead, casting little shadow. Occasionally, one would tuck its wings and drop into a dive, disappearing below the horizon, only to reappear with its prey in its talons.

"Once we find out if the man we're following is friend or foe, we can mosey on our way up there. In some places, we'll have to knot this rope and use it as a ladder to pull ourselves to the eagle's nest. They usually live where there are no paths. That's the only place where we'll find the feathers you want. You heard Potak. Only the greatest warriors wear such a prize. It's all part of the path to becoming a mountain man. Maybe while you're at it, you'll build a legend. This is about the task of risking such a climb to have the honor of wearing a bald eagle feather. For an Indian medicine man, it'll mean something else too complicated for us White folks to understand." Levi chuckled. "You already have your bear claw necklace. For such a young fella, you sure are catching on fast."

Without thinking, Levi rustled his yellow hair just like everyone else in the compound. He had noticed how Money reacted when the others did the same: he didn't like it. Still, when his mentor did it, he felt proud. He wasn't making a gesture like he was a little boy, but he took it as a sign of approval, which was what the apprentice wanted most. He wanted to become everything his mentor was and, if possible, more. His face broke into a smile, and it reached his eyes.

"I know Potak said it's all about that spirit world he's always talking about, but we're White men, and no matter how much we learn from the Indians, we're still Christians. Besides, that old medicine man is about as superstitious a fella as I've ever met, except maybe Rusty. Why, my old mentor believes in just about any strange notion. No matter how far-fetched it is. I reckon that's from livin' alongside Indians for so long."

Levi led as Money scrambled to follow. Sometimes, he forgot how little he was and had to take two or three steps for every one his mentor took. When Beaver shot a glance over his shoulder, he saw his apprentice grinning like a possum. He was utterly up to the challenge, even if they were going to climb some of the tallest reachable peaks in that part of Beartooth Mountain. Beads of sweat rolled down his furrowed brow, cutting white lines down his dust-covered face, but he didn't slow his relentless pace.

"You won't believe the view from the top." Levi used the flat of his hand to shade his face from the sun as he stared up and above where they stood. "Careful now, we still don't know who it is in front of us. We'll move slowly until he either moves off the trail or disappears. If he vanishes, we'll have to scout around and find out where he went to make sure before we continue. When in the wilderness, you can't be too careful. Don't worry, though, we'll be up there within the clouds soon enough. Some peaks are so high we'll look down on them from above. It's a sight you'll never forget."

"Whatcha mean if he disappears? He's just a man like us. You don't believe in ghosts, do you, Levi? I know I don't. I bet that Potak does, though. And maybe even Rusty Steel."

"We'll. I'm glad you don't because I don't believe in such nonsense, either. Now, if he vanishes, it'll mean he's better at this than I am, and we'll have to be careful in case he has bad intentions. For all we know, he could be a scout for a Blackfoot war party. Then again, if he's this good, I should have heard of him. Usually, the best trackers naturally get into the Indian gossip, so it might even be somebody we've heard of, so maybe he's heard of me. We'll know soon enough, partner. I doubt he's much farther ahead."

A hundred yards farther down the trail, they saw the first drops of blood. It contrasted with the inch of fresh snow from the evening prior. Again, Levi saw a faint footprint, but even Money saw this one, which was more recognizable. It looked like the man they were trailing was becoming slightly reckless. The tracks were easier to see with every step.

"It looks like whoever it is might be wounded. That's human blood, I reckon. Now, we need to be more careful than ever. There's little more dangerous than a wounded animal, be they man or beast."

Now, they saw more and more prints. At one point, whoever it was staggered and appeared to fall. Bloody red handprints were visible in the white snow. There was a wounded Indian in front of them somewhere, and they had no idea if he was dangerous or not. They proceeded even slower, moving through the woods at a crawl. The rays of the sun fell through the leaves like rain, sparkling yellow on the white ground. The only sound was the chattering of birds and small animals rustling the bushes in their escape.

"When I was a boy, we didn't have two pennies to rub together, but we got by just fine. I never went hungry for a day." Levi grinned. "I reckon for me that's a lot. It's too bad you didn't have time to grow up properly before being thrown into the world. Earth can be a cruel place. Especially in such faraway lands."

"We were poor, but I reckon you already knew that from my tattered clothes. I sure do appreciate the new buckskins the women made for me. My pa, you know, the dead one, heard that there was free land in Oregon, so we sold what little we had and headed West. But I've never been in a place as wild as the Rockies and Yellowstone Valley. Everywhere else I've seen, it seems tame compared to here."

"That's because there is nowhere else like here in the Rocky Mountains. This is God's country, Money. Never forget that it's a gift to have the privilege to live here. Not everybody can hack it or even get the chance. The captain and I were lucky men when Rusty Steel chose us and brought us up here from the rendezvous years back."

They had carefully walked for another hour when Levi held his hand out, and without a word, they both stopped in their tracks and crouched. Money tilted his head like a dog as he listened for out-of-place sounds. Suddenly, his hearing became acute. He heard the dragonflies as their wings flapped fifty times a second. When they took another step, the crickets went quiet.

A stone's throw away, they heard a man mumbling, which sounded like a prayer and wasn't in English. Money was so nervous that he had to remind himself to breathe. Even when walking slowly, Levi's legs were so long that, at times, he still had to scamper to keep up. To the small but brave boy, it was like following a giant. All he wished to do was walk in his footsteps, but he was still too small.

Johnson nodded, and they pulled their revolvers, following the barrels into the small clearing between towering pines. Still, they didn't detect any movement besides the branches on the trees as the wind whistled through the pines. As they crept closer, the mumbling sound grew louder with each step. As soon as they walked into the clearing, they saw the man they were following.

Beaver drew in a deep breath and huffed, "Potak! What happened to you?" He ran over, dropped to his knees, and put the medicine man's head in his lap. "Who did this to you? Can you talk?"

"Yes, I can talk. Didn't you hear me praying? It took you long enough to get here. I thought you would never arrive. You travel as slow as a turtle." He looked up at the heavens and said, "It took you long enough, too," as though he was speaking to the Indian spirits.

"Whatcha mean, Potak?" Money asked. "How would we know *you* were here, or how would you know *we* were just around the corner?"

"You two travel like a herd of buffalo." Mischief twinkled in the Indian's tired, pain-filled eyes. "I don't think the wound is mortal. The bullet went through and through. So far, it hasn't gotten infected, but time will tell. I cleaned it the best I could and didn't find any pieces of the bullet."

"You didn't answer me, Potak. I asked who did this to you. You know, in the end, you'll have to fess up."

The famous Tonkawa shaman removed the bloody bandage, exposing the wound. Two puffy red holes showed just above his hip. He packed both wounds with a fine green powder he always carried. Like the eucalyptus, he burned to ward off evil spirits, but this was to heal. The medicine man traveled with an assortment of concoctions and cure-alls.

Nobody knew where he found the bark because the trees weren't native to the Rockies. Eucalyptus was more common in the Andes Mountains in South America. God only knew where the rest of his potions and trinkets came from. Each one was stranger than the other.

"If I can rest for a few days, maybe a week, I should be able to travel again without losing too much blood. It is only a few days back to the Crow stronghold and my lodge. It had stopped bleeding before, but as you saw in the snow, it started again. I'm gonna have to lay up for a few days for the wound to dry and close. If I keep pushing myself, I'll probably bleed to death."

The medicine man said all this as a matter of fact, seemingly almost detached from the situation at hand, showing no apparent fear or concern. Of course, injured and in such faraway places, any wounds were life-threatening. Now that he had been found, he no longer considered dying like he had before. Even then, he didn't panic or seem surprised. Potak took everything in stride as though it was all predestined.

"First things first. We need to build a lean-to to keep you out of the weather. I doubt it'll snow much more this early in the year, but we can't take a chance. Come on, Money. Grab your knife and help me chop some limbs down to make a shelter. We can gather enough firewood to last for a spell as well. There's plenty of dead wood lying around on the ground. It's a good thing the snow hasn't covered it yet."

Levi grabbed a buffalo blanket from his backpack and wrapped it around the apparently frail Indian. Potak had always seemed impervious to the pain and suffering of mortal men. To see him seriously injured was a shock even for Johnson, although he seemed to try to ignore his injuries. The fact that someone obviously shot him made Johnson's blood boil. Nobody messed with his friends without him stepping in, despite the color of their skin. Levi wondered why he didn't fess up as to who it was.

In a few hours, they had a lean-to built against a rock face with the windward end closed. A fire burned at the entrance as the flames sawed downwind. There was plenty of room for all three of them to sleep. Levi lifted Potak into his arms, carried him to the very back, covered him in his buffalo robe, and wrapped a blanket around his feet.

"While I make a fire, you can tell me who did this to you and why they did it. I don't take kindly to people shooting my friends. Money, you can pull out the pot and kettle so we can make something hot to eat. Potak has to regain his strength to heal properly."

"I don't much like people shooting me either." Potak coughed into his hand. When he opened his palm, he saw phlegm mixed with blood. He grabbed a handful of snow, rubbed his hands together, and turned his face to Beaver's, ignoring his condition. He forced his lips into a weakening smile; his face was wracked with pain.

IN MINUTES, a pot of beans was heating over the fire, filling the air with the smell of freshly cooked food. Levi cut up herbs and ground chili powder and mixed them with a wooden spoon, releasing the aroma into the air. The fire popped and crackled as sparks flew skyward, disappearing above the tops of the trees. As the wind continued to blow, they swayed in the breeze.

"So, what's up, Medicine Man? Why don't you wanna tell us who shot ya? Who are you hiding, and why? To me, it just doesn't make any sense. I've known you for a good spell now, and it ain't like you to not speak up. You know how stubborn I am. I'll find out even if you don't tell me."

Both the Indian and the boy could see the steel look in Levi's eyes as his blood started to boil. Potak knew he wouldn't let up, but he held his ground just the same. He looked at his friend with defiant eyes.

"It's much more complicated than you think, Beaver. If I tell you, it will start something into motion that should never be awoken. Believe me when I say you don't want to know. Do as I ask and leave it be. Some things are better left alone. Have I ever asked you for a favor before?" the Tonkawa shaman asked with raised eyebrows. "Then leave it be."

"Go ahead then—don't tell me if you don't want to, but I'll go and find out myself. If I can track you down, I can track anybody. You know I'm not one to let people take advantage of my buddies. If the culprits are human, they left tracks, and those two holes don't look like they came from elk horns."

"Do what you must, but my lips are sealed. I can't find it in my heart to tell you who it was. It won't matter if I live. If I die, it will matter even less. I wish for no restitution. Consider it destiny whichever way it goes." He sat staring at Beaver, blinking, and nodding his head. Then he closed his eyes and a peaceful calm seemed to come over his being.

"You can wish for what you want, but we're not gonna let this one go," Money grumbled in his little voice. "Nobody is gonna shoot one of our pards and get away with it. Not on Levi's and my watch."

Despite the seriousness of the matter, both men chuckled when the boy spoke. The funny thing was that he was as serious as death—or at least as serious as an eight-year-old could be. Money sat there with his eyes spread wide, clearly confused by the situation but determined to help no matter what. Like Johnson, he had no intention of backing down, all this despite not knowing what he would be up against. Of course, there was so much he could do. He was only nine years old.

Until they laughed, Money felt like neither man had noticed he was even there. Now he saw he was wrong. How Potak could get shot in the first place was beyond Levi's understanding. Not with his reputation and skills. Who would be so crazy as to try to kill such an essential element of the Crow tribe? It would bring an uproar from the whole stronghold.

Almost as an afterthought, Beaver took a second look at his apprentice. His eyes locked with Money's, and the boy instantly knew he was not going to do as Potak requested. He would track the culprit down and probably kill him or at least bring him back to the Crow stronghold to stand trial before the elders, which would have the same outcome. If the culprit was caught, he would surely die. Despite Potak being a Tonkawa Indian, the Crow people loved him like their own.

"So, when are we going?" Money asked, trying to sound older than he was. He hitched his britches up, pushed his shoulders back, and jutted out his chin as he stood, getting ready to gather his things. Wherever Levi went, he followed like a little pup. Until then, he couldn't imagine it any other way.

"I'm afraid someone's gotta stay with Potak, Money. You need to feed him thrice daily, give him plenty of water, and stand guard at night. I know it sounds like a handful, but I know you can do it. That means if I take more than a few days, you'll have to hunt for some meat. There are still berries on the bushes, and we've got plenty of beans. Keep the scattergun handy, just in case. You two should be all right here in the shelter. You both know it ain't in me to let something like this go. It would be a lot easier if you told me who did it, Potak. You'll probably save me a lot of needless running around."

"You were the one who had made the decision. I told you I would prefer it if you didn't go. Still, I made a promise that I wouldn't seek revenge, which I can't bring myself to break. But remember this, Levi Johnson. You might not like what you find."

THE COMPOUND

AS SOON AS ANGUS GRABBED THE DINNER BELL'S STEEL bar and started banging it around the triangle, everybody dropped what they were doing and headed for the dinner table on the main cabin's porch. Twelve chairs sat around the aging timber. The wood plank floor groaned under people's feet. Chairs clattered and scooted as those present in the compound sat down to eat.

The logs on the cabin's walls were massive, three-foot-thick, made of large tree trunks. They disappeared around and into the hill behind it, leaving half the building underground. The roof was sod, and in the summer, it was green and full of weeds and flowers, and in the winter, it was snow-covered.

Both were meant to camouflage the cabin in the early days when all the Indians were hostile. Gun slats were visible in the door and single window, making it impossible for the fortress to be approached. Built into the hill and with such thick walls, it was nearly impossible to burn down, which they proved during the recent forest fire.

A large stone chimney crawled up the left side, and a thin line of smoke squirreled out the top. An aging gray-haired man walked out the front door with a gallon pot of coffee hanging from the crook of his arm and eight tin cups dangling from his bony fingers, clattering with each step. Despite his age, his eyes and smile were full of life and wisdom.

"Dinner's ready." Angus cackled. "Get it while it's hot. Careful now, don't burn your tongues. Then you won't be able to thank me later." The aging mountain man's eyes sparkled with mischief and fun.

Under the covered porch sat ten of the twelve members of Rusty Steel's compound. He had been the designated leader of the clan for the last decade. Some of the original residents had perished only to be replaced by others, despite being in the middle of the wilderness. As their numbers grew, they became more like a family than friends. Four White men, three Indian women, and one Black man sat waiting for Angus McFarlin's delicious food. Their mouths watered in expectation of their daily feast.

As the clan's elderly leader, Angus McFarlin's only job was to feed their growing family. Everyone was always treated equally, although they looked up to Rusty, their old leader, and Levi, the new head of the clan. Both men were famous throughout the mountains, across Yellowstone Valley, and even up to Fort Boise and across the Great Plains.

"Listen up, folks. We have squirrel pie for starters, then elk hindquarter steaks." He closed his eyes and took in a deep breath as his mouth broke into a smile. "It sure does smell fine, even if I say so myself."

"What's for dessert, Angus?" Captain Will Forrester asked. "I smell something sweet coming from the kitchen."

A gust of wind blew up, festooning his empty sleeve in the breeze. When he moved, his old saber clattered on the wooden floor. Sky-blue eyes sat under a beige hat, and he had a blond mustache over his mouth.

A middle-aged marshal, Joseph Walker, poured coffee all around as several added a dash of corn liquor from the jug in the table's center. Virgil helped Angus by slicing up the roasted meat into thick, juicy steaks and forking them onto tin pie pans. Everyone at the table sat with their knives and forks in their fists, ready to dig in like they were waiting for the signal to start at the beginning of a race.

Usually, Levi Johnson sat at the same table, and they all knew they had to quickly get their second helpings before he ate most of what was offered. Beaver almost ate them out of house and home at six foot seven and two hundred pounds. Despite his and Money's absence, out of habit, the others hovered over the food like wolves waiting for the kill. A low growl came from the barrel-like Marshal Walker.

"Remember your manners," Virgil grumbled as his white eyes contrasted with his dark brown skin. He laid his calloused and scarred hand on his tattered Bible. "While I'm here, we say grace before we eat. Come on, that means you too, Joseph. Up here, you ain't a marshal no more. You're just like the rest of us simple folks."

Christianity was something that the Crow wives,

Dahteste, Bar-Chee, and Pine Needle, didn't quite under-stand, but they respected their husbands and bowed their heads as Lovejoy said a few words with his eyes closed and his hand clasped around his Good Book. He believed he had the most to be thankful for since he was lucky enough to be freed by his old master, the Englishman, Fitzgerald Worcestershire. Virgil Lovejoy lived as a free man among his friends. In such remote places, it mattered more where a man's heart was than the color of his skin.

Rusty Steel sat at the head of the table. They brought one serving of food after another from the kitchen until everyone had a steaming piece of meat and a bowl of beans sitting before them. A gallon coffee pot sat beside the ceramic jug as brown bubbles popped from the spout. As soon as Virgil said amen, everyone dug in. Nobody said another word until they consumed every morsel. Afterward, they all drank coffee, including the Crow women. It was one of the most valuable trading tools with the Indian Nations, along with scarcely provided gunpowder. They traded them just enough to hunt, but not enough to turn against them.

"We've got piñon cookies for dessert. That's why I asked for all those sacks of pine cones. It's an old Spanish recipe I learned years ago from a Mexican cook in a fancy restaurant. They're mighty tasty. Lucky for us, I made four dozen, so we have four or five each. Y'all are lucky that Levi's not here, or he'd polish off half of 'em before y'all got started."

The wind whistled through the pines as Steller's Jays chattered from their perches on swaying limbs. The sound of knives and forks scraping tin stopped as they turned their attention to the cookies and coffee.

"I wonder how Money and Beaver are doing," Bar-

Chee said with a shaky voice. "I worry about my son. Lately, he seems to be gone more than he's here. His youth already appears to be slipping away from me just when I was becoming comfortable with motherhood."

"Now, we've talked about this, darlin'," Marshal Joseph Walker said to his Crow wife. "I know he seems too young for all this, but how old was your brother when he learned to shoot a bow and hunt? I doubt he was much out of his teens when he became a warrior. Just because Money's White doesn't mean he's dumb or ain't tough."

"It is different with the Crow people. We are used to such hardships and spend our lives on these mountains, surviving the harsh winters. We learn life's challenges from a very young age."

"And Money should be used to them too. He's had a harder life than any of us. He's eight going on twenty if it's experience that you want. If he's gonna live with us in the wilderness, it's best if he knows how to handle himself. Sheltering him isn't the answer, Bar-Chee. He'll be safe with Levi. He's brought him back every time up till now. As I always tell you, worrying about things is the biggest waste of time and never solves anything. Whatever's gonna happen is gonna happen anyway."

———

HORSES RACED around the corral beside a line of stables. Chickens pecked the ground by the barn for insects before the hen hut. They provided the mountain men daily with fresh eggs. Colorful birds flew from tree to tree. Two teepees stood between Rusty's cabin and Virgil's. At the north end of the compound stood a graveyard with a dozen white crosses. The third building was in ashes from the recent forest fire. A brick-and-rail fence surrounded everything. Two entrances allowed them access—to the south and Yellowstone Valley, and north toward the big Crow stronghold, a half-day ride up Beartooth Mountain.

Snow-covered peaks reached for the sky all around them as eagles spied for their prey's movement from high above. Wild turkeys gobbled as they spooked and scattered into the bushes. Vultures made lazy circles in the sky. A column of wolves showed their silhouettes on a distant ridge. The last large male stopped, stared momentarily, and sniffed the air before carrying on. They knew that humans were dangerous in numbers and kept their distance.

Rusty nodded, picturing the charred ruins. "When are we gonna rebuild yours and Betty's cabin, Will? Or have you taken to living in a teepee like Beaver and Dahteste? For her, it's natural because that's how she grew up, but for you, it seems odd to me. A West Point man living like an Indian. Who would have ever thought."

Angus chuckled humorously, shaking curtains of white hair. "Leave 'em be and let 'em live where they want. You lived with your Flathead wife in a teepee, didn't ya? And you boast of being the smartest of the bunch."

Lovejoy made a knowing smile as mischief continued to twinkle in his eyes.

"To be honest, Betty and I have talked about it, and we would prefer to have four walls around us. The teepee is fine for a few months, but for us, it's confining, especially in the winter. There won't be time this year, but I hope to build another cabin come next summer."

"We spend most of our time here in the big cabin in winter, anyway," Rusty replied. "All you need the teepee for is to sleep and to have some privacy with your wife. Silvia and I could use a little more privacy ourselves. If you move out, let us know, and we'll move right in. We don't need a lot of space, anyway, do we, Darlin'?"

Silvia looked at Rusty with star-struck eyes. Despite being younger, she looked up to him for everything and felt lucky to have married such a famous mountain man. It was the last thing she expected when she set out with her sister and brother-in-law on the Oregon Trail. She would never have guessed that she would fall in love halfway across and end up living high in the Rocky Mountains surrounded by Indian tribes.

In Charge & Alone

Late that night, Money sat exhausted from the tension as he stared into the fire while listening to stories told by his mentor and the medicine man. Instead of finding them interesting that night, they alarmed him even more, and he dreaded the hour when his mentor would depart and leave him on his own. The air smelled of woodsmoke and eucalyptus from the cinder of a piece of bark as a fine string of smoke snaked from the glowing ember.

For a moment, the young boy's mind drifted to his real family. Although he missed them, he knew that fretting over them did him no good. They killed his father before his very eyes, and he watched as slavers sold his mother. Still, he didn't know if she had survived, and although frightened to discover the truth, he was dying to find out. This lack of knowledge of her outcome left an empty place in his heart that even his new parents and Levi couldn't fill.

Lucky for him, Levi had decided to leave the following morning when he had plenty of light, believing he could catch up with whoever was responsible for wounding Potak before the end of the day. He would backtrack and didn't believe that the assailant's tracks would be as hard to find as those of the medicine man. Johnson was an expert and had learned to track back in Indiana as a boy.

When he was young, he hunted animals to put food on the table. Now, he tracks men to right wrongs and is taught by the best—his mentor, Rusty Steel, and the Indians he had lived with, along with his wife, Dahteste, a Crow war chief.

For a brief moment, Money didn't know if it was worse that Beaver hadn't gone off right then and there. Now he had all night to think about him leaving him in charge of such an important man. Little did he know, Levi waited to ensure their campsite was secure, at least for the first night. If nothing happened by morning, he would be on his way after the man who tried to murder his friend.

Johnson knew the layout of the land on this part of the mountain, and in his mind's eye, he saw all the possible places for an enemy to lie in ambush. He would have to be on his toes, or he might end up shot too, but he felt that whoever did try to kill his friend wasn't very good at what he did, or Potak wouldn't still be alive.

Dancing flames cast moving shadows on the stand of trees around them, making the fire hard to see from a distance. The medicine man snored softly as Beaver and Money listened to every sound, identifying them one by one. When the moon blinked onto the earth's rim, it cast silvery shadows across the landscape below them as stars pulsated in the heavens, light years away. The constant mountain breeze rustled the trees as an owl called out to its mate, and she responded in kind from a nearby nest. Somewhere in the distance, a pack of coyotes sang their nightly choir.

————————

AFTER A LONG, uneventful night, soon, the yellow disk wavered over the horizon as heat radiated from its core, and another new day was born. As quietly as possible, not to wake their wounded friend, Levi began to gather his things. Before the mountain man left, he checked his guns and ammunition and packed some dried meat and stale biscuits to eat while he ran. After three cups of coffee, he stood to leave.

Levi whispered, "I'm ready to go. You're in charge of things here, young man. Always keep that scattergun close to you, just in case. I doubt you'll have much trouble in such an out-of-the-way place. But if you do, don't hesitate to shoot. But you already know that from that grizzly bear that attacked us. Don't let anybody into the camp unless it's me—no exceptions, Money. That means anybody, even if you know them. Since we don't know who shot Potak, we don't know who our enemies and our friends are right now. I doubt anything will happen, but keep sharp just in case whoever did this comes back to finish the job."

Money's eyes looked as big as saucers as he watched Levi vanish as soon as he neared the bushes and dense vegetation. He disappeared like smoke in the wind without leaving a trace of his presence. He blinked, and it was as though Levi was never there.

Money looked down at the shotgun and saw his

white-knuckled fists as he squeezed the weapon for dear life. He had to force himself to ease up on his grip. The boy took a deep breath to settle his nerves, then walked over and checked their wounded friend. He carefully crept like Levi taught him, not making a sound. When he got close, he listened to his breathing. He had to listen hard, but it was there, although the rise and fall of his chest wasn't apparent.

"Is he gone?" Potak asked, startling Money so much that he pulled the trigger, but there was no click or explosion.

Lucky for him, the shotgun wasn't cocked. He pulled the Cold Patterson Levi had given him and laid it on his bedroll beside the Indian's, ensuring he was never out of arm's reach of either weapon. He knew how important a man Potak was, and Money felt the responsibility. It felt like a horse was sitting on his chest.

"You scared the daylights out of me, Potak! I thought you were asleep. Why, I couldn't even see you breathe. Yeah, Levi's gone all right, and I don't know when he's gonna come back. Why wouldn't you tell him who shot you? It seems you're putting your friend's life in danger."

"Would you have me break my word? Out here in the wilderness, a man's word is no small thing, Money. Sometimes, it is more important than your life. At least for Indians. Beaver understands. He is more like us with each passing day—maybe more than even *he* knows. We care what people think of us after we are gone to our spirit worlds. If a man is lucky, he will be in the elders' songs for generations. This recognition after death is only possible because we have the Indian spirit world that White people continue to deny."

"So important that you have to put Levi's life in jeopardy? That doesn't seem quite right to me. How would you feel if something happened to him because you didn't talk?"

"I didn't put Beaver's life at risk. That was something that he chose to do himself. Every man has the right to do what he thinks best, regardless of whether it's right or wrong. I am just an observer in the theater of life."

"Then I reckon you ain't gonna tell me either, and I'm supposed to stay here and make sure you stay alive. That just doesn't make sense to me. I know I'm young and all, but it didn't look like Beaver understood either."

"We each have our missions in life. It may seem as though it's true, but none of us control anything from the moment we awake to the moment we fall asleep. Destiny is what decides what is to come or not. We are no more than small pieces in the puzzle of life, moved around by the spirits."

"I don't know about all that Indian spirit stuff, but I don't like jeopardizing Levi's life. To me, he's more than just my mentor. He's the one teaching me how to live my life and become a man. What'll happen if he doesn't come back? What will we do then?"

"Then that, too, will be a lesson. Every day, we learn new things as we walk on the earth. Some are good and some, not so much, but together, they make us who we are. Every day, things happen that shape and mold your future without you even knowing. It happens so subtly that it is like a tiny flash of light."

Suddenly, Potak looked at the bright sun overhead as he fluttered his eyes, and again, he suddenly fell asleep. His snoring was deeper and more pronounced, as though the short conversation had worn him out. Sweat beaded on his dark red forehead as his fever once again reared its ugly head. Shortly after, he began to mumble in his dreams. Or were they nightmares? From the sounds, it was hard to determine.

"Please help me keep him alive until Levi gets back," Money prayed as his eyes gazed at the heavens above. "And keep my ma safe if she's still alive, too."

————

THE FOLLOWING MORNING, Money awoke with a start. He didn't remember falling asleep. He watched as a sliver of sunlight crawled onto the horizon, pushing away the stars and replacing them with a blanket of blue sky.

Unbeknown to the boy, Potak looked Money over, sizing him up afresh after all he had heard as he feigned sleep. For a moment, the Indian just stared at Money, all baggy-eyed, like he was confused. He had just awoken from another fever-induced sleep and had yet to get his bearings anew. He shook his head, shaking his tresses of hair. His beak-like nose sat above thin lips between large ears on his tall, thin frame. He swiveled his gaze and locked eyes.

"Many men wiser than me say worrying is for fools and horses. It's the opposite of faith, so how can you be a spiritual man if you worry day and night?" Potak laughed, then coughed into his hand, wiped his palm on a rock, and looked away. "Worrying is believing in trouble that may never come. Is it not obvious that it is a waste of time?"

The hint of a smile tugged at the edges of Potak's mouth. Even when at death's door, the famous shaman bore no fear. Life would work things out, whether they were in his favor or not, but the circle would continue.

Money struggled to mask his frustration and confusion. To him, Potak's refusal to talk and Levi running off half-cocked made little to no sense. Who could be so important that Potak would try to protect him after he tried to take his life? The more he thought about it, the less he understood.

Potak blinked his eyes open again and rolled onto his side with his head on a rolled-up blanket as he tented his fingers before his mouth, deep in thought. "Secrets can be troubling things at times."

"Maybe some secrets weren't meant to be," Money huffed. He didn't understand why Potak wouldn't budge from his decision.

"Just the fact that three of us know would mean that it would be less of a secret than when you and Levi arrived. Don't worry, such things have a way of getting known on their own, but I can't break my word. Once what happened hits the Indian gossip, everyone will know, but I will not have tarnished my name. Among the tribes, these things have a way of working themselves out."

Money sighed deeply and said, "I don't understand. How would that work out? If we're out here all alone, who's gonna say anything? Who's gonna know?"

"We will know, won't we? Is that enough to break an oath?"

"Yes, sir," Money said as he tried to manage a smile. He raised his chin and stared boldly into the medicine man's eyes. "Livin' in the wilderness is a lot riskier than growin' corn or having a ranch in Oregon like my ma and pa planned. They thought it would be like picking up gold nuggets scattered across the ground. I reckon they were about as wrong as a person could be." Money pondered momentarily, then said, "I wonder if my ma is still alive."

"Do you know what tribe the warrior was from who bought her?" asked Potak. He had to stop and take a breath. "When I am better, if that is my fate, maybe I can find out for you. I have a long tongue but long ears, too."

"I didn't know the difference then, but I do now. When I remember back, I know it was a Blackfoot warrior who traded my ma for hides and a pony. Now I can tell by the feathers and how they dress. Levi taught me that. I can identify the difference between the seven tribes."

Money was still too green and Potak too exhausted from his wound to notice the rustling in the bushes.

The grubby White men stared at them like hungry wolves but maintained their distance before skulking through the brush. They looked poor, dirty, and ragged, but they had expensive guns stuffed into their belts. Somehow, they had sneaked up on them without drawing notice. Of course, Potak was struggling to stay conscious, and young Money was still a beginner. He was just about to discover just how much of an amateur he actually was.

Potak gasped, just as utterly surprised as Money. Both their eyes spread wide as their chins dropped to their chests.

"Well, I'll be," the outlaw said, then spat a brown stream of juice into the dirt. "We found ourselves an old Indian and a young White boy. I told you we'd find something of value way up here where the White hunters don't go. We can collect on the old fella's scalp and sell the boy into slavery. There's plenty of Indians that would pay good money for a White, yellow-haired youngin'."

The leader of the trio of bandits smiled wolfishly, then balled his hands into fists. His expression was cocky and cruel. Money snapped out of the daze and frowned. He stood for a moment, chewing on what the stranger said. He tried to reject fear, but as an eight-year-old boy, it was hard. Yet, he knew he couldn't act like a frightened little kid.

A man needs to always plan carefully and act decisively.

He remembered that Levi had told him that. But what to do when there wasn't any time to think and plan? For the blink of an eye, he felt lost and didn't know what to do, but then his newfound instincts instantly gave Money the answer.

That was when the strangers felt and heard the deep discharge of both barrels of Money's shotgun. They tried to scatter as though the blast was the starter at a horse race, but they were all three too late.

He saw the strangers' faces twist with shock and disappointment. Then came the pain. Both barrels full of buckshot filled their bodies from head to toe. The distance between Money and the outlaws was perfect, and they received full power from the blast. Blood splatter speckled the boy's cheeks. He looked small compared to the heavy gun as smoke wafted from the barrels.

The boy abruptly understood the euphoria of war when you tried to kill your enemy and he tried to kill you. Money's body was suddenly racked with a tremendous shudder, nearly making him fall. He fought back the tears and put on a brave face.

"You don't get scared easily, do you, young fella?"

Potak huffed, out of breath as the blast still rang in his ears.

"Levi said he never saw much sense in it, so I reckon I feel the same."

Money stood there, his heart pounding as he prayed to God for forgiveness. Smoke wafted from the barrels of the sawed-off shotgun. He was pale white and glistening with fear. He looked down and realized that he had somehow managed to keep the gun in his hands despite the recoil. He ejected the hulls and slipped in two fresh shells just like he was taught. Levi said an empty gun was worthless if you needed it quickly.

"Roll the bodies off the edge of the cliff. That's the only way you can move them before they begin to stink. They smell bad enough already. Use that pole over there as leverage. But take their guns before you send them on their way to the White man's spirit world."

Potak could see the light in the boy's eyes, red-ridged. He appeared almost manic with concern. Worry lines creased his brow as his face tugged into a frown.

"Are you all right?" the shaman asked. "You don't quite look yourself."

Money recovered enough to hide his true emotions. He covered it with a mask of good-natured innocence. He didn't want to show weakness, just in case Potak gave Levi a report when he got back.

He hesitated, knocked off balance. "Shaw," he said, slapping his hand to his forehead after he tried to budge the dead outlaws, acting as nonchalant as possible. "I plumb forgot the pole." He had to turn his face to hide his disgust, but Potak was right. They were stuck there until Levi returned, and the smell and presence of scavengers were unwanted, especially by the boy.

———

ONCE HE HAD ROLLED the dead men to the edge and pushed them over, Money poured his patient a cup of steaming hot java, trying to keep his mind on the task at hand. Potak only drank real coffee and not chicory, which was unusual for most Indians. Then again, Potak wasn't like any other Native American that Money had ever met. He seemed to be some strange mix of cultures and races. He cocked a brow and looked at Potak like he couldn't quite understand his ways, but somehow, he knew it was important that he carefully watch and learn.

Potak lit a long-stemmed pipe, inhaling deeply as he observed the situation. His wounds had stopped bleeding, but he still had to be careful not to break the scabs. With each passing day, his pale face regained more color, and his appetite soared. His recovery seemed nothing short of miraculous to the boy.

Sometimes, when Potak looked, Money appeared like a frightened animal cowering at the end of a boxed-in canyon with nowhere safe to go. Then, as soon as he felt the medicine man's eyes on him, he put on a brave face. He seemed to be more concerned about how the shaman perceived him than the dangers around them.

That evening, everything was hazy, as though Potak's thoughts covered his eyes with a blindfold, and he didn't speak. Despite looking better, all night long, he went in and out of consciousness, although he was as lucid and sharp as always when he was awake.

On the fourth day, the medicine man could sit up and eat by himself, and his bouts of dizziness and nodding off to sleep became less frequent.

"I wonder when Levi is gonna get back. He should have returned by now if he was right about catching up with them by the end of the day. Whatcha think, Potak? So, you think he's run into trouble?"

"It appears that finding my assailant is proving more difficult than Levi thought. Sometimes, our egos are too big, and we say we can do things when we don't know if it is possible. Especially when you don't know who you are tracking. He's located his signs by now. Time will tell. If he doesn't return soon, we may have to go and find *him* and not him *us*. I should be able to walk in another week. By then, we'll know for sure that there has been a mishap."

The medicine man said everything as a matter of fact, as though he felt no emotion or curiosity about what might have happened or what would be. Money wondered how it would feel to be free of all fears as he walked through life. He felt the ragged, edgy feeling in his stomach and knew he couldn't imagine such a thing.

———

IN THE MORNINGS and late afternoons, Money visited a small pond to fetch water. He also hid in a blind he built a few days prior to hunt. Now, he waited for dinner to appear. Just as he was about to feel heavy eyes and become sleepy, he suddenly saw something brown moving through the trees. The six-point antlers of the mule deer appeared over the bushes. It couldn't be over two years old.

Levi had given him a bow and taught him how to use it, although he was far from an expert. Especially since he wasn't strong enough to pull the string back without holding the bow with his outstretched feet pushing and his small arms pulling the string until it reached his chin. He let the arrow fly with a twang as it zipped through the air and drove into the mule deer's chest, dropping it to its knees. It struggled to get up as blood began to spew from its mouth. After what seemed like minutes but was probably only seconds, it toppled over, dead.

"Gotcha!" After looking all around, Money jumped up and ran for his kill. "Now, we'll have plenty of food for when Levi returns."

He quickly sliced off the hindquarters, backstrap, and removed its liver. Then, he struggled to drag his kill into the bushes. That very night, the coyotes would clean up his mess, and nobody would know he had been there. Only the flies lighting on the drying blood gave the true scene away.

Lucky for him, the deer was small. He slipped a rope around its back feet and dragged it into the dense bush, slipping on the snow and falling several times during the struggle. When he finished, he rubbed his hands with the cold white powder to clean away the blood.

When he looked up, Money saw that the buzzards were already lingering overhead. Their presence gave him a sense of urgency. If anybody else were around, they too would see them making lazy circles in the sky. With every dip and swing, they came lower and closer to food. All the scavengers were drawn to the smell of fresh blood, so he knew that soon it would be a free-for-all. Blowflies buzzed around his head, landed on his face, and even tried to walk into his ears, nose, and mouth.

Money grabbed the burlap sack with the steaks and

tied it to a stick he slung over his shoulder. He grabbed a branch he had broken off a low limb and used it to sweep away his footprints. Still, the acrid smell hung heavy in the air.

When he was close to their camp, he cupped his hands around his mouth and cawed like a raven, which were plentiful from the mountains to the valley floor. Potak immediately quacked like a sandhill crane, and the boy knew it was safe to enter.

"Who is it?"

A boy's voice answered, "It's me, Money."

Another Colt Patterson lay beside the recovering Indian as he locked eyes with the boy. Money saw humor in his gaze when he didn't see anything funny. Then again, Potak often said that life was no more than a folly, whatever that was supposed to mean.

"My mouth is as dry as a corn bin after a drought, and I got the jitters in my stomach, but they won't go away. Do you ever feel like that, Potak?"

"Not for a long time, I haven't, but I can still remember when I was young and how I felt about different things. Maybe I'm not as old as you think."

"To be honest, I can't tell if you're young or old. I have the same problem with most Indians."

"That's because you haven't been around us long enough to become accustomed to our faces, but after a while, you will see that we aren't so different once you get past the clothing, hair, and paint." The shaman chuckled and gritted his teeth as a pain shot through his side.

BRENDA PENNY

BRENDA LAY AWAKE, STARING AT THE STARS, AS SHE shivered under a tattered blanket full of holes. Tears streamed down her face, cutting white paths through the dirt. When she glanced at her master's teepee, she saw silhouettes of his other wives, warm and under shelter. The smell of freshly cooked meat floated through the air, making her mouth water and her stomach grumble, but she knew there would be none for her.

Her blond hair, the color of the sun, and her skin, white like snow, had urged Acha to buy her in the first place. The extravagance of having such a woman for his own was more than he could resist, and he ignored it initially when his current wives complained about the price. They all said that she was vile, smelled bad, and they often spat on her when they passed her outside.

They all three believed that buffalo hides *and* a horse were too high a price, especially for a White woman. But after several sessions of violence and the three wives' beatings, she now looked worse for wear, and apparently, Acha had lost interest in the beaten and broken women. Especially since she seemed to have started talking to an invisible person.

At first, the superstitious Indians thought she might be speaking to the spirits, but soon, they realized that Brenda, little by little, was going stark-raving mad. Her eyes batted uncontrollably as she pulled at the edge of her mouth and constantly hacked like she had a catch in her throat.

Money's mother picked at the bones her Blackfoot husband gave her, breaking them with a rock to eat the marrow. She chewed on them like a dog. Grease covered her hands and mouth, and grime was deep under her fingernails. Despite all she had been through, she still fought to stay alive, hoping that her son wasn't dead and that she might reunite with him again by some God-sent miracle.

She had no idea where she was, let alone where her *son* was. The thought made her fall deeper into the mentally depressing hole she was digging for herself. She knew that soon she would block out daylight and be nearing the end. Brenda understood that if she discovered that something had happened to Money, she would take her life. Other than him, she had nothing to live for, and it was only for him that she continued, despite the physical and mental torture and her state of mind.

She wore old hand-me-downs from Acha's other wives, but the buckskins were torn and tattered and were three sizes too large. She made her own makeshift moccasins to protect her feet from the snow, but they were numb, and she feared getting frostbite and losing her toes when the temperatures dropped.

The first white blanket had already fallen, and it was getting colder with each passing day. Her scarce meals weren't helping the situation as her energy was being slowly depleted, and her life was slowly being sucked from her soul. She was losing both energy and drive, which was also making her lose her focus.

While she sat there as if in a daze, a large hand grabbed a fistful of hair and pulled her off the ground. She held back a scream, lodging it in her throat before it could escape. She didn't plan to give her vile husband the pleasure of hearing her shriek in pain again. Only on the first day did she give in while he took her repeatedly, leaving her bloody and unconscious.

When he reached the teepee, his oldest wife threw back the door flap while Brenda fought for all she was worth to escape. She knew what awaited her in her husband's dwelling. The other three wives sat there watching as they giggled while Acha raped the White woman over and over.

When he finished, again, he dragged her out by the hair and into the fresh air. Brenda gasped as she tried to gobble oxygen and kicked her feet, propelling herself backward, before he pulled her hair out of her skull. Finally, Acha pushed her face down into the snow near her tattered bed like so much trash.

Money's mother wondered if they would allow her to seek shelter when the weather got worse or if they would force her to stay outside, where she would freeze to death alone. As it was, she had to clamp her teeth shut to keep them from chattering. It left her jaw muscles so sore she could hardly talk.

She would rather die than be raped again, but she had to stay alive for Money. Maybe he was out there somewhere, lost and all alone, and she felt she was the only one who could ever save him from their wicked world.

She had no idea it would be like this when they left back east. They had condemned their family to slow and torturous deaths. She was constantly confused but still aware enough to know that if things didn't change soon, she would either freeze or starve. Then who would find and rescue her little boy?

Sometimes, she could hear the wolves at the edge of the Blackfoot camp as they snapped, snarled, and howled. Until then, they hadn't dared enter the boundaries of the encampment, but Brenda believed it would just be a matter of time. One dark night, they would sneak into the camp and drag her off for a late-night dinner, and she knew that nobody would lift a finger to help her. On the contrary, they would probably laugh, cheer the wolves on, and watch as they ate her alive.

The captive White woman involuntarily shuddered as goose bumps rose on her arms and hackles grew on the back of her neck. She remembered her first days there at the Blackfoot camp. In the beginning, Brenda was allowed to stay inside the large tent while her new husband abused her, but soon, the other wives became jealous, and her owner was bored with the White woman's ways.

They banished her from the warrior's large teepee. To avoid their annoying complaining, Acha went along with his wives' wishes, or he knew they would make his life a living hell.

That night, it snowed again, and when Brenda

awoke, cold white powder covered her tattered blanket. That was when she saw movement at the edge of the camp, four teepees away. At first, she thought it was the wolves that she feared so much. Finally, they had gotten up the courage to come and get her.

Then she heard the Blackfoot battle cries. She had been there long enough to have learned enough of their language to know when serious trouble existed. They were coming under attack by a hostile tribe.

She glanced at her husband's lodge and then back again, into the eyes of several Shoshone warriors. She felt faint as her heart exploded in her chest, hammering between her ears. Brenda closed her eyes tight and curled up like a fetus, praying, making herself as small as possible while she prayed that God spare her any more violations. She preferred to die rather than to go through more of the same. Finally, she gave up.

The prisoner White woman was surprised when she felt no blows or heard any gunshots. She pinched herself to see if she was dead, but she was still with the living. It appeared the intruders weren't interested in a weathered, skinny White woman in ragged clothes.

Her heart nearly burst through her chest when she heard her husband's screams as they scalped him and dragged his three other wives away. They left him there for Brenda to watch as he bled out. The hint of a smile touched the edges of her lips, and then it vanished as quickly as it appeared. Still, something evil remained deep in her eyes if you looked closely.

It was a raid to gather women for a depleting population of Shoshone. Lucky for Brenda, their standards were too high to steal a broken-minded White woman covered in cuts and bruises, accompanied by two black eyes and swollen lips. They preferred the younger women who had few or no children. If there was a pretty one with a child, that would be fine, too. If the baby were a nuisance, they hit the head with a rock, toss it into a gully, and carry on their way.

TRACKING UNKNOWN ENEMIES

LEVI JOHNSON MOVED THROUGH THE FOREST AT lightning speed. Still, he was surprised when he found no signs of tracks on the first day. It had snowed lightly the previous evening, but not enough to cover any existing footprints. As he moved through the dense woods, he kept his eyes glued to the ground and bushes around him. His sharp sense of smell and hearing was focused on his surroundings.

Something as simple as a broken leaf could be enough to give Potak's assailant's position away or indicate the direction he went. Every hour, he stopped, dropping off the trail and doubling back to ensure nobody followed him. Until then, he hadn't seen another living being. Eventually, he found a few scattered footprints. The man he was tracking was fair, but no match for the likes of Johnson. He could track a cottonmouth snake across a river.

The mountain man crossed a stretch of bear grass toward the shadows of a stand of pines. Beaver ran for the clearing, zigzagging through scattered piñons while searching his surroundings for danger. Still, he saw no one, but wasn't used to taking chances, so he continued to refrain from recklessly charging forward. He would catch him tomorrow if he didn't catch up with him before nightfall. In the wilderness, patience was a virtue you couldn't afford to disrespect.

As soon as Johnson confirmed it was safe, he continued at a run. As the sun sat squat on the western horizon, he realized that he wasn't making the progress expected. Since the moon wouldn't rise for a few hours, Levi decided to catch a few winks of sleep even if he wasn't tired. You never knew what you would run into when tracking down dangerous men, so he wanted to be as rested as possible just in case. If this man was capable of shooting a medicine man, he wouldn't hesitate to kill Levi were he given the chance.

———

LOOKEE THERE, *fresh horse droppings on the trail. Maybe he's closer than I thought. For some reason, I never expected him to have a pony. Not way up here. Maybe it's not who I suspect.*

Johnson continued to follow the trail when he suddenly saw the tracks he was looking for, and they were on the same path Potak had taken up the mountain. It seemed obvious that it was whoever had followed him, or so it seemed. At the moment, he had only found one set of tracks, and it appeared that whoever it was no longer trying to hide his presence. Footprints became easily seen, but Levi knew that that too could be a trick to make him think the man fleeing was no longer concerned when he could be waiting for him right around the next corner, waiting with an ambush.

Beaver stopped, squatting on a hill covered by waist-high bushes. He scoured his surroundings for feasible places to lay in wait for an attack, but he saw no such place. In the same token, he saw he had little place to hide as this part of the trial was in the wide-open spaces of the higher parts of the mountain.

When he looked up, he saw orange cinders disappear just above the treetops. He stopped, sniffed, and harrumphed. The smell of chicory lingered in the air. That was when he knew he had caught up with the man he was tracking. Now, it was a matter of sneaking up on him without getting shot. From the looks of Potak's wound, he had a muzzle-loading musket. He had already assumed it was an Indian. White men wouldn't be so sneaky and usually rode in more than one. Numbers meant safety in the wilderness, but to men like Levi, it also meant it was hard to hide.

Levi moved into a crouch as he neared a clearing on the other side of a bunch of ponderosas. As he closed in, the smell of woodsmoke became stronger. Occasionally, he caught glimpses of a fire through the wavering bushes and trees as the wind continued to blow. He was so close he could hear the fire pop and crackle.

As soon as Beaver felt he was close enough to have a good target, he raised his rifle. Wanata heard the metallic sound made as he slid the rifle's bolt home, making his head swing back with his eyes spread wide. He was cornered like a rat.

"Go ahead and make my day, Chief. But remember, if you do, it'll be the last move you'll ever make. What are you up to way up here? Up to no good, would be my guess."

A 50-caliber Sharps rifle was in his fists as Levi stared at his longtime adversary. He knew it would be too easy to pull the trigger and kill him. He had been a nuisance ever since he took charge of the Crow tribe after old Chief Hachta's death. Until then, as the stronghold's leader, he had blundered through one issue after another, alienating many friends and a few peers.

The power of being chief had gone to his head, and he now believed he was special above all others. Levi thought about it quickly, but he saw no reason for a Crow chief to be alone in the wilderness unless he was up to no good. He would only go without his usual guards if he wanted to hide what he was doing.

"How dare you barge into my camp and point a weapon at me?" Chief Wanata spat. "Who do you think you are?"

"What are you doing out here all on your lonesome, Chief? What do you have to say for yourself? Are you lost for words?"

"I don't have to answer to you. Remember, I allow you and your people to live on Crow land. I could ask you the same. You, too, are alone, aren't you?"

"Remember is a funny word, ain't it? It seems to me that you should be remembering me, not killing you, when you intended to bushwhack me up by Fort Boise. I kept my word and never talked about what happened. Maybe it's time I changed my mind," Levi replied in perfect Crow. "And right now, since I've got my gun pointed at you, I figure you're gonna answer a few of my questions. Have a seat, Chief. This may take a while."

———

WHEN JOHNSON first found Wanata buried in the shadows of the out-of-place foliage, he felt the war drums beating in his chest. He had expected the worst and was surprised their initial encounter didn't end in bloodshed.

Levi was a narrow-hipped man with large hands and wide shoulders. His rugged, square-jawed face looked as though it was chiseled from granite, but he was still handsome in a rugged sort of way. As his anger grew, his eyes glowed orange like branding irons fresh from the fire.

Right then, Wanata felt like he had iced water in his intestines and a blazing fire in his brain. Instead of offering to shake his hand, the chief sneered with disdain. It was Levi Johnson whom he hated the most above all the White intruders, and he considered the Crow women who married them to be traitors too, even his sister, Bar-Chee, Marshal Walker's wife.

At one point, just before they were married, the chief had the chance to kill Joseph, but he mistakenly let it pass. Had he murdered him, there never would have been a marriage. But then his sister would hate him forever. For some reason, this mattered to him even though he wasn't clear about his feelings for his sister, even before she married a White man. He sensed something broken in his soul when it came to love and feelings. He had hardly anything other than greed for that which others possessed.

Wanata's voice was full of gruff challenges, and his eyes were full of fury, but he knew better than to test

Levi because he knew he couldn't win in a hand-to-hand fight.

"As soon as I met you years ago, I knew you were a rabble-rousing troublemaker," Levi huffed. "Even as a young man, you were always getting reprisals from the chief, if not the elders. To be honest, I know you have it in you to be such a leader, but for some reason, you don't want to. You sure don't act like you were cut out for the job."

Wanata returned Levi's glare like he was a dead tree, utterly free of emotion. He neither smiled nor frowned, and his eyes gave nothing away. Who knew what thoughts were churning in that complicated brain of his.

———

LEVI'S MUSCLES rippled up and down his arms and back. The veins in his neck looked like steel cords, ridged and hard as his mouth twisted into a snarl. Wanata looked into his eyes and took a step back.

Levi opened the 52-caliber, inserted a round, and levered it into the chamber. Then, he rested his finger on the safety trigger as he stared the Indian down.

Squinting, he studied his opponent. He finally made out his target's silhouette and centered his sights. Levi emptied his lungs, but just before he pulled the trigger, he pushed the barrel up, and the round sailed through the air two inches over Wanata's head. Levi watched as the Indian held his breath and tried not to lose it. For a second, he was sure he was dead. The blood drained from his face as he began to tremble and waver, but he bit his tongue and bucked up, trying not to show the shock.

————

THE FOLLOWING MORNING, the sun suddenly seemed to pop up from over the horizon like a big yellow rubber ball and hang there immobile for far too long. Surprisingly, nobody died that night. Levi and the chief quietly talked until late into the evening. When the first light of day graced Wanata's campsite, he was still alive, and both men continued their long conversation as they continued to whisper.

NOTICEABLE ABSENCE

RUSTY WALKED UP AND DOWN THE PORCH, PUFFING ON HIS pipe as clouds of smoke floated around his head. The wooden planks groaned under his feet with each step. Worry lines bunched on his brows as his frown deepened. Marshal Walker sat at the table with Angus, Will, and Virgil. They all had the same thing on their minds, even though nobody had yet voiced an opinion. No matter how they looked at it, something wasn't right.

"Do you think they could have fallen off one of those peaks up there?" the captain asked as he looked up at the snowcapped mountains. "I've heard that some of them are impossible to climb." He fiddled with his empty sleeve as it slipped through the fingers of his only hand. "I suppose it's about time we went to look for them. It's not like Levi to be gone so long for no more than to climb a mountain or two. If they're in trouble, maybe we can help them out. If they're hurt or worse, we can still do what we can to assist. At the moment, all we know is that they're too late and then some. It's not like Beaver to linger so long, especially with the boy."

"So, who wants to join the scouting party? I know I'm going, especially if something's happened to Beaver." Rusty glanced around the table. "What about you, Joseph? I figure the three of us should be enough muscle if it comes to violence. Maybe one of these fool Indians have gone on the warpath again, but I ain't seen any smoke signals."

"I'd go even if y'all didn't. This is my boy you're talking about." Marshal Walker hooked his thumbs into his suspenders. "I reckon the three of us can handle anything we're thrown up against. I've been chewing on this for the last few days, and now I feel like it's past time."

After three years in the compound, the marshal still wore his tarnished old badge from back in Leavenworth in the Territories, where he was a lawman most of his life. But here in the Rocky Mountains, he discovered a chance for a new start as a father, and he wasn't going to let anything happen to little Money Penny and take all that away.

He still wore his single-action Colt revolvers tied low to his thighs as he did back in the days when he had to go up against gunfighters, thieves, and bandits. When he was a young lawman back east in his home county, there was little to no law at all except for him and a few other marshals across the Territories. They couldn't deal with it all but were hard on those they caught to send a stern message, especially Marshal Joseph Walker. Most men who crossed him didn't have long to continue to breathe.

"Well, it's settled then. We leave half an hour before first light. Does anybody have a problem with that?"

Rusty eyed Joseph and Will, but neither man flinched. If the truth were known, they were both more warrior-like than Rusty ever was. He preferred to be the mentor and marksman, but all their skills might still be needed if Levi disappeared with the little boy, especially Steel's tracking skills, which were possibly second only to Levi's.

———

THE FOLLOWING MORNING, Marshal Walker lifted the gun belt from the wall peg and strapped it around his waist. He planted his feet wide as he blinked. Captain Forrester stank of duty and honor, especially when his best friend might be in trouble. His saber rattled in its metal sheath.

When he walked outside, Joseph spat out the stub of a cigar and turned his boot heel, grinding it into dust. As soon as he left his wife's side, his look changed from sweet and in love to a certain terrifying dread he instilled upon others as his eyes bore into their souls. When called on, the old lawman in him came back like it had never gone.

The old black dust-covered dog barked dispiritedly when the rabbit raced across the yard and got away. He lazily crawled under the porch and fell asleep again. As the years passed, Dog seemed to slow down and now spent most days dozing in the shade.

Steel's mouth was tight in thought, and his old face was scared, with crow's feet stretched around the corners of his eyes and deep lines across his brow. His skin was like worn leather, tough and sunburned.

The captain walked three horses from the stables, ready to ride under the twilight of the stars. A yellow circle of light surrounded the porch from the lamps roosted in the rafters. The men silently tied their saddlebags down and slipped their rifles into their saddles. Revolvers protruded from Rusty's and the captain's belts. At first glance, it looked like they were ready for war.

When Angus walked out onto the porch to see them off, his eyes were full of worry and concern. In the old days, he would have been one of the men riding out of the compound to save the day, but those days had passed for this aging mountain man. Still, he enjoyed their home lost in the mountains and didn't feel like he missed anything in life, but when it came time to defend the compound, he was on the front line, ready to risk his life for their homes and his friends.

He was lean but, with age, had become slightly stooped. Before, he wore a raccoon cap, but now he favored floppy, wide-brimmed hats that provided more shade. Curtains of white hair flowed past his shoulders. The wrinkles on his face looked like a roadmap, but the sparkle in his eyes was that of a younger man. Despite his years, he was full of spark and mischief.

When they rode out of the compound, Rusty led the way. The marshal was a fair scout, and the captain maybe a little better, but neither one held a light to the mountain man mentor. Captain Forrester rode in the center, with the marshal cautiously taking drag. They knew that the reason why Levi and Money hadn't returned could be hostile Indians. Lately, there had been a war between the Blackfoot and the Crow, although short-lived, but the hostile feelings were still there with such a recent incident.

They may have run into a runaway war party of young bucks who wanted to make their mark on history by throwing away their lives. All they wanted was to be sung in the songs of the elders. That, or, as Will had said, falling off a peak, so his was unscalable. Levi had the habit of biting off more than he could chew, but to date, he had survived. With a small boy included, such disregard for danger was unwanted.

Levi had told Rusty approximately where they were headed. When in the wilderness, it was wise to let someone know where you've gone so they had a vague idea of where to search if there was trouble. He believed they were headed for some peaks Rusty had shown his apprentices five years prior. It would be just like Beaver to tackle something he had seen him do in the past but wasn't ready at the time.

Would a little boy be up for such a venture, or would Beaver keep his head and see how he would endanger his life? He was usually one of the most responsible people in the bunch, but sometimes his desire for excitement overwhelmed his good judgment. Despite all three men telling themselves that Beaver wouldn't take such risks, for some reason, he was late, and in the past, he had taken risks that nearly cost him his life. The marshal just hoped he had the common sense to stick to the plan.

Up until now, Levi had always brought his boy back intact. Sure, sometimes he has the odd cuts and scratches, but no more than any of them when they venture deep into the wilderness to hunt. Still, he was eight going on nine, so he was totally reliant on Beaver for everything he did.

"If Levi's let anything happen to my boy, I'm gonna have his hide," Marshal Walker growled under his breath.

"Don't worry, Levi can take care of himself and Money too, so stop frettin'. We'll find 'em soon enough." Still, Rusty's voice wasn't as confident as he had hoped.

"Levi said they weren't going to go far, especially since they're on foot. We'll make better time with the horses, and if we have to, when the terrain gets too tough, we'll leave them behind and hope a mountain lion or grizzly bear don't get 'em." Rusty turned his head, spat a brown stream of juice, and wiped his mouth with the back of his hand.

Even though Rusty saw their tracks, neither the marshal nor the captain saw them. They didn't even see Money, who, due to inexperience, was easy for Steel to see.

"That boy's learning faster than an adult. He seems to soak up everything Levi says like a sponge. I wouldn't be surprised if he gets as good as Levi and even me. It's pretty much a toss-up between us two."

"He has to live that long first," Marshal Walker growled. It was clear that he wasn't in a good mood.

It was like there was a dark cloud hanging over the marshal's head, and Lord help the man who harmed his little boy. He was among the most dangerous of the bunch because of his skills with his Colt revolvers. Not that the captain was lacking in his capacity to fight despite his missing arm. He was a dead shot, and a terror when he pulled his saber, which White men and Indian warriors feared alike.

Then there was Levi Johnson, who was something else entirely. Sure, he wasn't quick with a revolver like Joseph was, but he could out shoot even Rusty, who had been the champion year after year during the time of the Rendezvous. All that ended in 1840 when top hats went out of fashion, and the beavers were all trapped out.

As they rode through the forest, they feared no one because they knew they had the best skills on Beartooth Mountain and even down on the plateau in Yellowstone Valley.

Rusty kicked his leg over his horse and slid out of the saddle, making deep footprints in the snow. He dropped to one knee and studied something invisible to the others.

I see our boys, but I see the tracks of another Indian, too. The way he walks even seems familiar to me for some reason. Maybe it's somebody I know. We all walk a little differently. When we sit on a horse, we all make a different print with the horse's hooves. What we've got here is someone wearin' moccasins like mine. The only good thing is that he's alone, but what would a hunter or warrior be doing up here all alone?"

"If my guess is right, whoever it is, he'll be up to no good. He's too far off the beaten path to be a coincidence. Nah, this fella's following Beaver and Money, sure as shootin'."

"You don't know that," Captain Forrester replied.

"Well, well, lookee here. I see a fourth set of tracks. These look familiar, too, but I can't place where they come from. Give me a spell, and I'll figure it out. Now what in the world would two people we know be doin' up here near the peaks for Heaven's sake?"

"How can you be sure you know them just by looking at nearly invisible footprints?" the marshal asked with a face full of doubt. "Sometimes, you claim to have some skills that are impossible to believe."

"You just wait and see, Joseph. I tell ya, they're both on the tip of my tongue. Don't worry, they'll come to me eventually. They always do."

LOST IN ANOTHER WORLD

BRENDA WAS IN SHOCK WHEN THE BLACKFOOT CAPTORS set her free. She had understood why they kidnapped her well enough. Her Indian husband had used her like a rag doll. What she couldn't understand was why they let her leave. It was almost as if they couldn't wait for her to go. The look in the Indians' eyes was something verging on fear as they watched how she behaved so strangely.

Little did *she* know that the tribe thought that evil spirits possessed crazy people, and apparently, this White woman was overflowing with devils and demons. At least that was what Acha and his wives thought, and now they didn't want to have anything to do with her. The sooner she left, the better, but now none of them had the courage to force her to go.

Lately, she had howled at the moon as she squatted like a beast and stared at the pale orb in the sky, her knuckles dragging the ground like an ape. Nobody had any idea what she was thinking or if she had any thoughts at all. Brenda Penny had crossed that blurry gray line between sanity and madness. Her mind had flown off with the wind as it swirled around and around in a whirlwind, never knowing where it would land or if it would land at all. The Indians hoped that at some point, she would fall off the end of the earth and vanish forever, but none of them were brave enough to give her the push she needed. They had learned all their lives how dangerous the insane were.

During the day, she hid from the sun in the shadows as though its rays were poison—if they touched her, she would melt. All day long, she would sit without moving until the sun set, and then she would go out on the prowl. Whenever someone tried to stop her, all it took was for them to glance into her eyes, and they would back away, wishing they had never seen what they just saw. She had no idea why her captors had changed so much, but she felt a strange power when she saw their fear.

It frightened them when she appeared to be talking to people they couldn't see. The Indians believed she was communicating with ghosts, and perhaps, in a way, she was.

Little did they know she was talking to her twin sons. One, she had seen murdered with her very own eyes along with her husband, but at this point, she didn't remember, as all her memories were fuzzy now and hard to discern. All she knew was that her other twin, Money, was still alive when they sold her to Acha.

She would never forget her blond-haired boy as the bad men separated them, and her wicked Indian husband dragged her away and took her while his other wives watched. The way Money blinked his robin-egg blue eyes as tears streaked down his face melted her heart despite her personal fear as she stepped into a nightmare and beyond anything a White woman could ever imagine in their darkest dreams.

Again, Brenda howled at the moon, and it sounded like a wounded animal full of pain. When the Shoshone heard it, they all ran away. After the battle, and losing twelve women to the raiders, the enemy disappeared into the forest without a trace. Of course, her Indian husband was dead, and good riddance, but now she hardly even remembered him. Her mind tried to block out all he and his three other wives had done to her, and their faces were now no more than blurry visions somewhere in the deepest recesses of her mind.

As soon as she could, Brenda escaped any possible recapture and ran into the dense forest full of wild animals, including wildcats and grizzly bears. Of course, she had no idea that she had already lost her mind, but she believed everyone else was acting strangely. To her, she seemed to be the only person trying to live a normal life when, in truth, she had resorted to living like a wild beast.

A flash in the forest revealed Brenda racing after a baby raccoon. She ran so fast she was like a blur, snatching the animal off the ground and bashing its head into the nearest tree as she growled like a rabid dog. She immediately squatted and began to tear the carcass apart with her teeth as her eyes shot all around wildly, and she ate the animal raw. Rivulets of blood ran down her mouth and dripped off her chin as her teeth glowed red in the moonlight. Again, she howled like a wounded wolf as red drops rolled off her chin.

Brinda suddenly grabbed her dead animal and scurried off into the bushes, back into the shadows, and out of the silvery moonlight. The only sign that she was there was when she occasionally blinked, showing the whites of her eyes.

That night, she heard someone on the trail. In the last days, she had become so wild that she shunned any other human beings, believing that everyone intended to kill her. She had been tortured and violated by Acha until her mind had snapped, and now all rhyme or reason had vanished from Brenda's thoughts. When she fled the camp uncontested, she had taken a chance and had stolen a knife from the cooking utensils. Now, it remained grasped in her white-knuckled fists, and she intended to turn it on anybody who neared her, and in the case she found her son was dead, she would turn it on herself.

Again, she heard the snap of someone stepping on a twig along the trail, and she instantly knew it was a human, and he or she wasn't being as careful as they should be. Brenda jumped up and dove into the thick brush, vanishing from sight. The leaves on the branches rustled, then fell still again. All that was visible of her was when she occasionally snarled, baring her white teeth.

When the Indian cautiously walked into the shaded clearing, he took a deep breath and slowly let it out as if trying to control his nerves. He wore a fancy headdress, which made her believe he was important to one of the local tribes. She saw he had a White man's rifle in one fist and a large knife in the other. A tomahawk hung from his belt. The warrior appeared to be ready for battle. That, or he was running from somebody or something.

Suddenly, Brenda's breathing and heartbeat

sounded so loud that she was sure the Indian would hear it. BOOM-BOOM-BOOM, it hammered in her chest as sweat beaded across her forehead. Her muscles tensed as she prepared to lunge at the stranger threatening her immediate territory. Now, she had truly lost her mind and believed herself invincible.

MONEY AND POTAK

"WHADDAYA SAY, MONEY? NOBODY CAN CLAIM WE'RE ALL mouth and no action. You're doing a fine job scaring up food for the cookfire, and as you can see, I'm feeling better. Soon I'll be strong enough to be ready to travel."

"You do have more color in your face, Potak. Compared to a couple of days ago, you look like a different man."

The medicine man had been around White men much of his youth while he, like many Tonkawa Indians, worked for the army as scouts. Working with soldiers day in and day out, he had perfected his English. At the time, most of the Native Americans working for the cavalry came from the Tonkawa tribe because all the other Indians considered them their enemy due to their unusual customs.

They had even joined forces to attempt to wipe them out. This made their banished tribe turn a blind eye to what was really happening and helped the people who were trying to run the tribes off their land and send them to reservations.

This fact just made most of the Tonkawa even more of an enemy. At least *most* of the members of their tribe, but for some medicine men, it was a different story. Potak was famous for his work curing people, whether from illness or evil spirits, and his leadership skills were an example.

He was also said to have special contacts with the Indian spirit world, which made him desirable to most tribes despite his origins. Only shamans could pass these boundaries without issues. The medicine man was welcome in all seven of the original Rocky Mountain and Yellowstone Valley tribes and most of those on the Great Plain, and all the way to Texas.

Money slid his tongue over cracked lips. "So far, I haven't seen any tracks besides ours, and I've done my best to keep signs of my presence minimal. It wouldn't do for some passing Indians to see such small footprints in the snow when I'm out hunting. I believe that out of curiosity, they would feel they need to have a look. Especially since I'm movin' around all alone, they'll surely wonder who or what it was that made my tracks if they do see them. That's something I doubt an Indian could pass on. They seem to be too curious of people to let it be. Especially if it's on their land."

"Up here is no-man's-land, Money. Nobody lives up this high because of the altitude, so no one has claimed it as theirs. If you get caught up here in the dead of winter, you probably won't survive, no matter how good a mountain man you are. Once the dead of winter hits, this part of the mountain is uninhabitable."

The boy looked at the strange Indian, blinking like a bird. Sometimes, he found himself lost for words. Potak always said things that surprised him.

"You aren't scared, are you?" asked Potak, peering at him from the corner of his eyes.

"I'm sorry to say, I'm scared stiff, especially now that I know that Blackfoot or Shoshone can come up here without worrying about being attacked. Maybe we aren't so safe after all."

Potak waited until the heat of embarrassment drained from Money's face. He could see the boy's guts turn to mud, and his body went rigid like an icicle.

The medicine man's drapes of ghostly black hair shook with his laughter. "You would be a fool if you weren't scared. I don't tell anyone, but I got scared when I was a little boy, too. The important thing is that you can function just the same. Most men in battle feel fear, but they push it aside or use it to energize their attack. That is something that you will learn when you are older."

Potak stretched stiffly on his bedroll and yawned so wide that Money could see his wisdom teeth. When he moved abruptly, Money could see the pain in his face, but he didn't utter a sound or complain. He gritted his teeth and took it like a man. He made the boy feel better than once upon a time when the medicine man knew fear, too. It made him seem more human, like him and his friends. Little by little, he learned to see past the fact that he was an Indian and a shaman. Now, he began to see the kind man behind those amused-filled eyes.

Money frowned. "Is all this gonna turn out to be really dangerous? I wish Beaver hadn't run off. Why didn't you stop him, Potak? He seems to listen to you for some reason, but you hardly tried at all."

"Sometimes waking up in the morning can be risky, Money. That's why we must enjoy every minute we are alive—even the bad times. You never know if you'll still be here in a day, an hour, or even a minute. Nothing is written in stone when it comes to death except that it will eventually come. As far as Levi's concerned, he's a man with his own choices to make, and we can't make them for him. I must admit, though, your mentor is as hardheaded a man as I've ever met."

Potak stopped for a moment and pulled at the half dozen hairs growing on his chin as he studied Money's reaction to what he had said. His mouth was in the shadow of his hooked nose.

"When Beaver decides to do something, nobody's going to talk him out of it. Some men out West are hard because they grew up in hard times, but Beaver had a fine family and a good ma and pa. Still, he couldn't resist the temptation of heading for the wilderness like many adventurous young men. Still, many fall along the way. But not Levi or the Captain, either. You'll be a fine man when you grow up and become like either of them, if not a little like both."

It was funny how a couple of words could bring up such a bitter memory. For a moment, Money's eyes blazed with hate. He hadn't talked about his parents much since his father was murdered and his mom sold like a bushel of corn. Constant change and a certain amount of chaos had kept the thoughts locked away in the back of his mind. Money looked at Potak, and his frown turned into a grin. He pushed the memories back into the darkest recesses of his mind and did as his Indian friend said as his eyes twinkled in wonder.

Potak's brow furrowed in concern when he saw the look of pain flash across the boy's face. He was growing up too quickly, but still, he was lucky to be alive and with people who not only cared but could teach him to stay alive if he decided to remain in the wilderness when he was older.

For then, he had no choice and seemed content with what life threw at him, at least after losing both his parents. For a moment, the medicine man wondered if he could find his mother and if she would be the same person she had been when they were last together.

The Indian had lived with numerous tribes and spoke various languages. In his time in the different camps, captured or bought White women didn't seem to fare well. Either their new husbands were too vigorous in taking what they wanted, or their wives became jealous. It was one thing to be invidious of one of your own kind and another to have envy for a White woman.

"I'm afraid what you said caught me off guard. Sometimes, it's hard for me to act like a man when I'm still really a little boy, but I'm doing my best."

"You're only as little as you believe in your soul. Haven't you seen little dogs with hearts so big they take on bulls or steers? Think of yourself as big, and you'll *be* big, just like those little feisty puppies. Sometimes, all it takes is confidence to win a battle or defeat a foe. All you need is a little dose of bravery mixed in."

"I never thought about it like that, Potak. I've seen little mean dogs whop big dogs and make them run away and chase horses that were twenty times their size. From now on, I'm gonna try to think like that, but the fact that I'm too little to do the job keeps worming into my mind."

"That's right, a little dog with a big heart. That's all it takes. Now, how about putting some more wood on that fire to warm my aging bones up? Today, I wanna see if I can get up and walk on my own. See that branch over there? Cut it down so I can use it as a staff."

When he sat up, Money could see that the side of the Indian's shirt was stained in dry, dark blood. His head wavered at first, then he took another breath and steadied himself. He fussed with his bowl, filling it with sweet-smelling tobacco. The old Indian exhaled a blast of smoke from his long pipe.

The dark-skinned Indian with the hooked nose and the small boy sat up, stretching their legs. They stared dumbfoundedly at their feet, the glowing coals, and each other, wondering what tomorrow would bring.

"Why didn't you speak your mind before Levi left? Maybe you could have talked him out of it. Or do you think he would have gotten angry if you interfered? It's *you* that he's doing this for, ya know. To be honest, to me, it's making less and less sense every time I think about it."

"A man can always speak his mind as long as he can run faster than the fella you've made angry." Potak chuckled. "And Levi's not doing this for me. Levi is doing this for himself and his sense of honor because he believes he should. It's like an unwritten code for him, like it is for some men, like the captain. That is what has driven him to do what he is doing. Of course, I didn't tell him who shot me because I cannot bring myself to break my word when I swore to silence. This is something that I must bear. Life works in mysterious ways, and things we don't understand often happen until we wait patiently and sit back and see the whole picture. So far, we've only seen a little peek of what is going on. Soon our visions will broaden."

There was a sudden rustling in the bushes. Money

froze, but Potak snarled as his eyes turned toward the intruder. He could hear small sticks crinkling under his feet.

"State your business or be off," Potak suddenly said with a growling scowl, catching Money off guard. His voice suddenly sounded like thunder.

Money found the Indian who stumbled on their campsite was so scary he believed he could frighten termites off rotten wood. His Adam's apple bobbed up and down as he tried to swallow, but his mouth was too dry. Even though the boy tried to hold his gaze, he looked away and down at his feet after two seconds as he dug a hole in the dirt with his toe. The hostile Indian scared him too much to lock eyes, but Potak didn't hesitate. He stared at him defiantly.

The medicine man pointed a crooked, accusing finger at the strange warrior and said, "Do you know what you're getting into? I am Potak, the Tonkawa medicine man. You may have seen me in the smoke signals and heard of me in the Indian gossip. Beware, if you enter my camp uninvited, I will cast an evil spell on you and yours. No one in your bloodline will remain safe."

A knot tightened Money's mouth. A forced smile remained on Potak's face, but now it had no longer reached his eyes and had lost its meaning. It made him appear even more dangerous than before. The friendliness he had just heard in his voice disappeared as it turned coldly polite. Money's mouth was so dry his teeth stuck to his lips as his heart roared in his chest and hammered between his ears. Sweaty palms clutched at his scattergun as rivulets of sweat ran down his back despite the cold.

Money had to tell himself to breathe slowly so his

heart would stop making flip-flops in his chest as he clamped his teeth so they didn't chatter, giving away his nervousness in front of an apparently hostile warrior. A white line was painted from his widow's peak, down his nose, and over his lips to his chin. Red lines spread from his nose at an angle, and white rings painted around his eyes. Even Money knew it when he saw an Indian painted for war.

During these few days with the medicine man, he felt he had learned a lot, although he couldn't put his finger on one thing. He appeared to be learning without knowing it, yet he knew something was happening inside because he could feel it grow in his mind.

Money's jaw was hanging open, and his eyes were opened as wide as his mouth. His sunburned face showed on his pink cheeks. He had his hat pushed back and his face was dirty and tired. His mouth slowly twisted into a smile, but his eyes belied his true feelings. He was scared to death and only tried to smile because Potak did.

They both watched as the Indian silently hesitated. He took a brave step forward but thought better and turned on his heels and vanished just as suddenly as he appeared.

"You better put the fire out for the rest of the night," Potak whispered. "We've drawn enough attention for one night. We better keep a cold camp for now."

Money raked his buckskin-covered toe through the dirt, pushing it over the dying fire. Instantly, the glowing orange coals extinguished, suddenly leaving them in the dark.

Overhead, the stars swung counterclockwise in the vast night sky as Earendel winked in the farthest distance. Falling stars left vapor trails streaking toward earth and then burned out in midair. Hours later, the sky burst into pink, rose, and crimson prisms as it stretched to the western horizon. The warrior hadn't returned.

CHRISTOPHER HOUSTON CARSON

THE MISSOURIAN RODE HIS HORSE THROUGH THE DENSE woods, leading a pack mule loaded with traps, mining equipment, and provisions. Rifle's stocks protruded from sheaths beside both legs, and a brace of cross-draw pistols hung from his waist. He moved in unison with his horse, indicating he had spent days, months, years in the saddle. By profession, he was an explorer and a scout. Despite his fame, he shunned the notoriety and found it to be in poor taste.

"Hello there! Are ya friendly, or should I mosey on my way?" Kit asked. "I'm mapping and writing reports on the Oregon Trail and thought I'd ride a couple of weeks south and check out this part of the country. I'd heard of Yellowstone Valley and thought I'd have a peek. From the looks of your cabins, I reckon y'all have been here for quite a spell."

Virgil was the first one to walk out onto the porch, while Betty, Dahteste, and Bar-Chee held rifles at the gun slats. The door and window were closed. Despite the faraway location, having guests wasn't all that unusual, but they were usually Indians or the army with a lost buffalo hunter or two.

"That might be, and then again, it might not, stranger," Virgil replied cautiously. "Of late, we're not all that big on uninvited guests. Before you think about steppin' down, do you have a name, mister?"

Kit was obviously surprised when a Black man walked out the front door. Most frontiersmen he found this deep in the wilderness were usually White. Some were Americans from the East, and others were Frenchmen from Europe or Upper and Lower Canada. The odd character from the British Isles popped up on occasion, too, but most of those were Scots.

The land officially belonged to the local Indians, comprising seven major tribes. How these people managed to live there long enough to build such a compound with the Indian threat was enough for a curious man to want to stop and ask.

Carson was another young fellow from back east who decided he wanted to be a mountain man. Kit struck out at the ripe age of sixteen and headed west in the 1830s. He was sort of like Rusty or Levi and was a man with unusual wilderness skills.

"The name's Kit Carson. I hail from Missouri. I'm a working man. John Frémont hired me to map and make reports and commentaries about the Oregon Trail and the surrounding areas. I know I wandered off my path some, but at times, my curiosity gets the best of me."

Little did Carson know the unwanted fame he would acquire after completing this mission. Still, he was already well documented to some extent and had publications of his earlier exploits in California posted in the national newspapers. In 1840, they numbered more than one thousand two hundred across the country.

From the first newspaper published in North America in 1704 by John Campbell, the postmaster of Boston, to over a thousand companies publishing the latest news, along with exaggerations and sometimes out-and-out lies. Little did he know that in the following year, he would find himself in the Mexican-American War, which would turn his life around like it would many others.

For the moment, he was doing what he enjoyed most: exploring new passages and beautiful landscapes. This time, rather than California, he sought out the Rocky Mountains over Yellowstone Valley. What he found was a country of such beauty that human eyes seldom saw it.

It all started with a single sheet printed on both sides. It made history as the first continuously published newspaper. Carson was also often depicted in the penny press, which only cost one cent, while others, like dime novels, charged a nickel or ten cents. Although it was the crudest form of journalism, it still made many men famous across the States. Especially individuals as unusual as Kit Carson. He even had a small write-up in the New York Harold, with nationwide distribution. But all this attention was completely unwanted as far as he was concerned. He shunned notoriety like he did the plague.

"Why, I've read about you. If I'm not mistaken, I've seen a picture of you in the newspapers." Virgil squinted to better see. "It's you all right. Ride on in and take your animals over to the corral. I'll help you with your horse's saddle and that aparejo pack. We rarely get a celebrity up here on Beartooth Mountain." He didn't notice the frown when he mentioned Carson's fame.

"That's mighty kind of you, Mister?"

"Virgil Lovejoy's the name. If you're wondering, I'm a free man, especially with you coming from a slave state along with Texas, Louisiana, Mississippi, Alabama, Florida, Georgia, North Carolina, Kentucky, Tennessee, and Virginia. I apologize, that was a full lung, Mr. Carson. I just like a man to know where I stand. I have papers to prove it too."

"Call me Kit. All my friends do. I hail from Missouri, but I'm not a plantation owner. A long time ago, I took one slave into my home, renamed him Juan Carson, and made him family. You don't have to worry about me treatin' you colored folk badly as many do. I'm not that kind of fella. For me, the same goes with Indians. There are good ones, and there are bad ones, just like us White folks. I figure it's the same the world over."

"Well, I'm glad to hear that. You can come on out, girls! Stop pointin' that gun at Kit, Angus. He's come in peace."

Carson was surprised to see five women and an aging White man with flowing White hair shyly walk out of the cabin's only door. Three of the females were dressed in buckskins and wore their hair in long braids.

"This here is Kit Carson." Virgil smiled. "Why, he's known from New York to California."

McFarlin looked down, and as soon as he saw the gun in his hands, his face filled with surprise. "I plumb forgot I had it in my hands, Mr. Carson. I didn't mean to be pointing it at cha. Beg my pardon. I'm Angus McFarlin. I do believe we crossed paths at the Rendezvous back in 1886 or 1887 or thereabouts."

"You can call me Kit, too. Like I said, only bankers and lawyers call me mister, and I don't hang around with either one."

"You don't say," Angus said. "I've read about your exploits in the newspapers. I'm an avid reader, ya know. Virgil too, he reads the Bible every night."

"Yep, I've been in a dime novel or two," Kit replied, insinuating he'd prefer not to make a big thing of it. Then his frown turned into a grin. "But don't believe everything you read when, in fact, I'm just an everyday sort of fella. Nothing to make a fuss over. I reckon I was just in the wrong place at the right time. To be honest, I don't take much to fame—never did, never will."

The thirty-six-year-old frontiersman wore short hair for a frontiersman. It was pushed back on his head over a thin, wizened face. When he removed his beaver hat, it revealed a receding hairline, leaving his forehead looking pale and snow-white. He was clean-shaven, save for his modest mustache.

Somebody from inside the cabin called out, "Look out! Hot coffee coming through." Betty was the only one who remembered her manners. "Leave the man alone for a spell. Can't ya see he's tired? How about something to eat, Kit?"

As soon as Betty broke the ice and half smiled, the others' doubts about the White stranger vanished. He was too well-armed to be a peaceful man, then again, that was the only way to go in the wilderness. The explorer brushed his mustache with his knuckles and politely smiled. He was used to the initial gibberish when it was first discovered who he was. After an hour or two, they would see he was just another man, and half of what was said in the newspapers wasn't even true.

"Sit down and excuse our manners," Angus grinned. "We don't have well-known folks who come around often, so you caught us off guard. I can make up some beefsteaks and frying pan biscuits before you can wash up. I keep the fire goin' all day long. When we're all here, I cook for twelve. Get ready to have one of the tastiest meals of your life. The best you'll find in the valley and up here in the mountains, anyway. That includes Fort Boise and Fort Hall on the Oregon Trail."

"Why, I just came from there. I had a word with Captain Harvey Crow after stoppin' in the McKay Trading Post for some supplies and a bite to eat. I can't say much about the food, though. Who else lives here?" Kit asked with raised eyebrows.

"Why, Rusty Steel, the mountain man mentor, Captain Will Forrester, and Levi Beaver Johnson," Angus replied. "The latter used to be Indian fighters in the Territories against the Comanche. Now they're mountain men like us."

"Well, I'll be. I've read about all three of those men, and if I remember right, Rusty was in the shootin' contests in the Rendezvous. I have the habit of trying to learn more about the folks with my same ways. I heard that Levi Johnson was the best shot west of Missouri. I read about the captain's and Levi's expedition being wiped out by the Comanche. Everybody in the know heard about that. It was a surprise to most that Levi and Will survived. If I remember correctly, everybody thought they were dead for a spell since there were no other survivors. I sure would like to meet all three if that's possible. We'll surely have a lot to talk about."

The mule and horse's lungs were tired from the altitude, which made them breathe through their mouths. They stood wavering, all sweaty despite the crisp mountain air. They brushed them down before hooking feed bags over their heads and letting them loose in the corral.

It was apparent that Kid didn't want to talk about his notoriety. Some men, like Wanata, did whatever they could to become known for their bravery, but it appeared that Mr. Carson was only interested in exploration. Secretly, he despised the reputation his work had brought him. He was a simple man who wanted most to be left alone to do the work he loved. In minutes, the explorer wolfishly shoveled food like he was starving. "Why this is some fine cooking, Angus. I never expected to find food like this way up here. Is there more of that gravy to spoon on my last biscuit?"

"Here, let me take care of that," Betty said as she poured another ladle of gravy on Kit's plate.

The women went silent momentarily, then Angus laughed to fill the void and ease the tension. Of course, the three men talked about places they had been all over the West, but the Indian women soon tired and headed off to tend to their chores.

Betty's face broke into a smile, and she said, "I met you as a young girl. You knew my Uncle Davy Crockett. If I remember right, you said you were twenty-six back then. That was ten years ago, and I was just a girl, and my uncle was still alive. That was before the Alamo."

"Oh, I remember your uncle well. He was a fine man, Davy. It's a shame what happened in that horrible battle. But then again, I reckon they all knew what they were getting into. Half the famous frontiersmen of the time died during those thirteen days. Your uncle was both brave and headstrong, I'll give him that. We lost Jim Bowie and William Travis as well. It was a sad, sad day in February at the Alamo Garrison. They hardly had a chance with six thousand Mexican soldiers against a couple hundred of our finest. Still, there are no odds to winning, no matter how skilled and brave you are."

Betty beamed when he remembered her family fondly. She had always been proud of her uncle and her family name.

Virgil and Angus chatted with him until midnight, when they changed the cool evening outside for their warm beds inside. Since the captain was gone, Betty offered Carson the use of her and Will's teepee until the men returned from searching for Levi and Money. But Kit sat on the compound porch for the remainder of the night, listening to his thoughts as they flashed through his mind at the speed of light. He apparently didn't need much sleep or rest.

THE SCOUTING PARTY

WHEN RUSTY SUDDENLY HELD HIS HAND UP, THE CAPTAIN and Joseph stopped in their tracks. He turned his head and mouthed, "Over there," while pointing his thumb over his shoulder.

He squatted and looked at the little tracks, but it appeared the boy was all alone. He instantly realized that something had happened to Levi.

"Are you in there, Money?" Rusty called out. "It's me, your father, and Will."

They heard the distinct sound of two hammers uncocking, and a young boy's voice said, "Boy, am I ever glad to see you guys." As soon as they pushed through the bushes, they saw him sitting beside a lean-to and Potak lying on a bedroll.

"Excuse me for not getting up, but I had a little accident." Potak pulled his blanket aside so they could see the bloody buckskins. Before taking chase after the man responsible, Levi had wrapped a long bandage tightly around his waist.

Rusty ran over and dropped to his knees, letting his horse's reins trail behind him. "What happened, old friend? That looks like a bullet hole in your buckskin shirt. Who did this to you, Potak? Is that where Levi's gone?"

"Oh, boy, here we go again." Money rolled his eyes. "Maybe you'll listen when it's Rusty askin' the questions."

"Tend to your horses while Money here heats up the beans and makes a new kettle of coffee." The medicine man pushed himself to his feet. At first, he was a little wobbly, but he soon got his bearings. He was obviously doing better. "After we eat, we can talk. It is impolite not to care for your guests' needs first. Remember this, young man. These are the Indian ways."

Luckily, all three men were starving after traveling hard. Curious eyes glanced at the shelter they had made. Rusty shoveled the last spoonful of beans into his mouth and wiped his lips with his hand.

"Well, tell us then. Where's Levi, and what happened to you?"

"How is it you're taking care of a gunshot man all on your own?" Joseph asked, as concern filled his voice while staring at his adopted son. "Y'all had better have a good explanation for all this."

"He's after the man who shot me. Lucky for me, he spooked and ran off before he finished the job. I reckon he'll figure I didn't make it anyway. I'd probably be dead if it weren't for Levi and Money here. They found me and built a shelter, and Beaver left Money here to feed and care for me, and he's done a fine job."

"Hold on for just a minute." Joseph's face was

turning red as his anger rose. "You mean that Levi left you here to tend to an Indian all on your own, out here in the middle of nowhere?"

"The boy did fine, Joseph. Don't blame him *or* Levi. All this is my fault for making a promise and keeping it. I know it doesn't make much sense. To be honest, I thought that Beaver would have returned by now. What's happened to him, I'm not so sure. I promised the man who shot me I wouldn't tell. That's probably the main reason he let me live, so it wasn't for nothing. I'm proud of the fact that I've never broken my word, but I guess there is a time for everything."

"Go on then, spit it out. Who's Levi chasing over you getting shot?" Captain Forrester's eyes suddenly became deadly.

Forrester wasn't impressed with the medicine man like the others. He was still a military man despite five years of being inactive. It had been born and bred into him along with all the first males of his family. It was a tradition that went back generations, and even though he ended up living in the wilderness, he could never shake that side of his personality. That made him and Levi as different as night and day, but still, they were best friends. Some say opposites attract.

"If anybody's harmed Levi, you're gonna pay, medicine man. I don't care if you gave your word to God, you better tell me right now, or I'm gonna cut your tongue out and you won't have to worry about breaking your word ever again."

His little speech shocked Rusty, but Joseph clapped him on the back and urged him on. "Come on then, who was it?"

"It was your wife's brother, Wanata, Marshal. Now you can see why I didn't want you to know. Starting a serious problem with the Crow chief could cost you all your freedom to live on Beartooth Mountain. When the chief asked me to swear I'd never tell anyone, I happily agreed. I was already shot, so he couldn't take it back. Mind you, I doubt he has a sorry bone in his body. He was just afraid of facing you boys, especially Levi. I don't know if you know, but there's bad blood between them. The chief tried to kill Beaver unsuccessfully, but Levi let him live just the same to protect you and yours in the compound."

"Why didn't you say so in the first place?" Money asked, already hanging on his dad's jacket. His head only came up to his chest. "I thought you were just being stubborn. Levi must have suspected all along what happened."

"I'm sure he did, and he had a clue who it was and all. I was out here looking for a rare stone only found near the mountain peaks when Wanata snuck up on me. Lucky for me, it went right through, front to back. I should have been more careful, but most Indians don't take to shooting shamans and medicine men. I knew that the chief and I had our differences, but not so as to try to kill me."

"The question is, did he *really* try to kill you, or was it actually a scheme or façade?" Will thought as he pulled on his blond mustache. "Maybe it happened just like he wanted. Who is the man Wanata hates the most of all of us? It sure isn't Potak, is it?"

"It's Levi if it's anybody. We all know what happened up by Fort Boise when he planned to ambush Beaver, but he wasn't smart enough. I always knew not killing that man when he had the chance was a mistake. Sometimes Levi forgives people too easily." The marshal turned and spat brown juice into the white snow to make a point.

"I don't think he ever forgave him," Will said. "I think that Levi was looking out for all of us. He worries about our hides more than he does his own."

"So, what's the plan?" Joseph asked. "I know *I'm* going after them. I'm not gonna let this stand."

"But don't you think it's best if you stay here and protect your boy?" Rusty removed his hat to block the sun and tell the time. "I know it's not your way, Joseph, but it ain't right for you to run off and leave your son alone with Potak again. Not when we know that the chief is up to no good."

The marshal grumbled. "I reckon you're right. I guess I can stay back here and make sure Potak continues to recuperate until you all get back. Do me a favor, Captain, and bring him back to me so I can strangle him with my bare hands. I got the feeling he took advantage of him being with the boy and planned all this to catch Baver out on his own."

"Lucky he's your wife's brother, or he may not have spared the boy if he is out there somewhere."

Rusty stuck his finger in his mouth, pried out a worn-out tobacco plug, and spat. "He might have lured Beaver off to God knows where so he and his boys could bushwhack 'im." Hopefully, he's still alive."

"I guess I unknowingly helped Wanata set the trap. I never guessed he would be that devious as to shoot me to trick Beaver. I know he is terribly jealous of Levi's fame since it dwarfs his, but he doesn't know what he's wishing for. I reckon it's time to get rough. It's time to put your brother-in-law in the ground, Joseph. You can't be part of this, or your wife will never forgive you. If my guess is right, they won't be expecting you to show up here looking for Beaver and the boy for a week or two more. By then, they'll have returned to the stronghold with nobody the wiser. At least, I reckon that was their plan."

Joseph gave Rusty a gruff look. It was hard for him to let Rusty go without him. The look on the marshal's face when the captain and Rusty rode out was almost comical. Clearly, he was torn between his duty to his family and the game of the chase. He had been hunting down outlaws most of his adult life and struggled not to go along anyway. Then again, he had come to love the small boy with a big heart and quick wit, so he knew he had to take care of his family responsibility first.

The medicine man pulled his bear coat tight across his shoulders to ward off the chill. He had lost weight, so the cold penetrated his body, making him shiver involuntarily. Still, his lips weren't purple any longer, and the color had returned to his face. He would be healthy enough to travel to the compound in a few more days. He could stay there for a spell longer to rest before they rode with him back to the Crow stronghold. That is, if they were all welcome after what they were about to do.

———

STILL, nobody knew for sure what was going on, but they suspected the obvious. There was no way that Will and Rusty would ever leave Levi behind, no matter the danger. They were betting their lives on their success.

The more they thought about it, the more certain they were that Wanata and his personal guard had taken him prisoner.

Rusty rode ahead, keeping an eye on the tracks, but they didn't have much trouble following Wanata's. He wasn't making it so obvious that it would be suspicious under normal circumstances. Still, now he had the feeling he was leaving too much track, making it impossible for Levi not to discover them and follow. At first, they were few and far between, but soon, they became reckless. The two mountain men could hardly see any sign of Beaver, but one was his best friend, and the other was his mentor, so they would track him over the mountains, through a jungle, and across a desert if necessary.

After a long day's ride, Rusty swung down from his saddle, pushed his fists into the small of his back, and arched away the stiffness. Will stayed seated hand over hand on the pommel as he searched the trail for signs of trouble. His Appaloosa stomped its feet and twitched its ears, whisking at flies with its tail.

———

THE FOLLOWING MORNING, an hour before dawn, they discovered where they were camping. A guard was out, but Rusty easily navigated them around him. "Let's get in front of them so they'll come to us. If we don't move a muscle, we should catch them by surprise. All we'll have to do is wait on them with our guns ready. It should be over before he realizes who it is. But remember, nobody kills Wanata unless it's unavoidable. I know he's brave, but he thinks too much of his life to take too many chances. This makes him weaker than us."

They watched the black specks that gradually grew as they came nearer. Eventually, the dark silhouette turned into six horses and riders. Two warriors rode point, and two were on drag with the prisoner in the middle. Another rider led the way. Rusty instantly knew it was Wanata by the way he sat on his Indian pony. Levi sat on the back of a small horse, dwarfing it with his feet nearly dragging on the ground. Fire blazed in Rusty's eyes like branding irons fresh from the fire. Just as they suspected, it had all been a trick.

Beaver's face was bruised and battered, but he wasn't the only one. Only Wanata didn't have a scratch on him, but his personal guard looked like they had been beaten with a stick. Levi had a large bump on his head, which was circled in black and blue skin. He had a sleepy daze in his eyes. It looked like someone had worked him over.

Stillness held heavy over the men sitting under snowdrifts as they watched the Indians approach, but they knew they were impossible to see. Rusty had covered the captain with snow, leaving a thumb-sized hole leading directly to the trail so he would see the riders, but they wouldn't see them. Rusty found a small snowdrift and wormed his way into the back, using a hollowed-out flute to pierce the wall so he, too, could see them coming without being discovered.

It was obvious that they were being careful, but it was also apparent that they didn't expect Rusty and the gang to have caught up with them yet. They probably believed they had another week or more before the dead body was discovered, so they rode lazily without rushing. Maybe it was Wanata who enjoyed seeing Levi all trussed up like a hog for the slaughter, and he wanted his enjoyment to last. He looked back every so often and smiled a wicked grin.

Levi's hands were bound together and to the saddle horn, and a rope ran under the small horse's belly, tied to each foot. As an added measure, he had a thick hemp rope wrapped several times around his chest, leaving his arms and shoulders immobile, making him less capable of escape.

When the sun neared the snow-covered horizon, a breeze stirred. It whispered through the trees, giving relief after the glaring white light of daylight.

A hint of a smile softened the straight lips of Rusty's mouth as he slowly let out a breath. He felt the weight of his revolvers in his hands. He was poised, ready to jump to his feet and take two deliberate shots, and Will would take the others. Only if forced would they kill Wanata right then and there. There were some questions they wanted to ask him before they sent him asunder.

They heard the soft squeak of saddle leather and the muffled sound of hooves clopping against the ground, making white puffs of snow. They watched as they neared, unaware they were being spied on. Rusty's and the captain's pistols were already cocked, so there would be no warning, however short. The Indians wouldn't even have the chance to defend themselves, but then again, they knew the consequences of messing with Rusty Steel's family—especially a man who had it in for Beaver for months.

Wanata's intentions were clear. He wanted Beaver dead and silenced forever. He held secrets that would damage the chief's position if the tribe's elders were ever to find out. The chief despised Levi even more for catching him out, being the bigger and better man, and allowing him to live, something the chief would have never done.

This time, that was what Wanata didn't intend to do with Johnson. He wanted to see the coyotes rip his body apart and the rodents eat his guts. He planned to tie him to stakes and watch his demise from the safety of a tree as his four guards kept watch while the scavengers of all species devoured him to the last finger and toe.

When the time came to shoot, Rusty clicked his tongue. Immediately after, four gunshots rang out, and four warriors tumbled off their horses and into the snow. Each one had a bullet hole in the middle of their hearts and was dead or dying before they hit the ground.

"Don't move a muscle, Chief, or it'll be the last move you'll ever make," Rusty growled. "Go ahead, fool, and make my day. I dare you to twitch a finger."

The blood drained from Wanata's face as his body went rigid. Four of his best men lay dead around him, and their horses had scattered to the wind. Frantically clopping hooves disappeared into the distance. Levi's horse was so overloaded it couldn't even run. It was as steady as a rock while under gunfire, but the chief's mount pulled and swung its head nervously, and then it reared, flattening its ears along its head.

Wanata nearly panicked and made a run for it, but another gunshot whizzed through his hair, and he pulled his Indian pony under control. His moment had appeared, but he had been too slow, and the White men were too fast, and now it was too late. He had been caught in the act. Failure was something that had never even crossed his mind. He was sure his plan was too clever to not work. Still, there he sat on his horse with three guns pointing at him, and both men were dying to pull the triggers. The cold look in the captain's deadly eyes made him involuntarily shudder.

LIFE & DEATH

ONCE BRENDA WAS FREED, SHE STILL DIDN'T KNOW WHERE to go or even what to do. The only place she knew to call home was with the people who had captured her. She didn't even know exactly where she was, except in a large valley surrounded by gigantic mountains. A light cover of snow had fallen in the last days, leaving everything white, but the temperatures still hadn't begun to fall. Soon, the heavy powder would accumulate several feet deep, and then it would get too cold.

When she neared the camp, nobody tried to stop her. They averted their eyes, acting like she wasn't even there. That was because they were terrified of what she represented. They now believed the devils that possessed her were who brought the Shoshone warriors to come and steal their women as revenge for them taking Brenda. For Indians, the spirit world was complicated, dark, and mysterious, and crazy people had one foot in each world, making them even more dangerous. Now, they all cursed Acha, even though he was already dead. He was the one who brought the witch to their stronghold, but the members were too scared to throw her out for fear of repercussions from the other side.

Their superstitious nature outdid all others in America. Not even Rusty Steel was so extreme in his beliefs. Others found these absurd, like Levi Johnson and Captain Forrester. They didn't have a superstitious bone in their bodies. Both agreed that this was their mentor's only fault. But then again, he had lived with the Flathead Indians for years and then became a blood brother of a Crow chief. It wasn't like he had converted from Christianity either because he still felt he was a staunch Christian, but he had let the ways of the Indians slowly brainwash him, mixing both beliefs when he found no logical answers.

Brenda had now been there for days since her husband's death. His other three wives disappeared with the Shoshone warriors during the raid. For the tribe, that was even more proof of her magical powers, and they believed that she had concocted all that had happened. She brought the enemy into their homes to get revenge for what they had done to her, and now they were paying the price.

So, now everybody in camp stopped what they were doing and looked away silently whenever Brenda walked by. All the tribe's members were worried about their futures, but they knew if they killed the crazy White woman, she might come back as an evil spirit, and things would get even worse. All they could hope was that at some point, she would disappear and go where all the other insane people went to die.

But to their surprise, instead, she claimed a cave a couple of miles from the Blackfoot camp and moved in for what appeared to be a permanent residence. The first days, she worked frantically, cutting limbs to make a cage-like door at the entrances since the fifteen-by-fifteen-square-yard new home was difficult to enter. He put smaller logs as crossbeams to close them securely against both local Indians and the wild animals scattered across the mountains, including mountain lions and grizzly bears.

She locked the beams in place with pigging string from the inside wall so it would be impossible for someone outside to reach the latches, tying them closed. As she brazenly walked through the Crow camp, she now felt the fear they held for her. No longer afraid, she took what utensils she needed from her dead husband and his three wives and supplied her new home.

None of the neighbors dared interfere. She had every right to what Acha owned as she was the last surviving wife. They would have never complained. They were too afraid to become one of her enemies with her living so close.

Even the Blackfoot medicine man was reserved in his comments. He was a knowledgeable shaman, but he knew he was no match for such a possessed White woman. He didn't even understand how normal White people thought.

Soon, the very adaptable Brenda Penny had all the comforts of home in her cave, and nobody dared to bother her. It was apparent she had installed herself permanently, and all the tribe could do was try to live with her presence and try not to insult or cross her.

They all knew the punishment for killing a possessed woman was much worse than tolerating her —especially since she had expressed no aggression to anyone in the tribe. They believe it was better to let a resting beast lie rather than wake something they would later regret.

Meanwhile, the smell of elk stew floated on puffs of air from the forbidden cave. Brenda was adapting fast, learning on her own to use her lance proficiency, and was currently learning to use a bow. She carried her perpetual Bowie knife on the side of her belt. She had taken it from her husband, Acha. It was his prized possession, and now it was hers. She went nowhere without it. With her newfound skills, she had no problem providing herself with food.

Strangely enough, some mornings, she would awaken and find baskets of offerings from the frightened people in the Indian stronghold. Some of them obviously believed that if they pleased her, when the judgment day came, they might be spared or even favored. Each person left a personal trinket, hoping she would have seen them wearing it as she made her daily strolls through the labyrinth of paths between fifty teepees.

Unfortunately, she was mentally rendered to a wild animal. The defense mechanisms in her brain had helped her adapt to her new environment in record time, but the blond-haired woman had slowly forgotten all that had happened before she was sold into the Blackfoot tribe. Her last memory was the warriors coming to kill her husband and kidnap her hated co-wives.

At night, she would climb the cliff above her new dwelling, sit on her haunches like a wild animal, and howl at the moon. None of these actions went unnoticed by the members of the tribe, and after a short time, they called her the Wolf Woman—part wolf, part human. For the tribe's members, she was quickly becoming a legend with invented stories in the Indian gossip depicting her doing the same things to other tribes for decades, long before she was born. Such was the imagination of the local tribes. Isolation from the world made them feel that only *their* beliefs were based on the foundation of truth.

Sadly, Brenda was so far gone by now that the chances that she could adapt to the White man's ways again were nonexistent. Most women who endured such treatment at the hands of the American Indians were never the same, and some didn't even acknowledge their families and friends. Their minds had blocked out the past as a safety measure to save the little sanity that remained.

What would happen if the medicine man, Potak, was good to his word and did find Money's mother? What would happen then would be anyone's guess. She might pop out of it at the mere sight of her child, or she might disregard him due to her life change. She possible could have completely forgotten her twin children and her dead husband. At this point, every eventual factor was unknown, and nobody could guess what would happen.

Only time would tell if Potak, hopefully with the help of Levi, the captain, and the small five-foot-tall boy, could find her and she would snap out of it and remember all that had happened and become the mother she once was. Of course, this was something that would bother Marshal Walker because he already loved him as his own, but he also knew that his blood mother would have all the rights in the world to little Money.

Lucky for him, he was tall for his age and appeared more like a ten—or eleven-year-old than his actual age of eight. In the short time since his father was killed, along with his twin brother, and his mother was sold, he had hardened unbelievably. With his sponge-like brain, he absorbed everything he was told or saw, knowing his life depended on it.

Time would tell if the boy and his mother ever rejoined again, but his friends seemed determined to see if they could find his mother. Potak alone could cross tribal borders without any repercussions. He was both respected and feared in all the valley tribes.

THE RESCUE

LEVI LOOKED UP INTO RUSTY'S EYES. "I FIGURED YOU'D come when we were gone for too long. I knew you'd find Potak and Money first, too, so I wasn't worried. I expected you boys to arrive and rescue me at some point, so I wasn't in a hurry. I've been thinking it was time to get to know our chief here a little better. When y'all rode up, I was just pondering on what Wanata's next move would be."

"We figured we'd run into Wanata, too, but Potak's wasn't very friendly about giving up the details," Will said. "He said he'd made a promise and claimed he couldn't break it."

"After someone shot Potak in the side, I knew he'd need a couple of weeks to mend before he could travel. That's why I left Money in charge. In hindsight, I reckon his pa, Joseph, might not have liked what I did too much, but it was the only way."

When Levi looked up and into Wanata's eyes, he could see how the hate surged, leaving them a fiery red.

Still, he didn't utter a word for fear of blurting out something he might be sorry for later.

"Are you all right, Levi?"

"Step down, boys, so you can all take a breather for the rest of the day. I've got plenty of food and firewood for us all, and there's a creek on the other side of that stand of trees. I believe I saw a few trout in there and all. The water is crystal clear. I reckon with Joseph taking care of Money and Potak, we don't have anything to worry about, but we shouldn't take too long to get back in case some fired-up warriors run across them."

Rusty nodded but didn't comment. He was still torn between killing Chief Wanata on the spot and waiting to hear what he had to say. Plus, he was already worn out, and they still had some country to cover before they could get back to the lean-to and could get Potak the attention he needed to mend properly. That meant getting him back to the compound.

"So, are ya gonna tell us what that fool chief had to say, Levi?" Rusty growled. "How dare he try to kidnap my apprentice and think he could get away with it. I know he's the one who shot Potak. I can see now he planned to ambush you by the tracks of his four dead guards. I figure that's all we've gotta know."

Levi twisted his body to face Rusty. "We've gotta remember the politics and whose land we're living on. Also, I wanna know the reason Wanata tried to kill Potak and if he really meant to finish him off, of which I'm not so sure. It would have been too easy to kill him while nobody was around. I think it's more complicated than it appears. That's why I just spent the last two days hashing it out, searching for a solution. Like I said,

Potak wouldn't say who did it, and now I wanna know the truth."

"It's time you coughed up what you know about all this," Rusty said as he eyed the chief. "Refusal to talk with such a flimsy excuse isn't gonna cut it. You're just postponing the inevitable future because, as far as I'm concerned, we're gonna play this out to the end whether you want us to or not. I won't stand around while my friend gets shot by anybody. He could have bled to death and died hadn't Money and Levi found him."

"By the by, how's the boy doing? How is he holding up through all this?"

"Just like everybody else. Doin' the very best that he can." Rusty grinned. "That boy is getting more like you every day, Levi. Don't worry about Money Penny. His father is with him, and I doubt the marshal will allow anyone to harm him without taking off his head first."

"For such a small fellow, he sure does have a hell of a big heart." Will gave them one of those crooked smiles he makes when he's pleased, which was rare. "Hopefully, he'll continue to grow like a weed, so he looks a little older. In my book, he could pass for ten, but with a couple of more inches, you'd believe he was twelve or so. The constant increase of cattle drives across the Oregon Trail has many young boys his age working cattle when the ranchers have a shortage of hands. Maybe we should buy him some spurs and chaps to look more the part."

"I don't like using steel spurs on my horses. I figure if your horse doesn't respond without them, you've done a shoddy job of training," Levi huffed as he touched the bump on his head and winged. "You don't need to cause the animal pain to get him to do what you want." Levi looked Will straight in the eye. "If and when he has some extra money, he'd be better served by buying another pistol. You'll find that you never can have enough guns or bullets in the wilderness. He's not learnin' to become a cowboy, anyway. He's gonna become a mountain man like us."

When they heard somebody trudging through the snow with a horse in tow, Rusty and Will swung around with their pistols in their hands. Levi with his long rifle, which he had retrieved from one of the dead Crow guards.

"From the drag marks and dried blood, I figure you have already killed the man who shot me," Potak said from the back of a travois. "He was one of the four that was going to set up the ambush. I must admit that the chief's intentions were bad. He intended to kidnap me and try to make it look like it was Blackfoot or Shoshone. For what purposes? I can't say because I don't know. The man lies through his teeth, so it's hard to weed out the truth. I have no idea what his plans were from then on, but he wasn't the one who pulled the trigger. I might be tight-lipped at times, but I don't ever out-and-out lie."

"So, why in the world didn't you tell me in the first place?" Levi asked, surprised.

Potak shook his head wearily, clearing his throat before speaking. "You would not have seen the difference between Wanata doing it and one of his men. One of his personal guards got scared when I turned my eyes to him and stared deep into his soul. He pulled the trigger on his muzzle-loader. I don't know if he did it in anger or fear, but it scared Wanata enough for him to panic and call it off. That's why he left me there to die. He didn't know what else to do. He's not the smartest chief I've ever met."

"Of course, he didn't consider taking you to camp to patch you up," the captain growled, pushing his hat from his forehead as he ran his knuckles across his mustache. Beard stubble populated his face. "As far as I can tell, he left you to bleed out."

Money ran for his dad and wrapped his arms around his waist, but they didn't reach. Still, the marshal patted him on the head and clucked soothingly. The boy's eyes were glued to the dead Indians on the trail.

They all studied the scene stoically beneath impassive eyes, imagining what had happened in their minds. On the ground at the chief's feet lay four dead bodies. The veins on the captain's temples pulsated like fuses as his jaws clamped, and he ground his teeth, and fury flared in his eyes. He had to fight the urge to swing his gun toward Wanata and shoot a bullet into his brain, ending all this once and for all.

———

THERE WAS little talk for the rest of the evening. Everyone was thinking about all that had happened and trying to figure out the puzzle. Why would Wanata want to start another war with the Blackfoot *or* Shoshone? Or was the motive something else entirely? So far, the chief wasn't talking. Especially with the famous medicine man lying on the travois before him.

After everyone else turned in, Levi sat perched on

the topmost rim of a hill like a misflown bird as he did night watch while the others caught a few hours of sleep. Beaver didn't seem to need much rest. As long as he had plenty of food, he would carry on all day *and* all night. He sat squatting on his haunches as he stared at the sky and listened to all the surrounding sounds, carefully identifying each and every one.

Under the moonlight, beclamored with yapping coyotes, amid cries of owls, a wolf lingered like a marionette from the heavens with his long mouth jabbering and saliva dripping from his jaws. His body stood before the moon's light as his silhouette continued to howl. The sound sent shivers up the night spines of anyone who heard it.

A retinue of wolves trotted silently in single file behind the pack's leader. The alpha male occasionally looked over his shoulder to ensure they followed. They cast long shadows in the silvery moonlight as they disappeared over the next ridge and vanished into the night.

Levi continued thinking about it all late into the night while sitting beneath the slow wheel of stars pulsating light years away. As the first sign of red showed on the skyline, they knew that their surroundings would be bathed in light in a few minutes.

Soon, the first hint of light showed on the eastern horizon as rays of red light wavered in the distance. The sun climbed into the sky like it was on a fishing line as it reeled heavenward. At first, it appeared to move quickly, only to stall and continue to climb slowly into the clear blue sky.

As soon as they finished breakfast, Levi stood and said, "Don't just stand there like twelve o'clock half-struck. Get those horses saddled, and let's get on our way." He scraped his boot along crumbly earth, kicking snow onto the fire, making it hiss as smoke rose heavy and thick for seconds.

When they finally pulled out and headed home, a dust cloud followed them like a dog chasing a rabbit. They squinted through the morning glare from the cover of sparkling snow and the end of the trail. As they rode, Levi and Rusty took turns slipping off their horses to their hands and knees and putting their ears to the ground to listen for Indian ponies.

Once they got moving, Levi took point. For a second or two, he was a barely visible blur, and then he would disappear into the next shadow, horse and all. Even though Beaver had already surpassed his mentor's skills, only Rusty knew where he was. Despite knowing Johnson was out front, they rode cautiously from cover to cover without a sound cutting the stillness.

They rode slowly under the windless rays as they reflected off a blanket of white. They had to keep from moving too fast to ensure Potak's wound didn't start bleeding again. As Levi scouted out front, he made no more noise than an alighting bird. They couldn't hear him, but still they knew he was there.

They crossed before the sun, vanishing over a hill one by one. When they reappeared, they were black dots on the horizon.

Under the bright sun, the shadows of the horses' legs were like elongated sticks, leaving animals and riders painted black on the ground. The shaman removed his eye shield, which was made of a crow's wing and a rosary of fruit seeds. Strange trinkets clicked from bracelets on his wrists.

A faint wisp of black smoke curled skyward in a line so thin it was nearly invisible as the smell of woodsmoke filled the air. Now, they were on home ground and almost home. It was the meridian of the day when they arrived and rode through the north gate of the brick-and-rail fence.

WANATA'S ESCAPE

THE CROW CHIEF STOOD TIED TO A TREE AS HE SNORED lightly. He had been hanging there for the entire afternoon as Levi, Rusty, Will, and Joseph argued about what to do with him. The captain believed it was time to take his life before he took the life of one of them or innocent others, and the way things were going, they probably wouldn't have too long to wait. He had a nervous tic when he was riled. He drummed his fingers on the wrapped grip, making it rattle in his metal sheath.

After a hard day's ride, they stopped to rest and had a heated debate about whether the chief lived or died right there with Wanata watching. His wide eyes showed his level of fear. Every time the captain got near him, he traced his face and neck with the tip of his saber. Wanata was convinced he would feel the cold steel enter his body at any moment, or it may even lob off his head. Above all, he feared the captain the most. He knew he could kill him without blinking an eye and only refrained due to the arguments of the others. Every time he looked at him, he felt like he was seeing his own demise.

Rusty Steel had another plan, though. He wanted to scare the daylights out of the chief, warding him off in the future. He knew if they killed him, there would be hell to pay, and they might find themselves being escorted from their compound on Beartooth Mountain. If they somehow let him escape while believing they truly intended to take his life, hopefully, it would ward off future schemes to harm or kill one of Rusty's clan members. After losing his four best guards, the other warriors would walk on eggshells. They knew that things in the tribes could change from one day to another because of a silly mistake.

When they let him down, Wanata lay beside the fire with one eye swollen shut and both top and bottom lips split. When their backs were turned, the captain used his sleeved saber to beat some sense into him, but was stopped by Beaver, his best friend. But he was still conscious and listened to every word said during the last hours. He knew his life depended on it. At first, he was too dazed to enter the conversation, but later, as his head cleared, he wasn't sure what to do. Had they let him live, hoping that he would change his ways? But now, the chief had tried to kill one of their friends after his failing attempt to murder Levi. Now they were going through the same thing again, but Beaver meant this to the last, no matter what they had to do, including killing the chief. The thought had crossed all their minds, even if only fleetingly.

"Give me one good reason why I shouldn't run him through with my saber right here and now, Levi. Just say the word, and I'll take his ugly head off. Had you not stopped me, I'd have beaten him to death."

Wanata's mouth opened and closed like a goldfish in a glass bowl. He tried to swallow, but his mouth was too dry. Blood stained the white snow red where their dead bodies lay. His foolish plan had cost all four of them their lives, maybe even his own. However, his hatred for the medicine man and Levi Johnson was such that he appeared to lose his senses and took many more risks than he should have.

"Remember who I am," Wanata warned before losing his last bit of courage. He was shocked when he realized his voice wavered and sounded shaky, and his hands trembled as he spoke. When he turned his eyes on the captain, he quickly had to turn them away.

He wasn't sure of himself without his warriors to protect him and knew that he had pushed Beaver too far. He looked from Levi to the marshal and back to Rusty again. Each one glared at him as if he were already dead. That last glance led him to believe he had made his ultimate and final mistake. The chief suddenly realized his own stupidity was to blame.

After all he had experienced, seen, and heard, he had underestimated these men yet *again*. It came to him like a hot kiss at the end of a wet fist. He had never had a chance with such mountain men, but he was too full of ego and cynicism that he didn't see the truth until it was too late. Now he was going to pay for his sins.

The day moved into a fast-falling gloom. The dimness clung close to the ground as the air continued to dry. Wanata's feelings matched the weather. He felt all damp and moldy but with a chill to his bones. His self-confidence had been shattered.

Beaver looked at Wanata with sternness. "I'm afraid you're gonna have to die for what you've done, Chief. I let you live once, only to have you come for me again. Haven't you learned anything during this time? It would appear not, so I suppose it's too late. Now I see it clearly. You'll never change your ways."

"I give you my word. I won't try to kill you again, Beaver."

All six foot seven towered over the Indian as his black hair and beard fell across his face, making him look more like a wild animal than a man. "Your word is worthless to me. You begged for your life last time, too, and I let you live only to regret it. At least we will have killed you before you can cost one of us our lives. You're a reckless man, Wanata. What are your people gonna do when they find out you shot your own medicine man and tried to kill me, again? What will the elders sing in their songs after you're gone, or will the tribe be forbidden to speak your name?"

"You can't treat me like this! I'm the chief of this mountain, not you, Rusty Steel! You and your kind are barely tolerated. If I had my way, you would be run off immediately, and I would forbid any of your kind to trespass on our land on the threat of death. I believe that all White men should be run off our land."

Rusty looked at the chief and spat a brown stream of juice at his feet, speckling his moccasins. "That's because you've changed as a man after Chief Hachta died. He told us what he wanted when he passed, but you're not holding up your end of the bargain. He would turn over in his grave if he knew what you were doing. You're not honoring his agreement with me and Levi like your leader had wished. Now, because of you, we are always on guard. Can't you see that now we cannot allow you to live? You've forced our hand, and now it's too late."

"You might be boss around your compound, but you are not in this part of the mountain. Once you left the stronghold and came all the way up here, you entered no-man's-land," Wanata snarled. "How long do you think you'll last even if I were to say you could go? Blackfoot warriors come up here, too, and at times, Nez Percé and Shoshone. I'm sure they would love to run into some White men for a little campfire party, and you will all be the ones on pickets. Everyone in the stronghold knows who you all are. Do you think you could hide? And you all out here all on your own with a hundred warriors on your trail. I think this is a message and a gift from their gods. The Crow spirits always come to their leaders when in need."

The captain chuckled at the chief and said, "I've got a better idea than shooting him. Why don't we personally deliver him to the Blackfoot Indians? If we have Potak with us, they won't dare kill us. He has a free pass to visit all the tribes. At one time or another, he's helped them all. Who knows, they might reward us for bringing them their direst enemy. Then we won't be the ones who kill him. We can say we heard he was found alone out here by hostile warriors, and they carted him off, and we can all walk away without a guilty conscience. What do you say about that idea, Chief? How would you like to visit your worst enemy, tied hands and feet, and with no weapons to defend yourself?"

The captain threw a loop over the Crow Indian's head and pulled it tight, trapping his arms at his sides. Will jerked the rope around Wanata, dragging him to the ground. He pushed himself to his feet, swearing before he remembered his current situation, then bit his lip. He was so used to striking out without repercussions that it slipped out before he could stop.

"You're just digging a deeper grave, Wanata. Keep it up, and I'll think of something worse to do to you. What were you gonna do to Levi? Maybe you can tell us, and we'll do the same to you."

"He said he was gonna tie me to stakes face up so the scavengers could get to my soft belly. He said he was gonna sit in a tree overhead and watch as the buzzards and crows pick my eyes out and the coyotes and rodents tear me apart. That's what he said he had planned for me. How's that sound to you, boys? I'd feel a lot better not having someone else have the pleasure of finishing him off when we deserve every minute. Why don't we do to him what he was going to do to me while we watch him from a tree?"

———

THAT NIGHT, the mountain men sat around discussing the current Indian situation as they got deeper into their whiskeys. Money fell asleep hours before. He was dead tired from the ride and all the tension. They passed the corn liquor ceramic jug around until it was empty. Finally, the marshal, captain, and Levi called it a night. Joseph held the jug up in the air over his mouth as the last three drops fell onto his tongue, and he smacked his lips. They slouched on their bedrolls, and shortly after, they were all three snoring from the liquor-induced sleep. Rusty moved his feet like he was having a dream.

All the while, as Wanata carefully watched, he twisted his arms to see if the binding was too tight to wiggle free, but it was impossible to remove, even with his teeth. The hemp rope was rough and thick. But he found the bindings on his feet a shoddy job, like the man who tied him was too confident that he wouldn't escape. It took half an hour, but he managed to chew through the hemp like a trapped rat. That one lucky break was all Chief Wanata needed to sneak away into the night.

A few minutes later, the first hint of daylight appeared in the eastern sky. Twinkling stars hovering overhead began to roll back like a dark-blue glowing carpet westward until it went out of sight and onto another part of the world. Wavery red light showed as the first rays stretched across the sky, creating a prism of colors on the rim of the world. Finally, the fiery globe exploded into yellow light, quickly rising into a cloudless sky.

A wildcat roared in the distance on his way home after a long night of hunting. Brewer's sparrows, roosting in stunted shrubs and krummholz near the tree lines, spooked, fleeing the trees like dragon-like clouds swirling through the sky. A string of six wolves crossed a nearby ridge to their deep dens for the night. They scurried away before the heat of the day arrived.

Levi was the first one to start chucking. When he pushed his buffalo blanket off, it revealed he had two guns hidden in his fists, with the hammers cocked and ready to fire. The captain sat up, his saber in his white-knuckled fists. The expression on his face was that of disappointment accompanied by a frown. He wanted his moment with the Crow chief, but knew it wouldn't be today.

"It rubs me raw to let that fool brother-in-law of mine walk away scot-free when what we should have done is string him up like the outlaw he really is."

"It would be too easy for them to discover it was us, and that is something we can't let happen. That would mean an all-out war with the Crow Nation, not just the stronghold on Beartooth Mountain," Will whispered.

"You and your clan could never survive such attacks. At least, it is still a local issue with a man we have a lot of dirt on," Potak added. "He also knows that now Levi means business. I doubt he thought for a moment we planned to let him get away. I'm sure he thought he was going to die. With his ego, he's convinced that he outsmarted us. All the better. He'll think he has a handle on things, so he shouldn't start any more trouble, but we'll be waiting and watching for him when the time comes.

"What I want to know is why he didn't kill me. I admit I've seen him shoot that old musket, and he's not much of a shot, but at such close range, he must be blind, too. Either that or it was all in a plan we've yet to see play out. Even if he was a bad shot, he could have shot me twice. I was down, but he had plenty of time to reload. He knew he hit me in the side and that it probably wouldn't kill me, at least not for a few days. Maybe he couldn't pull the trigger while looking me in the eyes. I doubt the shock of what he did shook him up so much, although his face did go quite pale."

"Maybe that was the chief's plan. To let you suffer out here with no food or water until the scavengers get you. Hadn't Levi found you, you'd have been more food for the coyotes and the vultures." The marshal hooked his thumbs on his gun belt as he grumbled. He moved his chew to the other cheek and spat. His jaw was so full his lips hardly moved.

"So, what do we do now?" the captain asked as he rubbed his beard stubble and frowned.

"We need to get Potak back to the compound where we can keep him a couple of weeks inside beside a fire. The nights are beginning to get chilly now, and it wouldn't do if he got a cold or even worse, pneumonia. With Virgil tending to him and the strange green powders and powerful-smelling oils he puts on it, it'll heal well enough. Angus can help him gain weight again. I'd hate for him to arrive back in the stronghold like this. The Crow people will see him as weak and would suspect that something happened. I wonder what excuse Wanata's gonna have when the medicine man shows up in camp."

The men suddenly remembered little Money sitting by his adopted father's side. None of them remembered him being there, so he heard some things he probably shouldn't have.

Levi pulled Rusty to one side and whispered, "I don't know if this boy seeing so much violence is good for him."

"Seeing so much bloodshed isn't good for me or you either, but this is the life we chose, so we will have to play the cards we're dealt with like we always do."

"I know he's young, but after what happened to his ma and pa right before his eyes, I doubt that much will shock him anymore. He's already gone through the test of fire." The marshal ruffled his yellow hair, making the boy frown, but the marshal didn't notice.

"You weren't all that much older when you think about it, Levi. Remember, ten years old back in Indiana, you were a lot younger than many a man out here. Even at that age, you had your grit tested, especially if you came by way of Comanche country. All that experience turns boys into men despite the size of their bodies. If the young boy wants to be the best, there he is, just like you wanted. The younger he starts in earnest, the better. How old were you when you started to hunt in the forests by the Ohio River? If I remember right, you told me you were eight when your pa gave you your first shotgun, too."

"We might as well get started with the sun already up and all. The sooner we return home with our Tonkawa friend, the better chance he'll have of a fast and full recovery," Levi replied. He knew Rusty was right, even if the marshal wasn't convinced. Still, *he* respected his son's desires, even though his mother and he didn't see eye to eye on the matter.

"You stay there on that travois, and you'll be fine. The first part of that old path is a tad rocky, but it won't last for long. We'll have you in the girls' hands before you know it." Rusty's eyes softened when he spoke to the medicine man.

"Wait a minute," Potak said as he reached out with his bony arm. "I promised Money that I would try to find his mom if she was alive."

"Until you're well, you're in my charge," Rusty growled. "Put it out of your mind. It's been a spell now, so it won't make any difference if we go ten days or so from now. She's already been in the camp for weeks on end. But when the time comes, we can go and have a look anyway. We'll have to wait until Potak is ready to ride that far if we wanna go to the Blackfoot camp in Yellowstone Valley. If we go on our own, they'll kill us for sure. There ain't any lost love between them and us White men. I'm sorry, Potak, there just ain't any other way. We can't go it alone because they'll shoot us on sight without you."

In an hour, they were gone. Now, they weren't trying to cover their tracks because with the mule pulling the travois that carried Potak, a blind man could follow them with his hands. Soon, the traverse's wooden frame scraped against the rock trail and the horses' clops were heard in the distance. Little by little, the sound vanished as they disappeared.

————

THEY COULD HEAR old Dog howling long before they could see the thin line of smoke rising from the main cabin's chimney. Then came the piercing ringing of Angus's dinner bell echoing off the canyon walls. They were a stone's throw away from home.

"I never knew that thing made such a racket way the heck out here." Rusty huffed. "That's enough noise to wake the dead. We might wanna stop that so everybody that passes by doesn't know who we are and where we live."

"Be my guest to inform Angus about that little change in his habits.," Will laughed. "I can't even imagine what kind of fit he'd throw. I don't know if he loves that bell or if he's just trying to be mean to us with all the racket."

"I reckon he likes that dinner bell more than his guns." Marshal Walker chuckled. "I think it's because he knows it annoys us, and he can get away with it because he's such a good cook. The alternative is to return to Rusty's cooking, but none of us wants that."

"I'm not all that bad of a cook," Will added. "We wouldn't have to suffer Rusty's cooking."

"He *is* better than Rusty—it's pretty hard to be worse." Marshal Walker laughed and winked at the compound mentor.

"I can hear every word you're sayin', people. Don't you know you cut me to the quick with your criticism?" Rusty asked. "Why to hear the way you all talk likes to break my heart. I did the best I could, and nobody died, did they?"

"Yeah, but all you know how to make are beans and hot cakes. A man can live on it, but you might die from boredom quicker than starvation. Angus is the best cook on the mountain, bar none. Isn't that right?" Marshal Forrester nodded as he laughed, pulling his horse to a stop at the main cabin porch. Will and Rusty helped Potak off the travois and inside. The women saw he was wounded and raced to help

"Thank ya, Virgil" Angus replied. "At least you really value me. How about I cook a special dessert for you tonight, Money? But just for you and me, boy. Let these complainers eat store-bought licorice while we have a treat. How do you fancy that, son? I bet you'd help me eat a whole blackberry pie, wouldn't ya."

"But blackberry pie is my favorite," the marshal complained like a little boy being punished.

"You can't have your cake and eat it too," Angus retorted.

"And what the heck is that supposed to mean? We

all said you were the best cook, didn't we? We were only sayin' Rusty can't cook."

"It's too complicated for your delicate little brain, Marshal. Let your boy have a treat that's just for him. It'll make him feel special."

"And I imagine you're gonna eat the pie too, ain't cha, Angus?" the marshal asked.

"Of course, I am. Mmm...can you smell it, Marshal?"

The old lawman involuntarily let his nose follow the smell toward the back of the kitchen until Angus rapped his knuckles with a large wooden spoon.

"Mind your manners, or you'll go without dinner, too."

AN UNUSUAL WELCOME

EVEN THOUGH THE RIDERS CAME IN TIRED AND WERE ALL worried about Potak's wound busting open and bleeding again, they were surprised when they met a man whom most had only read about in the newspapers. A stranger was sitting in Levi's chair at the head of the table as the women, Virgil, and Angus hung onto his every word. They could tell the story's intensity when the only one to turn around upon their arrival was Money's Crow Indian mother, Bar-Chee.

She jumped up, knocking her chair over as it clattered to the wooden floor, and turned and ran for her boy. She pulled him out of his saddle while the men tried to figure out what was going on. She, too, ruffled his yellow hair as tears ran down her dark red cheeks. She didn't notice when Money's neck went red with embarrassment, but the men were all focused on the visitor.

"Ain't y'all even interested in our return?" Rusty complained before he realized who was sitting in his chair. "Here we've been gone for days rescuing Levi,

Money, and Potak, and y'all ain't got nothin' to say? We're in a hurry to have the medicine man mended before he loses too much blood, and we end up where we began."

"Tend to your horses, boys," Angus replied without even looking. "We're in the middle of a story. Don't worry, we'll still be here when you get done." His best friend didn't even turn his head, barely acknowledging his presence.

They rode their horses the short distance to the stable. They always tended to the animals first, especially after such a hard ride. Pulling off their saddles and harnesses, they let their mounts tiredly clop into the corral, where their companions came over to check out any new smells and welcome them back.

They unslung the travois and helped Potak to his feet. At first, he wobbled but then got his balance. Fresh blood contrasted with the white bandages Rusty had wrapped around his waist. The Tonkawa Indian limped when he walked, but he was far from dead. Now, they had reached the compound and knew he would be up and around soon enough now that the danger had passed.

At first, Steel shot the stranger a suspicious look while raising a questioning eyebrow. Nobody sat in his chair when he was in the compound. Rusty was still the figure leader of the clan, even if Levi took charge of most of everything else. Then it dawned on him who it was, and a grin grew across his face from ear to ear. He blinked his eyes like he wasn't quite sure who he was looking at.

The last Rendezvous was back in 1840. Back then, Kit traveled with the likes of Jim Bridger and Old Bill

Williams. They were some of the many frontiersmen trapping beavers in the vast mountains. That was before he began working for John Charles Frémont on three 1847expeditions and became famous.

"Well, I'll be. Is that Kit Carson sitting at our table? Where in the world did you come from? And all alone, I take it?" Rusty was so pleased he couldn't hold back his laughter. "Why, you're a sight for sore eyes, Kit. I heard you were there when I won the shootin' match when Fred Country oversaw the Rocky Mountain Fur Trading Company and sponsored the shootin' match prizes. These here are my men too."

"So, you're the leader of this fine group of people, are ya, Rusty? No need to mister me, friends. All my pals call me Kit, you know that. It's a pleasure to meet you. Your friends here have told me a lot about you."

"Virgil, get over there and tend to Potak. He's been shot. He needs some serious doctoring," Levi said. "I've got him this far, so he's in your hands now. You're as close to a sawbones as we've got. There seem to be no internal injuries, so you should be able to handle him fine."

"Nothing life-threatening, I hope," Virgil replied. "Why, you look like death rolled over, Potak. Let me help you to my cabin and onto the spare cot. I'll build a fresh fire, so you don't get a chill. We're gonna have to tend to that wound before you bleed to death. Is it a bullet wound or what?" Virgil helped the medicine man down from the travois.

"Musket shot," Potak huffed. "It went all the way through, so I don't have lead poisoning, and nothing inside feels busted, so there's no bullet to dig out."

"I would imagine there's plenty of dirt and mud in

there, though. How many days have you been riding, anyway?"

"It's been a while," Rusty replied. "Probably too many days of riding, but it couldn't be helped under the circumstances. We found Potak and the boy, then had to hunt down Beaver. He was trackin' the folks that shot the Tonkawa medicine man. You know how he is. Once he gets the scent, he's like a hound dog, and it's almost impossible to call him off."

Virgil Lovejoy wasn't only the Christian spiritual guide for the clan, with his occasional Bible lessons and grace before most meals if he caught his friends in time. He was also the compound doctor—degreeless, of course. Potak continued to cover his wound with his green, smelly powder, but first, his Black friend had to clean the wound properly and wash it out with distilled alcohol.

"Anyway, I believe it's best that it opened again. It needs to be cleaned out properly with dispenser spirits and sewn up with catgut. Those old musket balls leave jagged holes. Rusty will suffice as a field medic in a pinch, but he's a long way from being a doctor. Now, I don't claim to be that knowledgeable either, but I can take care of most broken bones, arrows, or bullet holes if they ain't hit an organ. Come on now, let's get you inside, horizontal, and cleaned up. Help me out with him, Marshal."

"But I wanna see who this Carson fella is. Have one of the women help ya."

"It can wait!" Virgil snapped, surprising the marshal into action. "First, let's take care of our friend. Mr. Carson seems to be a long-winded fella with lots of stories to tell. There'll still be plenty to hear when we get back. First, we've gotta tend to our friend. Then comes the yarns."

He shoved his small and tattered Bible into his shirt, and then Joseph grabbed the medicine man's other shoulder as they guided him inside the second cabin while the others hurried across the worn path to the main cabin. It was twice the size of the other. It was where they sought refuge when hostile Indians came snooping around and had saved them countless times from warriors from all tribes. A group of White men living in the middle of the wilderness stood out like a bunny rabbit in a den of vipers.

Rusty took three strides across the porch with Levi right behind him, their arms outstretched for a friendly handshake. Beaver levered his arm like a hand pump from a water well. Kit grinned at the friendly welcome.

"Pleased to meet cha, Kit. I'm Levi Johnson, and this here is my partner, Captain Will Forrester. That big fella helpin' Virgil is Marshal Joseph Walker. I reckon you know everybody else. When did you arrive? I must say that this comes as quite a surprise."

"Rusty and Angus, I know from coinciding in the Rendezvous back when I was still a trapper. Steel and I have known each other for years, although not well. Right now, I'm working on an outline of how to improve paths across the Oregon Trail. But I got tired of life in Fort Boise. Every time I go there, it's twice as big. I reckon soon it's going to develop into a city. I've been in this part of the country before, but it's been a long spell, and I figured it was high time I came to revisit Yellowstone Valley. Once I got that far, it only seemed reasonable to climb a mountain so I could get a better look at the country from a higher perspective. I must say, it's one of the most beautiful places I've ever laid my eyes on. Unlike most other places, it ain't changed a bit."

Kit took a moment to sip his coffee to wet his tongue. Since he arrived, they hadn't stopped asking him questions and details about stories they'd read. For them, Carson was the epitome of a frontiersman and had done just about everything they ever dreamed of doing. Still, they had no idea what was yet to come.

"I even got to see one of those geysers once I reached the Yellowstone Plateau. When all that hot water blew up from out of the ground, I nearly fell off my horse. To be honest, I just ran into your compound by accident, although I had heard that a group of White folks lived somewhere up here. I figured it must be Rusty, Angus, and Mountain Dennis. At least that was what Charlie Fox said from McKay's saloon back in Fort Boise. Then again, there must be more folks than you. I've been watching folks heading west for a few years now, but with each passing day, they come in larger numbers. I wouldn't be surprised if the whole country isn't settled in five or ten years at the rate things are going." He shook his head, showing he thought it was a shame.

"Mountain Dennis passed last year, may God rest his soul. As far as I know, there are no other White folks living up here. Sure, the buffalo hunters come through during the season, but they stay together and try not to upset the Indians any more than they're doing shooting their food and hides," Levi replied.

"Not here on Beartooth Mountain, there ain't any other White folks that I know of. There used to be a couple of fellas halfway down Beartooth Mountain, but they're dead," Rusty huffed, then made the sign of a cross and kissed his thumb. "The only way to survive here for a long stay is if you're in numbers and have a solid cabin to protect yourself from hostiles, bad weather, and wild animals. It's not easy getting permission to stay and even harder to keep it, especially of late."

"Back when we first got here, fifteen years ago or so, we had a grand relationship with the Crow, who had a large stronghold a half-day ride up the mountain," Virgil explained. "The old chief, Hachta, and Rusty were blood brothers, but when he died, things began to get complicated, and we found ourselves having to sort our arrangements out more often. As a matter of fact, the trip we just came from had something to do with that. And that's with three of us having Crow wives, one of 'em is even the new chief's sister. The one with the boy there. You'd think that would make a difference, but it doesn't."

"Ya don't say. I'm lucky like that. I ride in a big procession of mapmakers, scouts, botanists, biologists, and half a dozen more specialists, of one thing or another. Then, of course, they've gotta have guards with so many greenhorns running around the wilderness. Then there are the jobs like I have now, where I am all alone with nobody to look out for, which is my preference. Since I'm a pretty good tracker and know how to cover my presence, I'm rarely discovered if I don't want to be. I reckon once I get back, they'll make a fuss about this trip too. They seem to raise a ruckus every time I have something new to report. Fame isn't something that I'm comfortable with. To be honest, I'd rather just get on with the job. Knowing new things is satisfaction enough for me without all the fuss."

"I never thought about fame that way." Rusty pulled

his hat off, holding it up to block the sun. "I thought all famous people were fine with all the attention. Now that I think about it, I can see how it might not be all it's made out to be. I doubt I'd like folks badgering me everywhere I went."

"Why, I've had people walk in on me to ask me questions when I was in an outhouse. It left me speechless. It's much better to travel to a country where you're not known too much. Then you don't have people you don't even know taking such liberties."

"So, how did all this happen?" Captain Forrester asked. "When you discovered you were famous, I mean."

"To be honest, Captain, I have no idea. One night, I went to sleep, and everything was normal, but when I woke up the next day, my life had changed. All because of a picture and article on the front page of a bunch of penny press newspapers named Quincy Daily Morning Courier. From that day on, I've had no peace. Mind you now, it don't bother me answering you and your friends' questions because we come from the same stock. Rusty and I go way back. Frontiersmen have always been big storytellers, especially around a nice campfire, and I appreciate that. I reckon Rusty, Levi, Joseph, and the captain will also have a few tall ones to tell *me*. But that's something altogether different. We're friends, and the others were all strangers."

Carson was a man of medium height with broad shoulders and a deep chest. He had steady blue eyes, frank speech, and was generally unassuming. He had thinning hair and was clean-shaven, save for a mustache.

"Are those deerskin clothes you're wearing?" Captain Forrester asked.

"Yep. When I cure them, I leave them outside to freeze so they get stiff enough to reflect most arrows—especially when you're discovering unexplored trails. It saved me from a puncture wound on more than one occasion. In my business, hostile Indians are a constant. Especially if they're Blackfoot. I kill every one of them rascals that I can find. I believe they're the most violently aggressive, hostile Indians in all the West, except maybe the Comanche. Even the Apache are more trusting and they're a dangerous lot. I've traveled from the West Coast in California to Washington, DC, and have seen all kinds."

Money sat as mute as a tailor's mannequin with his eyes spread wide as he took in every word and filed it in the memory banks in his mind. Thunder muttered somewhere in the distance as heat wavered on the horizon. Now, everyone from the compound was sitting around the table as they listened to one tale after another, each member contributing. Since there were only twelve chairs, the boy sat on his father's lap, although he suddenly felt too big for such things.

CLEANING THE SOUL

A WEEK AFTER THEY ARRIVED, POTAK WAS ALREADY UP and around. With help, he and Money were building some sort of structure at the back of the compound on the other side of the entrance beside the graveyard. Over a dozen crosses blessed the lush green grass freshly covered in half an inch of snow. Summer was still attempting to survive the inevitable. Soon, fall and winter would come and destroy all the greenery that the long summer had taken to grow. Then everything would turn blinding white.

Now snow fell from the trees' bows, and the first cover showed on the cabins' roofs. The dog's tracks ran a ring around the brick-and-rail fence as he made a big show of protecting the compound. Not a sound got by the old hound. He was the first to hear them returning, even though shortly later Rusty's sensitive nose scented cooking food and woodsmoke.

"Come on, Money," Potak said as he walked with a staff to keep his weight off his bad side. "I am going to teach you how to make something you will enjoy like most Indian boys."

"But I'm not an Indian boy. You know that, Potak."

"You are already more of a young Indian than you will ever imagine. I see things in you that others don't. You are like an imprint of Levi Johnson, but imagine the difference. Beaver has only been here in the wilderness for five years and fought his way across the West for another. You are eight, soon to be nine, and have your whole life ahead of you. Who knows the limits of such a young man who starts his life so early? As you grow up in the forest, you will not have White man's ways drummed into your head before you can understand the good of both races of man through the ways of my people. I like Levi's plan to keep a sharp eye on your progress. We both have many things to show and teach you. First, I will teach you to build something enjoyable, which makes you feel good *and* improves your health."

"And what's that, Potak?"

"Wait, and you will see. First, we must build a lean-to with walls and a tight door. Then, we will pack the cracks in the wall with mud. You will be surprised how handy this will be in the middle of winter. We can get plenty of smooth stones from the creek bed, and Rusty has plenty of firewood cut and stacked."

"I have no idea what you're talking about, but tell me what to cut and how long you want it. I'm good at following orders, and I'm a willing worker. I might not be as fast as you, but I'm young and don't tire."

————

THE FOLLOWING DAY, as the sun sat squat on the edge of the world, steam streamed out of the hot box's door when Potak and Money entered. At first, the steam was so thick that the boy couldn't see his hand before his face. Then his eyes adjusted, and he navigated toward the glowing coals. A wooden water bucket stood in the corner. As soon as they were seated, Potak spooned a ladleful and poured it over the hot stones. Steam rose in waves, making them both break into profuse sweat.

"This takes all the poison from your body and makes you cleaner than you have ever been. It also relaxes your mind and soul. It is good for everything that ails you."

"I don't know how long I can take it. It's getting hard to breathe, Potak."

"Wait a little longer. Close your eyes, relax, and let the heat do its magic."

"Magic?" Money asked.

He closed his eyes as he was told and tried to relax. It came easier than he ever imagined. As his breathing steadied, he smelled the eucalyptus bark the medicine man was always burning from some faraway trees he had never seen and, before him, had never even heard of.

"Are you ready?" Potak asked, breaking him out of his trance-like state.

The medicine man grabbed his hand, pushed the door open, and pulled him as he hobbled. Before Money knew it, they were plunging into the icy water of the freshwater stream just behind the compound.

"It doesn't feel cold at all," Money cried gleefully as he splashed in the icy water. "This is fun. Let's go back and do it again."

The shaman held his side but smiled despite the pain. He was amazed at how fast the boy learned everything he was taught.

A Promise Kept

Two weeks later, Potak miraculously recovered and was at the point where he wanted to keep a promise he had made to Money back when they were waiting to be rescued. He had sworn he would try to find his mother, be it for better or for worse, and the shaman didn't give his word lightly. Even though he knew that sometimes it was best to put some things behind you and let life take its course—especially when it involved a captured White woman in any of the Indian tribes. But he had given his word, and there were two things he never broke: his word or his stones.

With rare exception, captured Indian women were treated poorly and were usually hated by the other wives just because they saw them as weak and different, having an immediate mistrust for the unknown, especially if they happened to be White. The women were outsiders, and for the men, something to use like a toy until they tired and became bored. Of course, there were some cases of true love between Indians and whites. But usually, when someone was kidnapped, as was normally the case, things didn't go well for the captive, even if they managed to survive.

All this Potak knew, but for some reason, he felt compelled to find out the truth as a favor for this unusual, young, but remarkable boy. Somehow, he knew that he had to discover the truth so that he could put it behind him, forget what had happened, and get on with his life. The shaman felt Money could only do good if he put that one knowing question safely into the darkest recesses of his mind and got on with his life. A boy didn't see his mother as gone until it was confirmed, and he knew it chewed at his stomach and gnawed on his brain because he didn't have an answer.

Potak planned to provide this to him whether he was ready for it or not. Somehow, he knew it was important for his progress as Levi's apprentice. Plus, when the Tonkawa Indian made a promise, as long as he was alive, he kept his word no matter what the risks. That didn't mean that they would find her because she might have been killed weeks ago. It was hard to say how each captive fared. It all depended on how lucky they were in their lottery ticket of men. Since they had no choice in the matter, they had to make do with what they were given, be it fair or not.

That morning at breakfast, Potak surprised everyone by saying, "So, who's going with me to find Brenda Penny? Money and I plan to leave as soon as we finish breakfast. I made him a promise while he was taking care of me, and I intend to keep it. He kept his word and stood by my side, never shying away from danger, and I plan to return the favor."

"Whatcha mean you and Money are gonna go and find his ma? Don't you remember she was bought by a

Shoshone warrior? I doubt they'll take too kindly to us showing up and reclaiming something they believe is theirs. I know it sounds hard because it is. These situations rarely work out, though. You know as well as I do this might turn out to be a bad idea. Why, you know, White women don't fare well while captive in Indian camps."

"Does that mean you're going with us?" The hint of a smile curled the edges of the Tonkawa's dark lips. "Who else is going to go? I know it might not be what you'd normally do, but I feel that Money deserves to know the truth. Then he can deal with whatever it is and not have it gnawing at his mind for the rest of his life."

"If you think I'm gonna let you take my boy to do something so dangerous, you're out of your mind."

"That's why you must go too, Joseph. It's your adopted son we're talking about. You know as well as I do that the Shoshone has no problems with me, and I can come and go as I please, just like I do with the other six tribes here in the Rockies. As long as I don't bring a war party with me, they won't stop us from finding out what we need to know. It might be as simple as watching the Crow camp that I believe she is in from afar. We may never need to let them know we were there."

"And how did you find out about all this?" Kit Carson asked.

"Why, from the Indian gossip in the smoke signals, of course. How else would I know? We have our own newspapers, so to speak. The messages arrive faster, too. I sent up smoke, asking for information as soon as I could walk on my own. Since they knew it was me, I heard from three tribes. I don't have anything concrete, but I have some ideas and think I know where the camp is. It is a couple of days' ride west of here. I hear there are fewer than a hundred people, including women and children. Twenty-five to thirty teepees or so."

"We'd better go along, Levi. Three of us should be enough to keep the boy safe, even if we're walking into the lion's den." Rusty frowned, but he understood where Potak was coming from. It would be hard if the boy learned his mother was killed, but then he could put it behind him.

If she was alive, he would know that the Blackfeet didn't intend to kill her. Whatever they found would give the boy some closure, which was the medicine man's intention. Then, he could put the issue to rest and carry on with his learning. While working to become a mountain man, you had to be focused and couldn't let your mind wander to mysteries about your past.

Everyone else turned and looked at Kit, but he was busy scribbling in his journal and didn't say a word. There was no need for more men either, as it may save the boy an embarrassing moment and the Blackfoot camp wouldn't feel threatened with too many White men with guns.

It was one thing to cry in front of your family and another to cry before a stranger, and a famous one at that. Money sighed a breath of relief when only his closest friends in the world would be going through what he expected to be a devastating experience. But he, too, knew it was something he had to do to put all that ugly past behind him.

———

AN HOUR LATER, three mountain men, an Indian, and a little boy rode out of the south entrance of the compound. They would make better time on horseback and expected to be there in a few days. It was halfway down the mountain to the valley floor. Levi immediately disappeared as he raced out front while they were still on their land, knowing no enemies were near. If there were, Dog would have given them plenty of notice.

He rarely let anything pass without barking up a storm. Although most of the time it was a nuisance, sometimes it saved the day. Knowing this first stretch was safe would allow Beaver to distance himself from the main group and gather intel as they went.

That first night, Rusty, Joseph, Potak, and Money sat around a fire as the sparks sawed downwind in the constant breeze. Everyone was startled when Levi silently entered the camp. They saw his shadow in their peripheral vision before they heard a sound. He made no more noise than a ghost. Since their mission was just about as serious as it got, they all sat in a glum silence, waiting to see what the following days would bring. One by one, they fell asleep without a word.

When they got up to leave the second day, Beaver was already long gone. He had headed out under the light of the stars, hoping to surprise anyone who might be ahead of them or even lying in ambush, but it was an uneventful trip, making their arrival much quicker than expected.

During the day, they passed dying sunflowers hanging limp, no longer following the trajectory of the sun as they dried. Their seeds fell to the ground, sowing new flowers for the following spring.

The marshal's horse stomped his hooves and

stretched his neck as he squealed, ready to charge. The animal was as willing to ride into battle as its owner. Now more than ever, Joseph was dangerous because he had Money to protect, like a mother hen to a chick. Before, it was all about the law, but now it was about his family.

A waterfall thundered out of the warming noon and into a large pond, spilling off downhill in several quick-flowing streams. They heard the soothing sound of water trickling over the rocks. The horses refreshed themselves as they dipped their muzzles in the water, and beads streamed off their chins. The men filled their waterbags, and then off on the trail they were again.

That second night, they huddled around the fire as a light sprinkle made the flames hiss. The drizzle soon stopped, and the dark clouds vanished from the dark night sky. Little Money's face shone pale, like the moon. The pack of wild dogs shied and backed away, save one. It stood its ground and barked at the strangers. Once it felt it had fulfilled its duty, it turned, running to catch up with the others. It was dangerous for a lone dog in the darkness of night.

The next morning, the sun sprayed orange rays of light from the earth's rim, blinding them momentarily. They turned their backs to the sun and continued to ride westbound until they finally saw a dozen streams of curling smoke rising into the sky. It looked like they had located the camp. Now, it was time to do some spying and see if they had caught sight of Brenda Penny.

They climbed high above the camp so they could observe the morning activity below. Clusters of snow-covered bushes provided cover, allowing them to spy without being seen. They watched as an Indian turned his head, pinched his nose with thumb and finger, and blew twin strings of snot onto the dirt. He wiped his fingers on his buckskin shirt.

That was when he appeared to feel that someone was watching him and stared right at the mountain men, although they knew their blinds were too thick for his vision to penetrate the dense brush. Still, goosebumps sprouted on their arms.

It was early morning, and the small camp of some thirty teepees came to life. But as the mountain men sat there from sunup, three hours later, there was still no sign of Brenda Penny or any White women as far as they could see. Potak felt sure they should have seen her by now. She would be in charge of the dirty work to start a new day, carrying heavy firewood to make fires and clean up after the previous night.

"I suppose she didn't make it after all," Potak whispered as his eyes continued to scour the Indian village below. "Then again, there's always another possibility. All we must do is find out what it is. Let's circle the camp while it's still early. Each one of us makes a ring around the camp, everyone a little farther away than the other. I don't know why, but I feel that she may be somehow still alive. What I don't know is where she could have gone. I doubt she even *knows* where she *is*, if she is still with the living."

The medicine man pushed his braids of hair out of his eyes and gave Money a hopeful smile. "We haven't found her yet, but that doesn't mean that she isn't alive. Have patience, and we will see what we can learn. One way or another, you will have your wish fulfilled if it is in my powers."

Rusty took the nearest ring, Levi the second, and

Joseph the third, which was safer because he had Money with him. Potak wandered around on the very edge of hoofprints and the main trails to and from the Indian stronghold.

When the first three finished, they met back, where they hid the horses in a stand of dense trees. It not only made them impossible to see, but it would also block the sound when they neighed or nickered.

"Where did Potak wander off to?" Joseph growled. He didn't like the feeling of failure, especially when it was so important to his son.

"You never know with medicine men, especially him," Levi replied. "We might not see him again for days."

They all turned when they heard rustling from the bushes on the other side of their blind. Snow began to fall from the trees.

"Who goes there?" the marshal barked as he pulled his guns.

"Who do you think? Were you expecting someone else? I thought we were the only ones out here, but now I have discovered I was wrong."

"Whatcha mean?" the marshal asked.

Money looked up at his dad and blinked like a bird as his stomach tied in knots.

"I found a woman like you described, but she no longer acts like a White woman. To be honest, I don't know exactly what she is."

"You're not making any sense, Potak," Levi huffed. "Settle down and speak your mind. You appear to be a tad flustered."

"Flustered? I know the word. Yes, I would say that is a good description for this. Let's sit and have coffee to rest and calm our nerves, and I will tell you everything I saw. I think I need to prepare you, Money, before we go and spy on her."

"Spy on her? What's that supposed to mean? Are you sure it's my ma and she's alive?"

"I doubt there be any other White women up here living in a cave. She has blond hair like you and blue eyes, too. I saw her face up close with the spyglass Beaver gave me. I felt like I could almost touch her if I tried."

"Did you say my ma is living in a cave? That's good, ain't it? Maybe the Indians let her go."

"Patience, and you will see. It is not a finger from the sun. We will be there in minutes, but be very careful not to make any sounds. I feel she is like a deer and will leap and bound away at the first sight of humans."

They ran for a few minutes before Potak put out his hand and had them slow down to a slow walk. For the last yards, they crawled on their stomachs until they reached the edge of an overhanging rock. Below, they saw a double-entrance cave with bars made of sticks and branches. The door was closed tight with a tether. It looked like nobody was home until they saw blond hair flow behind a woman who passed the nearest entrance.

Joseph carefully extended his spyglass and looked before passing it to Money, who lay snuggled up to his side. The boy grabbed the telescope and carefully focused on the cave. At first, he only saw her hair, but he instantly recognized how she moved. That was something that he had never noticed before. It looked like he was already learning from Levi's teachings.

Suddenly, Money gasped as both eyes spread wide, and he dropped the spyglass to the ground. His mouth opened and closed like a goldfish in a bowl, but no words came out.

Finally, he managed to speak, "I-I-I saw her face. My ma, I mean. She looked right at me like she knew I was watching, but the shocking thing was that I didn't know who she was. She's not the same person she was when I last saw her. Now she's somebody else. I didn't recognize her at all. Somehow, I felt sure she wouldn't recognize me. I reckon I lost my mother after all, just like my father." He looked up into Joseph's eyes and said, "You are all I've got now."

"I know that's not what you wanted to see, but it's best to know these things firsthand so you can put them behind you and continue with your life," the medicine man said through hooded eyes.

Despite the shock, it surprisingly took a weight off Money's chest. Now, he knew his mother wasn't somewhere out there waiting for him. She was just the shell of the person he saw, living like an animal in a cave.

"I believe the Blackfeet left her alone because her mind has gone astray. Most Indians fear people acting strangely, like your maternal mother."

"You mean to say *crazy*, don't ya, Potak?" Money said outright and without fear. "I have the grit to take what it means."

"You can put a thousand words on it, Money, but it will still be the same. When people don't act like everybody else, they put a brand of one type or another on them so they can believe they know what it is, when it's the fact that they don't understand that scares them so much. Just like that woman living in the cave. They don't understand, so they call her crazy when, in fact, maybe she's the only one that's sane."

UNINVITED

WHEN WANATA STORMED INTO THE COMPOUND WITH SIX mean-looking warriors, he caught Angus by surprise. It happened so fast that they didn't have time to sound the alarm and hide in the main cabin. That was the usual drill, but this time, things were different. McFarlin instantly knew it was intended to be a surprise and had been perfectly planned. Angus swore under his breath.

When he was young, they wouldn't have been able to catch him out, but now he was an old man and evidently losing his touch. With Rusty gone, he was the one in charge of the compound's safety. It looked like this time, he failed miserably. Strangely, Dog was nowhere to be seen.

"*Sho'daache Kahee*," Dahteste said, greeting her chief in Crow. The shock was visible on her face. He had never dared enter so brazenly with their weapons pointing threateningly.

"Where is that old medicine man hiding? Where's Potak, the Tonkawa witch? I know he was here. I saw the smoke signals." He angrily spun on his heels and screamed, "Where is that evil old man? I know that you know where he is, so tell me before it's too late. I'm not going to ask you again."

The click of the lever of a bolt-action rifle broke the brisk cold air even above Wanata's voice. Everybody heard it and quickly figured out what it was. Five more hammers from muzzle-loading muskets clicked when the hammers were drawn back. Each of the women, Red and White, had a long gun in their white-knuckled fist.

Dahteste had Angus's Sharps prototype, which was aimed at the chief. One round from the nine-and-a-half-pound rifle with a .52-caliber bullet and a thirty-inch barrel would blow a hole in his midsection the size of a water bucket. Her hands were solid around the grip and foreshock as her finger slipped into the safety trigger. It clicked when it released the firing trigger as she moved her index finger forward.

"I know you are my chief, but I demand you show some respect when you enter Rusty Steel's compound. It would be unforgivable if he were to do it to you, wouldn't it? This is our home. How would you feel if we were to do the same to yours? It is a sign of disrespect. I am still your war chief, Wanata. Remember, the elders listen to me, too. What do you think they would say about your actions today?"

"Nothing, if you're dead." The chief's tone was hollow and flat.

"How dare you talk to one of your people like this. All I must do is pull this trigger, and you will be no more."

"I know you would never kill your chief. You have sworn an oath to keep me alive. Put your gun away. It's not in you to murder your leader."

"Maybe she won't shoot ya, but I sure as Dickens will. You ain't my chief, and if you don't think I can shoot straight, just try me. I come from Crockett stock, and my uncle Davy taught me when I was ten." Betty's hands and gaze were as steady as rocks. "When I lived in Tennessee, I backed down bigger Indians than you."

"Stop it right now!" Bar-Chee yelled as she stormed out of her teepee in the middle of the yard. She still held her rifle in her hand. "Be careful what you do next, brother. Do not tarnish our family's name, or your father will punish you from the spirit world. I do not know what has become of you. Do you know how dangerous it can get if you continue to badger the shaman, Potak? I know you have already shot him. Just because one of your men did it doesn't mean that you didn't give the order. I don't know how you will explain that to the elders who picked him as the tribe's head medicine man. Now, what are you going to do? Kill him so he doesn't talk? Then, you will have to kill all of us, too, won't you? And for what? Your ego? Is this what all this is about?"

"Watch your tongue, sister, or maybe I will have my braves cut it out," Wanata spat before thinking.

Bar-Chee saw a look in her brother's eyes that she had never seen before, and it showed on her face: she was frightened. When the chief saw it, it immediately gave him pause, making him listen to his own words.

Finally, he realized he was terrifying his sister, so he eased off. He seemed to be shocked by his own sudden aggression. But there were two men on Beartooth Mountain that he hated, and neither one was from there. The Tonkawa shaman and the White mountain man, Levi Johnson. Both held secrets that could doom his future as chief. One lived there in the compound, and the other in his stronghold. Despite their promises never to talk, he didn't trust either to keep their word. Of course, a man like the chief thought everyone was the same as him, and he would do almost anything for power.

Wanata took a deep breath and tried to talk calmly. "You know I would never hurt you, but you must watch what you say to me in front of my men. I am chief, you know. Things have changed, and they will never be like they were before. We remain brother and sister, but before that, I am your chief, and you must do as I say, even if you choose to live down here with White people. Remember, this is still my mountain."

"And here I thought all this land belonged to the Crow tribe and not you, Wanata. It belongs to your people. I'm beginning to realize just how much you have really changed. I believe the power is going to your head, and that's all you think about anymore. Why are you so angry with Potak? You talk aggressively with Levi, too. The tribal elders picked the Tonkawa Indian as our medicine man, and while excellent offers came from other tribes, we were lucky enough that he chose us. And now you want to run him off or, even worse, maybe kill him? And what will our tribe do without a spiritual leader? What has gotten into your head? I don't understand your actions."

"Beaver and I have made our peace, at least for now. As far as the medicine man goes, for me, he will always be a Tonkawa Indian first, and all tribes seek to kill them to the last man. Why should I be any different?"

"I don't understand you either. Something has happened to you since Hachta died, and you were made chief." Dahteste's voice trembled, and the anger in her eyes was impossible to hide.

The other women kept silent. Pine Needle knew her place, but Silvia was scared. Every time they saw the chief, he seemed more out of control than during the previous visit. Nobody knew what to expect next, not even his sister, who had the same blood running through her veins.

"Potak isn't here, Wanata," Angus said in perfect Crow. He acted as if nothing had happened. "Have a look around all you want, but you will be wasting your time." The intrusion had shaken McFarlin up and thrown him off his game. He bunched his lips and shrugged. "To be honest, I have no idea where he is. You know, Potak. He might get a notion to head for the Great Plains, and we won't see hide nor hair for months. He's the most unpredictable man I've ever met." Angus knew that further escalation would do no one good.

"Why are y'all carrying on so? The medicine man's never done anybody any harm," Virgil chimed in. "What can a mere shaman do to a famous chief like you? Your name is in the elders' songs. His skills are nothing compared to yours. You're the leader of the largest stronghold in the Rocky Mountains."

"Sit now. I just finished baking a raspberry pie." He closed his eyes, took a deep breath, and smiled. "That does smell like some fine cooking, if I have to say so myself. Don't it, Chief?"

Angus knew the best way to calm down an egomaniac was to compliment him. It also showed just how vain he really was.

Wanata still acted arrogantly as he slid off his pony's back, dropping to the ground and making deep footprints in the ever-increasing snow. His look was lit with pride and elation, and vindication was there too.

"Keep an eye on 'im, ladies," Angus whispered when he turned his back. "He's crazier than a dog humpin' a pig. Keep those guns handy, too. Let's see if we can't talk our way out of this."

Angus turned back to Wanata and smiled. "I don't know what you're talking about, Chief. You know how Potak is. You might find that old fool just about anywhere. I don't know why you're worried about such a silly old man. You must be half his age."

Suddenly, the truth settled in, and he blew his top. "He's off somewhere with Levi, isn't he, Angus? Tell me the truth! What are those two up to now?"

"Like I said, how would I know where your medicine man is? It's *you* who should know, being the chief and all? Don't you think?"

Fear kicked up a notch and got everybody's full attention. The members of the compound all knew that Angus was filling him with hot air, hoping he'd ride off and leave them alone. Nobody was afraid for the captain and Kit Carson, and they were even less concerned about Levi, Rusty, and Joseph, who must still be with Potak looking for Money's mother, wherever she was.

Still, there was no point in revealing the truth if they could help it. They all knew how much Wanata envied Beaver, who bested him every time he tried. Even when he attempted to ambush him way up by Fort Boise, he tried and failed again. Lucky for the chief, Levi was forgiving and didn't shoot or kill him unless forced. Then, when he had the chance, nobody would have known.

Betty wondered if the chief could hear the bass drum hammering in her chest as she squeezed the rifle so hard her knuckles turned white. She was so worked up that she had to tell herself not to shoot. Her anger was just about to overwhelm her dread.

Wanata looked at her and curled an amused smile. Suddenly, he became bored and saw he wouldn't get anywhere with Angus there. He also noticed the scattergun in Virgil's hands. Something in the Black man's eyes told the chief he had better not tempt fate. If he pulled both triggers, the blast would cut him in two. He didn't believe the red-haired White woman would shoot, but he didn't doubt the Black man would.

"If you want to find him that bad, you might as well be on your way because you're not gonna find the medicine man here." Angus forced a half-smile and swallowed appreciatively when he saw the chief's eyes wander.

Wanata pinched one nostril and blew snot onto the ground near the mountain man's feet, but he didn't flinch a muscle. He was the only one who was not armed, but his big Bowie knife was within reach in his belt, and the chief knew it. Angus was as deadly with a knife as he was with a bow and arrow after spending so much time in the Crow camp. Despite his age, the chief knew that they were at a standoff.

Nodding his head, Wanata mounted his horse, and the five raced for the west fence. They easily jumped it before racing for the forest at the tree line a couple of hundred yards away.

FAMOUS EXPLORER

WHEN FORT BOISE SHERIFF TOM HAND SUDDENLY showed up unexpectedly with a posse, everyone in the compound got the jitters. They knew if the law came all the way from Boise, something serious was going on. Ten men rode behind the leader with the star on his chest. Everyone was deputized, but they didn't have enough spare badges to go around. The odd shiny piece of tin flashed in the sunlight.

Normally, the army would be sent to hunt down the culprits, but this was McKay's Trading Post that was robbed, so the owner demanded that it be handled by the local law. His faith in the army returning with all his money was next to nothing, so he preferred men from the town whom he knew could be counted on. Men who lived and thrived behind the success of his isolated trading post.

"What in the world are you doin' way up here, Tom? You're a long way from Boise." Captain Forrester stepped down from the porch, the spaghetti grass crunching underfoot. "Is that a posse you have with you? That's a bunch of riders, so you must be after some bad men."

"Four desperate outlaws robbed the trading post and made off with most of Mister McKay's money. Why, it was the entire season's earnings of gold, silver, and coins. We chased them west on the Oregon Trail, but they turned back and headed east. When we nearly caught them again, they turned south, and we've been on their tails ever since. I reckon they got their bearings crossed when they headed for Yellowstone Valley. We almost ambushed them at the base of Beartooth Mountain, and that was when they fled for higher country. I doubt they have any idea of how many hostile Indians live on the plateau. If the warrior braves don't get them, the weather will."

"What's this all about? I remember you, Sheriff Hand. I'm Kit Carson. What were you saying about robbers and thieves? It sounds like it's right down our alley, doesn't it, Captain Forrester?"

"Everybody knows who you are, Mister Carson. Why, I'd be honored if you would ride along. You and the captain should be enough. Where are Rusty and Levi? It looks like the marshal's gone too."

"They're off doing a friend of ours a favor. We've been left behind to defend the compound, but I doubt Angus would mind if we disappeared for a while. What do you say, old pard?" Kit was biting at the bit for a new adventure.

"Oh, go on, Will. I might as well say yes because you'd badger me until I did. Virgil and I, along with the girls, can handle anything that gets thrown our way. All we've gotta do is hide in the cabin if somebody comes snoopin' around."

"If you're coming, time is of the essence, gentlemen. I figure they're a few miles over that way." Tom jutted his chin. "We've been right on their tails the whole time, so they can't be too far ahead of us. It will ruin Mr. McKay if we don't get that money back. He's paying a handsome reward, too, but I can pay you two from the town funds. Fifty dollars apiece for doing nothing but riding along and maybe tracking these boys so we can nab them once and for all."

In an hour, they had their horses saddled and were riding out of the stables and through the corral. As they rode out the gate and down the trail, their silhouettes became smaller and smaller until they became little dots against a blanket of snow.

———————

CLOUDBANKS STOOD AMONG THE MOUNTAINS. The four riders wound down the trail carefully as they bunched and halted. Sections of the same trail were far below where they saw the warriors. Carson rode right beside the captain to make sure the others didn't fall behind. A few posse members rode drag to make sure they weren't being followed. They planned to circumvent the hostiles without being seen, so they had to keep their distance.

A gunshot rang out from a heavy-caliber rifle. The frontiersmen's horses bared their teeth and swung their heads from side to side with their ears flattened against their skulls. Smoke squirreled out of Will's barrel, putting them all on edge. A White man on horseback broke into a run and fled as the round hit a tree beside his head.

When will glanced down again, he said, "It's all four of 'em, all right. The problem is that those Blackfoot warriors got between them and us. I reckon the one I took a shot at wasn't winged. It was too fast for me to tell for sure."

They angrily rode with their rifles across their thighs. Nobody knew exactly how far ahead the outlaws were, but everyone was aware that if they weren't careful, they could run right into them before they could stop and open fire. A dozen hardened men were after nonprofessional's so they weren't sure what they might do. They showed how little they knew when they turned back twice and headed south, hoping the Indians would stop following them and give up the chase.

The posse traveled like migrants following a falling star as the string of men carefully rode the trail behind Will. He was the only one who seemed to know exactly where he was going, although they could all see the tracks. When they looked up, high above, they saw straw nests lodged in crevices. Buzzards used their towering perches to spy on prey below. They launched, tucking their six-foot wings into a dive, as the earth floated off in a long curve to the end of the world. A dozen circled overhead as they hoped to locate dead bodies.

The first bad sign was when wild dogs began to howl at the edge of the clearing as they bared their teeth and snapped jaws. The Indians released domestic dogs into the wilderness to form packs and live off the land, making them mean. Their offspring were feral and were as savage as wolves.

A column of Blackfoot Indians wound down the trail less than a mile below them. They could see how they alertly marched on in monotone unison, never missing a beat. They all knew they had to have heard the gunshot. Perhaps they thought it was one of their rear trackers to ensure they weren't being followed.

The horses bucked their heads and sniffed the air. They all knew the smell of the Indians and their ponies. Fresh droppings covered the trail both from ponies and horses.

Lank light-colored hair fell around Carson's tiny ears, but his eyes were sharp and full of fire as he looked around with an experienced glare. One hand hung limp at his side with a pistol in his fist.

Suddenly, hostile Indians screamed across the countryside with blood in their eyes as they bared their teeth. One Blackfoot warrior ran into sight, beating his pony into a whirlwind, and rode right up, taking bead on the White men. He must have been the bravest man in the war party or completely mad.

Kit promptly shot him twice in the chest, then he removed his hair, leaving them raw-skulled just like the Indians did to friends in the past. His actions shocked everybody there and left them speechless.

When Carson turned his eyes to his friends, they were empty and dead. "Like I said before, I don't tolerate Blackfoot Indians and shoot them wherever I find them. If that one had the chance, he would have killed us, so I don't hesitate, *ever*. That's the way of the world—to bloom, wither, and die, and none of us makes it out alive."

Kit spat, wiped his mouth, and stared at his new acquaintance, wondering what he was going to do.

"Me personally," Will said, "I don't shoot anybody unless their aimin' a gun, a bow, or some sort of life-threatening weapon at me. But I can see your point. Most men don't turn the other cheek. The biggest problem here in the mountains, especially down in the valley, is with the Blackfoot tribe. I reckon they're the most warlike. Maybe they might back off some if we are all harder on them."

———

A FEW HOURS LATER, they made camp. The four bandits were still racing for their lives. They felt they were just about to reach their goal and freedom. Little did they know the posse was still on their trail.

Until they ran into the Blackfoot warriors. They were just about to catch up, but now the outlaws gained a better lead again. They rode all day until an hour before dark. It was dangerous to wander in the forest, foraging for firewood with no light. An Indian might sneak up on you and remove your hair.

A pumpkin moon ascended and grew until it seemed so big that it felt within their reach, and soon, it would block out the sky. Then, it rose higher into the heavens and turned silvery white.

Every night, as they sat by the crackling fire, Kit's pencil scratched his parchment momentarily. Then he stopped, put his hand to his brow, thought, and began to write again. He sat in somber silence for the hour or so it took him to record everything that happened that day. Carson even included what they ate and the mood of the expedition. He recorded it precisely as it was. He kept a finely detailed journal of his journeys, which was later published in the dime novels and even in a few newspapers with national distribution.

They huddled around the fire as a sudden sprinkle made it hiss. The men drew their hats down low and pulled up their collars, but it soon turned into snow again as large flakes floated toward the ground. Their bedrolls had gotten wet that night, and with the temperature drop, they all drew up to fires, eventually drying out their clothing and stopping their chattering teeth.

The following day, about noon, Will came riding back and said, "I just saw them over that rise. They're about a half-day's ride ahead of us, and there's no more sign of the Blackfoot war party. Mind you now, that doesn't mean that they're gone. If we push it, we can catch them before dark. Whatcha say, Kit? Should we throw caution to the wind and run these fellas to ground once and for all? Well, Sheriff? You have the last word. It'll be on you if any of your men get killed, though, pard."

"That's what we rode all the way from Fort Boise for. I never intended to let Mr. McKay's money get away. Why, it would ruin the town, we'd dry up and blow away in no time. Everybody's job depends on his trading post." They roweled the horses forward as they cantered nervously.

Will was right. As soon as they rode over the next summit and looked down the other side, they saw desperate-looking White men turning in their saddles with guns in their hands.

As soon as the gunfire started, they pulled their reins, sliding to a stop. "Jump down, grab the reins, and take your horses into that arroyo over there. Understand? Lucky for us, I doubt that they're very good shots."

The marshal wheeled his mount, gigged its flanks,

and raced after the posse. They were too far away to risk another shot, but he saw enough from afar.

The posse immediately heard the reports of Colt revolvers and knew they belonged to Kit and the captain. The sheriff watched as they gunned down the outlaws to the last man. Carson made a point of making sure all four were dead. The last man shot, kneeling, sank to the ground with a pneumatic sigh as he died on the spot. Pink froth showed on his dead, colorless lips. A brave and brazen vulture hobbled out to pick at the dead with yellow beaks despite the presence of the men.

"Did you find the money?" the captain asked.

"Yep, there must be a thousand dollars here. If the trading post goes, so does my job and, most of all, the jobs of the army. And the only reason they're in Fort Boise at all is to protect us from the hostile Indians. Had we not recovered this, in a year, Fort Boise wouldn't have been there anymore."

"Occasionally, the grizzly bear needs to show the jackals who he is," Kit said solemnly. "I can assure you *they* won't be stealing anymore. When you make your choice to cross the line, you have to be ready to pay the price."

"Well, you've got your money, so let's get back home. We've done what we came here for.

"Ain't ya gonna bury 'em, Mr. Carson?" Sheriff Hand asked, frowning. It all seemed to happen so suddenly that he was still slightly confused.

"Be my guest, but do you wanna get scalped by those Blackfoot wandering around out there because you wanted to tend to those kind souls? You do know they won't be alone, don't you? Do you really want to die for an outlaw?" Kit eyed the sheriff in an almost challenging manner. "They got what they deserved. Let the varmints eat what's left."

They finished collecting their guns and personal possessions for the sheriff to take back to his office and two cell blocks. There wouldn't be any prisoners to be put in jail.

The dying man listened until the last hoof-clop died in the distance. There was one that Cason hadn't finished off. Then he, too, took his last breath and whispered, "Mama."

MONEY PENNY

"I'M SORRY THAT YOU HAD TO SEE YOUR MOTHER LIKE that, Money," Joseph whispered. "I doubt she'd remember who you were had we gone down to the cave and tried to talk to her. Between that and the risk of being discovered, it wasn't worth the chance. I feel for you, son. I know it must be hard to let such a thing sink in. But I promise you, you'll get over it. You have two loving parents now, so you have nothing to worry about. Neither of us is going anywhere, so don't push all that out of your head. It won't do you any good thinking about it. Just be happy that you *have* a family. Most orphans ain't all that lucky."

"He's right, Money. After going through what your ma went through, you can't expect her to be the same again. Even if we asked, I doubt she'd understand who we are and agree to come," Potak said. "I've heard of cases where the woman was captured and tied and taken back even though they didn't want it, and things always worked out badly. It's not all that unusual out here in the wilderness. Especially along places like the Oregon Trail."

"To be honest, her face looked just like my ma's, but there was something that I didn't recognize in her eyes. They belonged to a stranger. She was so different. I know she's another person now. My ma died the day that I saw them take her away and sell her to that Indian brave. The woman living in the cave like a wild animal ain't my mother. That much I know, so I can handle it. I had already given her up for dead, only to find that I was right all along. She might be alive in body, but she is certainly dead in spirit." Money took a deep breath and shuddered when he let it out. "It's hard growing up so fast. Everything happens so quickly, it makes my head spin."

"Sometimes the wilderness doesn't leave us any other way but fast. Out here, it's the survival of the fittest, so youngins of every sort of critter are at risk. A good part of all wilderness babies fall to some ill fate before they've reached full growth. Sometimes men fall into that category too, especially mountain men."

Potak had recovered in record time and was already fiddle-footed to get back to his work as a medicine man.

"Thank you all kindly for patching me up, especially you Virgil. It's time for me to head home. Maybe I can find out more about Money Penny up in the Crow stronghold. That's where the gossip flies."

Now that they had their questions answered, they turned for home. Rusty. Levi, Joseph, and Money rode slowly through the vast forest. They were nearing the end of the day when they saw that the trail they were traveling on was well-trodden, with horses going and coming. There were so many hoofprints that it was hard to make out who was who, even for scouts like Rusty and Levi.

"Where did all these tracks come from all of a sudden?" Levi asked. "They weren't there when we were heading for the small Blackfoot camp. That means that they're between us and home. I wonder if that's intentional. I count six."

"I count five," Rusty replied, "but either one of us could be wrong with this mess. One thing's for sure: they aren't trying to hide. It's almost like they want us to see their prints in the snow."

"Maybe they're trying to spook us, but if they are, they've picked the wrong White men. Keep close to *me*, Money. Don't worry, this is only a little bump in the road." The marshal grabbed Money's reins and led the way.

Despite what the adults said, Money was still shaken. If they were right, several bows or rifles could be waiting for them down that path, but he wasn't sure if they could beat the odds. He knew better than to count his shotgun into the equation. The boy felt that no matter how you looked at it, if they had to stop and fight, it would be close, if not impossible, to win if the Blackfeet gave it their all. It was obvious that the mountain men weren't sure if they would stand and fight or cut and run to save their lives. Blackfoot Indians were notorious for being one of the most dangerous of all the tribes and possibly the most aggressive.

Near the end of the day, when the sun sat four fingers over the world's rim, they saw what they had expected and what Money had dreaded all day. Six Blackfoot warriors sat abreast of ponies blocking their path. They knew no matter what they did, they would attack. If they ran, they would charge them on instinct as the game began, and they raced after their prey.

If they stood their ground and waited, they might give their new enemy a chance to flank them, and they would be in an even worse spot. All three adult White men saw that they only had a third choice: to charge. That would be the last thing the hostile Indians would expect. Now, they wondered if the posse would show up too. If they did, they could only hope they had enough respect for their sheriff and would brave it out and join the charge. Everyone knew they were all workers in saloons, ranches, or stores, and none were professional Indian fighters. They could only hope they had the grit.

"Pull that shotgun out and cock the hammers, but do it as slow as maple syrup so you don't spook those boys over there. I'm afraid we're gonna have to rush 'em, so stay right behind us. If one of those Blackfoot gets close, give him one of those barrels, but save the second one because you won't get a chance to reload."

Now, things seemed to be going even faster for Money. Everything appeared to be spinning out of control. When his father told him to cock the hammers and follow close, his heart pounded so hard it felt like it was ready to pop out of his chest. The gun was slippery in his sweat-soaked mitts.

Right before they charged, everything froze like in a black-and-white picture for the briefest of moments. They really didn't expect the posse to follow them. They all knew this could be their last charge. Levi and Rusty exchanged glances and saw the same look in each other's eyes. It was that of two men who were obsessed with their lives and what they did. They were both mountain men, and there was nothing that would ever change the fact.

All four stood staring blankly like they might never see their home again. It was like they were looking at their future but couldn't see past the negativity surrounding them. Money drew a deep breath, sniffled, shook his head, and frowned. He worried about the heavy shotgun slipping out of his hands.

"It looks like we've got ourselves into a mess again, don't it? What do you think those Blackfoot are gonna do, Levi?"

"Who has any idea what a Blackfoot war party is gonna do, Rusty? But I believe these boys want to fight. Maybe somebody's riled them up again, and they're after any White men they run across. It won't be the first time or the last. Then again, usually, they don't need much more excuse than Easterners being this far west. They believe they don't need a reason to seek revenge on anybody on Indian land."

"I guess we're just about to find out." Marshal Walker put his reins between his teeth and drew back the hammers on his brace of pistols.

"Well, whaddaya say, boys? Shall we have a go at it or not?" Levi asked.

"Ten dollars says I'm there before you two. It's time to separate the chaff from the wheat."

Suddenly, they were racing for the confrontation with a half dozen dangerous warriors, all of whom were armed to the teeth, albeit, lucky for them, bad shots with their rifles. Few Indians had the spare ammunition to use for practice.

Levi looked back, tossed the marshal a wistful smile, and winked like it was a big game. He had been doing this for the last six years, so he had all the confidence in the world and didn't show an ounce of fear.

The pallor of terror crawled into the Blackfoot warriors' eyes when they saw the crazed mountain men charging. A half dozen white hands held six repeating revolvers. The sheriff stopped for the briefest of seconds, deciding if he was ready to die that day or not. He finally wheeled his horse around and charged after them, waving his hand in the air for his deputies to follow.

"Don't just stand there like six o'clock half-struck! Get your butts moving!" Sheriff Hand yelled as he broke into a run.

The rest of the posse followed in a helter-skelter response, none of them as sure of themselves as the men racing before them. Despite their fear and hesitation, they knew they couldn't turn back. Finally, they beat their horses into a fury of hair, hooves, and teeth, closing the distance between the apparently astounded Indians and them.

Sheriff Hand's heart suddenly thumped in his throat as soon as he spurred his horse's flanks and screamed, "CHARGE!" But nobody heard him above the hammering of iron-shod horses' hooves. The earth rumbled as the posse finally pulled into some semblance of order at a full run.

One mountain man just fueled the others' resolve and made the blood race through their bodies as their nerves began to fray, making them ride all that much harder. They could already taste the blood of their sworn enemies. After the Comanche, they hated this tribe more than anything on the planet—especially Levi, for what they had done to their expedition back in the Territories. That was why they decided to act so aggressively. They weren't about to let the Blackfoot do what the Comanche had done before them.

Joseph watched as Levi and Rusty charged into the group of Blackfoot right before his very eyes. He spurred forward and was suddenly right on their tails. Their change to Indian fighters was so complete that Money hardly recognized the men he knew back at the compound. What he saw before him now was White warriors, through and through.

Levi, Rusty, and Joseph arrived first, clashing in a flurry of knives, bullets, and tomahawks. The chaos of battle overwhelmed those now fighting for their lives. They knew they would die where they fought if they didn't win. None of the three was the surrendering type. They were so brazening about how they rode into danger that the six Blackfoot warriors lost most of their metal before the fight began.

The riders clashing with them seemed to be White men from hell, and nothing could stop them. They saw the posse coming as they died, but they were too late to participate. Chunks of lead slammed into the surrounding trees and whined off rocks, zinging into the air as gun smoke hovered over the trail. The Indians' old muskets sounded like whipcracks popping. The Blackfoot Indians were all on the ground, dead or dying, before the sheriff reached the scene. The odor of blood was noticeable, but it was nearly overwhelmed by the smell of cordite.

"Are you boys all right?" Sheriff Hand asked as he tried to catch his breath after the fast sprint and he pulled to a sliding stop. "You're all so bloody I can't tell if you're wounded or not."

"I don't see any arrows sticking out of you, Rusty," Levi said with a lopsided grin. "What about me?"

"I feel like I've been hit in the chest with a hammer," Marshal Walker huffed as he gobbled for air. It was obvious it hurt to talk. Money's face went from jubilant to terrified in the blink of an eye.

"They're the ones who started it," Money tried to growl, like his dad. His voice was so small that they all startled and turned. Joseph nudged his horse over to his son and ruffled his yellow hair. His eyes were full of love despite the pain in his chest.

After it was all over, Joseph's breath was trapped somewhere in his body, and he couldn't breathe. It felt like a horse was sitting on his lungs. He was drenched with sweat, and his hair matted with blood. His arms were red from the elbows down to the tips of his revolver's barrels. He dropped off his horse, holding onto the saddle to keep from falling. He slipped his pistols into their holsters.

"Are you all right, Pa?"

When the marshal looked down, he saw a bullet hole in his thick cotton shirt as alarm bells began to ring in his head. He reached inside and pulled out his diary stuffed with old wanted posters. He hadn't made an entry since he left the wagon train, but never bothered to throw it all away. The lead slug was lodged between the covers, deep inside the pages. At first, he swore when he saw the damage, then stopped and smiled when he realized it had saved his life. A grin spread across his face as soon as Money saw the book.

After the slaughter, Levi swung off his horse and wiped his brow with his shirt sleeve. "Like I always say, be decisive. Right or wrong, go for it and stick to the plan. The trail is full of flat varmints. Because we didn't hesitate today, we won the battle hands down. Had we acted any other way, the odds would have beaten us, and we wouldn't be here to celebrate."

He knew the sheriff would have been reliable, but most of the men in the posse were simple ranch hands from the surrounding spreads or workers from town. Although they all knew how to shoot like most folks that far west, they were a far cry from the mountain men. Without them, no one doubted they would have broken and run.

"Yeah, you make a good speech, Levi." Rusty smiled, happy to be alive. "But it's a good thing the posse didn't balk, or you, Joseph, and I could have gotten killed. The charge and the backup spooked them."

"Well, don't worry. There, there, Money, it's all over now. Lookee here, your pa doesn't have a scratch on him other than a hole in his shirt. Your ma will have to mend it, though. I reckon we could all do with a wash too. Let's go find us a creek with a sandy bank to lie in the sun and dry off once we're clean."

"We better get out of here before some of their friends come looking for them when they don't show up," Rusty said as he looked all around. He felt like they were four white lambs in a herd of black sheep.

REUNION

WHEN ANGUS HEARD THE WHISTLE, HE KNEW THAT RUSTY was back. They had begun to use a secret code to enter the compound ever since Hachta died and Wanata was made chief. They had been jumpy ever since the new Crow leader had brazenly passed by the compound, and it wasn't for a friendly visit. As soon as he confirmed it was one of their scouting parties, he rang the dinner bell until they were nearly deaf.

As soon as they rode their horses into the yard, Bar-Chee ran for her son, pulled him out of his saddle, and hugged him. She grabbed his shoulders, looking at him at arm's length. When she confirmed he was fine, she hugged him again so hard that he struggled to breathe, but Money didn't mind. After seeing what happened to his real mother, he realized just how lucky he was to have another chance at growing up in a happy, loving home, like before his family died. He even lost his twin brother, but now he was adopted by a new clan three times as big.

"We've had some company while you boys were

away," Angus grumbled when he finally stopped banging his dinner bell. "That fool Wanata has a grudge against Potak, and it doesn't seem like it's going away. He was here all riled up, asking for 'im like he planned to kill 'im. He seems to still be ticked off with you, too, Beaver. Do you know anything about this trouble with the medicine man?"

"Nothing new that you don't already know about. Who knows what makes Wanata do the things he does? I know why he's angry with me, he owes me his life when I let him go after catching him trying to ambush me. Why he came after me then, I still don't know. I suppose most of his anger is envy-driven. Since he became chief, his power has gone to his head."

"I think we already know what's bothering him. He's angry with me for the same reason he's angry with Levi. He believes we hold secrets that if the elder heard, it could maybe cost his position as leader of the tribe. Still, I don't worry about him. If he kills me, he will be in more trouble than he ever imagined and will no longer be chief. He thinks that now that he's the Crow leader, no one can tell him what to do, but that is exactly what the tribal elders are for. They are often called on to keep peace within the camp members."

"But then you'd be dead, Potak," Rusty huffed, "and we couldn't have that. What would the Crow stronghold do without their shaman? Every tribe has one, if not more. Hachta thought that he only needed you since you were such a good medicine man and popular with his people. He claimed there wasn't a better shaman on all the plains, Yellowstone Valley, and the Rockies. You'd think the new chief would take it more seriously. It seems his jealousy overrides all his logic sometimes."

"That is true, but we all must die sometime." The shaman cackled, taking it lightly like he did everything. "Maybe it would be a good cause to give my life for. It would save the Crow tribe many problems in the future, not to mention you all and your compound. He is not half the leader Hachta was. It is a very difficult thing to be a fair and just chief when they are few and far between. Wanata doesn't know what it means to be honest, not even with himself, or he would never have accepted the job. But he was ready to kill for the crown. Now, we will see if he can handle its weight."

"Well, he's still the chief, and no matter what's happened up until now, he hasn't thrown us off the mountain, and that's all that matters to me." Despite Potak's casual way of talking about death, Levi's face was full of concern. "Sure, I know how you got shot, and he wanted to shoot me, but who knows what he had planned. It must have been something dodgy, or his men wouldn't have been so nervous that they spooked and shot off a round. Lucky for you, Potak, it didn't hit your heart or head. It could have just as easily killed you."

"Well, everybody go on and tend to your horses, and I'll fix us up with something to eat," Angus said as he headed for the main cabin and the kitchen. Black smoke snaked out of both chimneys, keeping their home cozy and warm. "I bet you boys could use a good home-cooked meal after a hard ride."

Everybody was standing out on the porch with coats they snatched off the pegs by the front door, watching, curious about how the trip went. It snowed again the previous evening, and three inches of fresh powder lay on the ground, making the yard sparkle white in the glaring sun.

Levi undid the horse's cinch, pulled down the saddle, and slapped the horse's rump. The mare trotted into the corral and straight for its feed sack. The other horses dipped their muzzles into the watering trough to quench their thirst.

The compound members present waited on the porch for their friends. An aging Rusty Steel smiled, showing his tobacco-stained teeth as he shuffled in the snow toward his home. After squinting for a moment, he spat a long stream of brown juice onto the ground with shining eyes.

Flames crackled in the massive stone fireplace on the left wall, nearly half the room's length. Another long, heavy timber table with benches running down both sides was in the middle. The only chairs were at the ends for the owners, Angus and Rusty. Hides hung, drying on the walls. Racks of elk antlers hung from the ceiling. A long rifle gun rack hung over the fireplace with everything from buffalo guns to shotguns and muskets—holsters with revolvers swung from pegs by the door, which had a single gun slat. The thick window shutter had two. Waves of heat emitted from the roaring flames as cinder flew up and out of the vent. Hot coals left the room with an orange glow despite the open shutter.

Near the far-right corner was a cast-iron potbelly stove they had brought all the way from Fort Boise on a travois pulled by a mule. Another small fireplace stood in the corner where a large pot of beans simmered. Meat sizzled in the frying pan as the aroma of biscuits floated on puffs of air from the oven. Angus toiled in the kitchen with a brace of pistols on his waist. Five-shot Colt Patterson single-action revolvers filled his holsters. Despite his age, he could still hold his own in a gunfight with rifles or pistols. He had been hunting in the Rocky Mountains most of his life—both wild game and sometimes even men.

Most of their home entertainment was confined to reading, board games, and, of course, telling tall tales, just like all mountain men.

Bar-Chee was the most concerned about what happened. She was worried that Money's mother was still alive and maybe wanted her son back. She knew she couldn't face losing the child she had always hoped for. Still, she couldn't build up the courage to ask her husband or her adopted son what happened. She sat quietly in her seat and forced herself to be patient. Money sat beside her and had no more than the usual scrapes and scratched that come with traveling in the wilderness.

"Come on, now that we've tended to the horses, I wanna thaw out a bit," Levi said, rubbing his hands. "How about you, Money? Are you as cold as I am? Ever since we washed off in that freezing stream, my teeth haven't stopped chattering. Come on over here, close to the fire."

CARSON & THE CAPTAIN

AFTER DAYS OF RIDING WHERE NO WHITE SOULS ventured, save Will and Kit, they were tired and needed a rest. When the work was done and the sheriff and deputies headed back to Fort Boise, the captain and Carson turned for the compound and a roof over their heads. It was getting colder each night, and although they were both used to enduring bad weather, they knew that a warm cabin was not far away and more of Angus's cooking was available. Kit closed his eyes and remembered all the different tastes and odors. He could almost smell the hot butter melting over a steamy piece of cornbread. Most of the time, Kit's heart was led by his stomach.

Finding fine dining in such a faraway place was truly unusual, and the Kentuckian was in no hurry to go anywhere. He was enjoying his small vacation and excursion into the wilderness while he was at it, visiting old friends and making new ones. He found the captain to be more like him than the others, so their little journey into the unknown worked out well. They had a chance to discover their weaknesses and strengths. That didn't mean that Kit wasn't a first-class mountain man because he was one of the best. Still, he had more soldier in him than Levi or Rusty, who didn't have an ounce. This just made their bond easier. They instantly understood how each other planned and thought.

The rock trail rang loudly under his horse's hooves. Will's Appaloosa sidled and rolled its eyes as he pulled back on the reins. The sand on the riverbank's edge turned dark with blood, but there was no sign of where it came from. Edges of ice had formed at the sides where it met the ground.

"Look over there," Kit said, glancing up and then down the stream. "Somebody or something was killed here. The body probably floated downstream, and whoever did it didn't come out of the water. Otherwise, we'd see their hoof prints on the muddy bank. It looks like maybe they jumped somebody when he was in the middle of the stream. See those mule tracks over there? That's where he waded in, but his animal didn't walk out either side. It was probably led down the middle by whoever shot, killed, and robbed him. They must have dragged his body to the bank to rifle his pockets."

"Let's ride downstream a bit. I got a hunch that's the way they went."

"And why is that?" Kit stopped, raising an eyebrow in question.

"Call it a gut feeling if you want. I don't know why, but I'd pick the course of least resistance if I were them while getting away. That means I'd go with the stream and not against the current."

The bright sun said it was near noon as it cast no shadows. They both looked up and saw vultures making lazy circles in the sky. Some tucked their massive spread of six-foot wings and dove into a dive, only pulling on the brakes and pulling up at the last moment as they settled down like a feather on a windless day.

"There's something below those buzzards that's dead or dying. Maybe this is what turned the water red. Careful now, we might bump into trouble there ahead." Will put his reins in his teeth and pulled his pistol as his empty sleeve festooned in the wind. They didn't have to ride long to find what the scavengers were after. When they arrived at the riverbank, a handful of coyotes scampered off. Some of them had pieces of bloody material in their chattering jaws. Bloodlust filled the air.

"There you go," Will huffed, slipping his pistol into his holster and sliding off his horse. He pushed the dead man over with the toe of his boot. His sightless face turned up with mud stuck to one side. A bullet hole punctured his ribcage.

"I wonder who did this," Kit said. "He's been robbed of everything he had, including his boots. What's a White man doin' out here all alone?"

"I travel alone, don't I?" Kit smiled. "I find that sometimes it's safer to travel alone because it's easier to go unperceived."

"Yeah, but not everybody's like you, buddy. I travel the wilderness alone, just like Rusty, but we know what we're doin', not like this poor fella. I reckon he's a miner from the dirt under his fingernails and calloused hands. If he were riding a mule, he's probably not a buffalo hunter."

While they were there, the horses dapped their hooves as they rose and lowered their dripping heads, drinking deeply from the crystal-clear stream as the water beaded on their chins. The men filled their cupped hands, slurped water upstream from the body, and then filled their goatskin water bags.

They froze when they heard the snort of what sounded like a horse coming from less than a stone's throw away. They left the horses to continue to drink as they squatted, pulling their weapons again and carefully moving toward the sound. Every few minutes, they would squat, waiting for a spell before continuing.

Kit pressed a finger to his lips and then whispered into the captain's ear. "We should get a better look at them any second now."

Will nodded and followed him, creeping up the rocky incline beside the stream. They didn't have far to climb. Thirty feet above them, they caught sight of three grubby White men. With them were four mules stacked high with buffalo hides, staggering under the weight. They apparently had a good hunt and had downed what looked like several dozen bison.

"That's what they were after. One of them mules," Kit said. "With all those furs, it was too much weight for them to bear and survive. See how they move under the bundles. Even with an extra mule, it's still nearly too much. I reckon that the one with aparejo backpack was our dead friend's animal. It's the finest one of the bunch. Then again, now it doesn't really matter which one it was. How do you want to handle this?"

"I usually walk right up and ask men like these what they're up to, face-to-face. I'm not very shy about my way of doing things. I like them to see what's coming. The surprise on their faces is usually priceless."

"Remember, it's three to two. You just never know when you're going to catch a bullet. I've caught a couple myself over the years, and I'm not old yet, but I hope to be one day."

"We outnumber them despite their numbers." Will smiled jokingly. "It would take five or six of those wicked men to make us break a sweat. But they were the ones who killed and robbed that poor fella back there. Nobody else around could have done it. In my book, they must pay for that."

"I like your style, Captain. Let's ride down there and ask them who they are. We can act like it's a friendly stroll. Maybe they'll be friendly and nice."

"I don't care how nice they are," Will said out of the corner of his mouth just before they rode into the camp uninvited.

"Howdy there, friends. You wouldn't have some extra hot coffee in that pot, would you? We saw the smoke from your fire."

"Who goes here?"

"Have y'all seen anybody? We're looking for a friend." Kit smiled like they were old amigos.

"They're all dead, save us. I reckon it was Blackfoot Indians that hit us." The leaders whined. "We lost a few of our men. Lucky for us, they didn't run off with the buffalo hides."

"Is that who killed the miner back there, too? We found him not very far from here. Or don't you know nothin' about that?" The captain re-pinned his empty sleeve to his shirt.

"They killed him, too."

"So, where's the other bodies? How many of your party were murdered? I didn't see any tracks of anyone else."

"Is that blood under your fingernails?" Kit asked. "Oh, yeah, I reckon that's from all those buffalo hides. I reckon it's too much trouble to unload the mules while you have lunch."

"None of you seem to have a scratch on you."

"Are you calling me a liar, mister?" the leader growled.

Suddenly, a stillness came over the Indian fighters. It was so ominous that the buffalo hunters' faces were tense, and their bodies stiffened. In comparison, the two strangers who barged into their camp looked as cool as a fall breeze and didn't fluster or ruffle a feather.

"Well, whatcha waitin' on, mister? We don't have all day to stand around. Let's get this show on the road. Or don't you have the stones?" Kit's smile was alarming, and his eyes were full of fire. "We know you boys shot that man back there to steal his mule. You were looking at losing part of your haul, weren't ya?"

"Why have you two come here, giving us a hard time? We never done nothing to you. If you know what's good for you, you'll ride right on out of here and not look back. Remember, there's three of us and only two of you."

Everyone stood as still as a stone, knowing the slightest move could set off something that could never be undone. The captain drummed his fingers on the handle of his Colt revolver, his eyes asquint, watching every movement.

Without warning, dozens of arrows lofted across a blue sky void of clouds. They whistled like ducks at unbelievable speeds. As they passed overhead, for a second, they blocked out the sun. In shock, everybody went for their guns. In two seconds, all three thieves were lying on the ground with bullet holes in their heads as smoke snaked out of the mountain men's barrels.

Kit and Will dove for cover among the rocks along the steep trail. They had the disadvantage of fighting from lower ground. The Indians must have followed the buffalo hunters, got lucky, and stumbled on the Indian fighters. Time would tell if it was good or bad luck for the Blackfoot Indians.

The soft blue of a cloudless sky was the only redeeming factor of the jagged, wild-looking mountain. The trail was steep, it nearly ran straight up. They could follow it with their eyes a half mile above.

The captain paused to catch his breath. He wiped the sweat from his face with his stump. His face glistened with oily perspiration.

"I'm not afraid of heights, snakes, or red-headed women, but I don't like being around Blackfoot Indians."

"From what you've said and done, I've gathered that. I can't say that I have much-lost love for them either. It's rarely we run into a party, and they don't put up a fight, but not just with White folks. They love to take on other tribes, fight with all their neighbors, and steal their horses."

The captain's face was a bronzed, hard mask that matured beyond his age. His long blond hair was stuck with sweat close to his skull when he removed his beige broadband hat. His mustache was so wet it drooped over his mouth.

Of course, the braves had been following the three thieves and the miner, so they weren't expecting to run into professionals. This, unfortunately, made the Blackfoot warriors careless with their brashness and need to make a show of the best fighters. They had no idea of what they were getting into.

Will suddenly felt tense in his breast, and his ears got tingly, making every muscle instantly tighten. He saw the Indians creep across the distance like animals, slow and with their backs arched. It looked like they were going to try to fight their way down the trail.

Kit heard the arrow whine past his ear and knew right then that it was on. The fight had started, and this one wouldn't be a deadfall like that with the robbers.

Their war paint contrasted with their dusty bodies. They looked like they had been trailing the White men for days. Their eyes were white, caged in ridged, red lines, and their faces were full of hate.

"How about trying to pick off the leader with that rifle of yours? Then again, he's probably too far."

"Since Rusty and Levi are kind of famous, too, Christian Sharps gave us five prototypes to test. We can give it a try. How far away do you think they are?"

"Five, maybe six hundred yards." Kit spat and wiped his chapped lips with the back of his hand. "In my opinion, it's *too* far."

"If Levi were here, using one of these rifles, he'd make the shot for sure. Me, I figure I can give it a try. If we don't try to kill the war chief, they're just going to come down here for us anyway. They'll feel superior now that they're above us. Now we've got to figure out which one he is. I can't even make a good count, but they're popping up all over the place."

"It's the one standing at the top, watching from above. I've chased enough Blackfoot warriors to know how to spot their leader. He's no fool. The war chief will wait to see what happens. For the moment, they don't know who we are and figure we're more dumb White hunters like those over there. Yep, if you can take him out, we might stop this before it gets started. If not, I'd say we have a hard nut to crack."

Will pushed his hand under the snow, grabbed a tuft of grass, and dropped it at arm's length to see the direction and strength of the wind. He removed his hat and shaded his face from the sun as he calculated the height. He usually shot from above and not below, so he wasn't sure how it was going to work out. After leaning his rifle against a boulder, the captain undid his cinch, pulled his saddle off his Appaloosa, and laid it on a small snow-covered rock so he could stand and shoot with something steady underneath.

The scope was a long metal tube. Although the glass rifle sight scope was more precise, it was too fragile to travel in the mountains. After levering in a buffalo round, Forrester made a deep sigh, letting out all his breath, controlling his breathing as he felt his heartbeat slow. A bead of sweat became a rivulet as it squirreled down the side of his face, cutting a white path and then dripping off his chin onto the snow.

The safety trigger clicked, and he moved his finger to the firing trigger. He breathed out one final time and applied pressure. BOOM roared a 52-caliber round out of the barrel and out of sight, followed by a flash of fire and smoke. Kit watched with his collapsible spyglass. They waited for the bullet to reach the target zone as they held their breaths. It felt like ice was injected into their veins as they breathlessly waited for the results.

UP ON THE HILL, the Blackfoot war chief watched as curls touched the edges of his lips. The warriors around him huddled for a parlay at his signal. They had been tracking the miner for days. He had one of the finest mules they had laid eyes on, and they wanted it for themselves. The blundering fools who killed him for the same animal had no idea that they had stepped into the middle of them. The Indians weren't quite sure who the two newcomers were.

For a moment, they thought they were friends of the three buffalo hunters. Then, when they shot their first volley of arrows, the newcomers gunned them down in the blink of an eye, and they saw they were mistaken. They dove for cover before the war party could respond. There were too many rocks below where they could take shelter from the arrows. The hostiles were going to have to climb down the steep path and go and get them.

"They are making it easier for us by killing each other. Now, we will have four mules *and* their horses. We can butcher them here before we leave, but the mules go with us, along with all their guns. Maybe we will be lucky, and they will have plenty of ammunition. My revolver has only three bullets. Stealing a pistol or musket is easier than boxes of bullets."

"When can we attack, Lone Wolf? We should take advantage of their moment of weakness. They will be dazed and stunned now that they have seen our numbers and have drawn the first blood."

"You're right. It is time to teach these cowards what we are made of. Take no prisoners. I don't want to bother dragging them along with us. We have enough with the animals to keep us busy."

"We can torture them first. It won't take long. Then we will take their hair and cut their throats. I have some of the young warriors with us, so this will be their first lesson. It is better if it is an easy kill, and two of them will have drawn their first blood. Today, we will see who is cut out to be a true Blackfoot warrior and who is not."

"We'll let the young men enjoy the glory of battle. I will sit here and watch. This will tell us who will be warriors and who will trade their lances for bows and arrows and become hunters. Only a real, live battle will give us the answers we need. It is good to have this opportunity to have a test. I will be the arbitrator. This will be interesting and maybe even fun. I don't know if I can resist joining in, though."

They were so drenched in the excitement of the contact that as it washed through them, it took all the nervous tension along with their reason for life or death.

When the heavy-caliber bullet hit, Lone Wolf felt like a sledgehammer had smacked him in the chest, making him rock back and forth as he struggled not to go down. It came out of nowhere, and suddenly, he was dazed and confused. He looked at his bodyguards and blinked before looking down. That was when they heard the buffalo round crack loudly. The young Blackfoot warriors scattered like roaches when light spilled into a dark room. The others smelled fear, and the riders struggled to hold their ground with their ponies.

Lone Wolf's horse was so well trained that it didn't

move, even with the smell of panic, which was strong in the air. Nobody was quite sure of what had happened yet. He looked down and saw black blood bubbling from a hole the size of his fist in his gut. He was quickly bleeding out from a busted liver.

BOOM rang out another shot, and the man next to the war chief was hit. He was lucky and was only winged. A few seconds later, the third shot sounded, zipping through the air and splitting a rock in two on impact.

When the second bullet hit the brave, it spun him around like a top. Even though he was only hit on the shoulder, he instantly went into shock and spiraled off his horse. He lay face down in the snow, breathing erratically. When Lone Wolf fell off his pony, he had been dead for minutes. He sat frozen on his horse until a gust of wind blew him over, and he toppled into the snow. A red stain grew below their bodies like it had a life of its own. As the war chief died, he was still trying to figure out what had happened, but then he was gone.

———

WITHOUT ANY ORDERS or organizational semblance, the entire war party wheeled around and ran. Below, the White men showed themselves, but only after they heard the clatter of trotting horses beating across the trail and when they were sure they had left. It looked like they had lost enough men for a day. As soon as they knew they were gone for good, their anger drained away like the ground after a flash storm, and they both felt exhausted. It was as much a battle of nerves as it was of arrows and bullets.

When the yellow disk neared the earth's rim, it sat squat, pulsating, and malevolent as sparks from the dying campfire scampered across the mountain, disappearing into the distance. The wind whistled through the pines. That morning, the dawn-broached sky was a hellish red. Sometimes, a quirk of fate made men into tigers instead of house cats.

A WELCOME RETURN

ON THEIR WAY HOME, THEY WALKED THEIR HORSES through the day, occasionally standing in their stirrups to peer into the distance, assuring themselves they weren't riding into an ambush. Kit watched with the palm of his hand, shading his eyes while he chewed on the end of a dead cheroot. He looked out at the climbing, stretching, never-ending wilderness before them as his tongue slid over his cracked, dry lips.

After riding all day, they stopped and made a cold camp so that if the Blackfoot warriors decided to seek revenge, they wouldn't be easy to find. They unsaddled the horses and ground-tied them before making camp. They used their hooves to uncover what was left of the grass, sliding their jaws.

Still, the mountain men took turns doing guard duty that night to ensure their safety, especially with so many Blackfoot warriors around. On the fourth and final shift, Kit finally saw the sliver of red in the blackness to the east and knew it would soon be daylight.

He nudged the captain with the toe of his boot and

said, "It's time to get up, partner. We should be back sometime today, but you know these parts better than I do. Whatcha think?"

Will sat up, rubbing his eyes with the heels of his hands as he blinked the sleep away. He stood, shook the snow off his buffalo blanket, and prepared his bedroll to tie on the back of his horse. Everything around them was covered in three more inches of powder, and it was much colder than the previous night.

"We'll get there today if we don't run into any trouble and this weather holds. I'd say some more snow is on its way from the color of the sky. This time of year, having a surprise blizzard to kick off the winter season is not unusual. Then, it usually warms up again, but from then on out, cold weather would set in until spring. It gets so cold here in the winter, we have to stay indoors for two to three months."

Kit continued to stare, tight-jawed and solemn. As they saddled their horses and prepared to leave, Will knew something was eating at him, but felt he didn't need to ask because he was sure Carson would say something soon enough. He was accustomed to his own ways, so he remained patient. The captain was the one who would grind on something he didn't like for days before bringing it up, but in the end, he always spat it out like a bad taste in his mouth.

When the glaring sun hit the horizon, Kit pulled his hat down, shadowing his eyes in the brim.

"Those Blackfoot trash weren't people: they're no more than ramped dogs," Kit spat. He had been chewing on what had happened all night. "They were just waiting to prey on the old man. I've been fighting them for years and ain't found a good one yet. As far as

I've seen, they're all kidnappers and murderers. Their mothers must have mated with scorpions."

"And you think that I'm supposed to believe that?" The captain spread his hands. "Not everybody red is bad: not even the Blackfoot people. In my days back in the Territories, closer to civilization, I've seen plenty of White men just as evil, if not worse. At least the Indians have the excuse that we're stealing their land and killing off their food. All those folks on the Oregon Trail are what have the Indian Nations angry and up in arms. How would you like it if somebody came and took your home away when you were young and back in Kentucky?"

"I can't tell you how many times I've heard that same excuse. For me, it doesn't hold water. No matter what you say, I doubt I'll ever change my mind. I've seen too much of their wicked ways. I know for a fact that they've invented more ways of torture than any other tribe."

The new friends looked tired and had curious eyes. It was clear that they didn't agree on everything, but they felt comfortable together just the same. The wrinkles in their faces were dirt-creased, and they both had a week's stubble, something that the captain hated, but Kit didn't seem to mind. Kit found it curious how the captain ignored the fact that he was missing an arm. He never spoke about it and, for all appearances, seemed not to notice.

You could see the iron will in the tight line of Will's jawline. Sun-darkened, thin-lined features beneath the wide brim of a faded beige hat slapped up on one side like the cavalry. He pushed his cover back from his forehead, easing the hot grip of the headband, and grinned, showing rows of straight, white teeth. He liked Kit well enough, but they just didn't see eye to eye on some things, like Blackfoot people.

As soon as they were on recognizable ground again, the captain sighed a breath of relief. It looked like they wouldn't run into any more trouble. With the weather getting colder, they didn't make as good of time as the captain had hoped, and it was dark by the time they arrived at the edge of the tree line near the north gate.

The captain whistled twice, then waited and whistled again. Each compound member had a code, and those they changed regularly so an Indian spy wouldn't know what the right signal was and trick their way in to steal something. Usually, Dog gave them notice of strangers, but as he got older, he wasn't as sharp as he once was. Since Rusty adopted him or the Dog adopted the man, he had no idea how old he was, but it became more obvious with each passing time that he was getting on in years.

Angus appeared in a circle of lantern light, but you could only see his legs and the end of the barrel of a long gun. In the dusk, his features were hidden in shadows, but he could make out the silhouette of his cross-draw revolvers wrapped around his waist. Levi reached the porch ceiling and lit both lamps over the long wooden table, bathing them in light.

At first, Johnson showed concern momentarily, but then he saw who it was, and he relaxed into a grin. "Well, I'll be. It looks like you boys made it back in one piece."

The captain stepped out of the saddle, letting his reins trail as he smiled. Betty ran to him like she thought she would never see him again. McFarlin's white beard and mustache hid his wide grin, but they could see it when it reached his eyes. The marshal stared at the new arrivals from the door with his thumbs hooked on his gun belt.

Kit stretched his neck and gulped cool mountain air as he kicked his leg over the saddle horn. He slipped off his horse, his boots buried in the newly fallen snow.

Dust danced in the light, falling through the window, making yellow squares on the floor, and more light slanted through the open door. The riders watched as people poured into the yard, their faces full of curiosity. A scattering of nervous laughter rippled through their clan. Bar-Chee had her arms wrapped around little Money so he wouldn't run out into the snow and spook the animals.

"Don't worry about your horses, boys. You look tired enough." Virgil climbed astride Levi's horse, which knew him, and he walked through the corral, ducking his head as he crossed under the barn door and into the stables as he led Carson's mount. He would brush them down, water them, and feed them before putting them to sleep in their stables. Then he planned to hurry back to Rusty's cabin to hear all about what happened. He knew it had to be engaging with Captain Forrester and Kit Carson together, telling stories of their last adventure.

Everybody headed for the open cabin door and the warmth of a fire. They could hear the women complaining that they were letting all the cold in and hot air out. As usual, the fireplace was roaring, and the smell of food came from the back corner of Angus's kitchen. A water barrel sat beside the stove, and a large ladle hung from the side. A small set of stairs on the far back right led into a dry cellar, and their last line of defense, were they to be so unlucky.

Levi sat pondering as he took a sip of coffee before speaking. He wondered if Kit would start first, but he sat silently staring at him. Everyone was waiting to hear what he had to say.

Will took a deep breath and said, "We caught the outlaws with all they stole and then some. They were all killed, but nobody in the posse died. Considering their inexperience, that's a small miracle. I believe they'll be safe and sound back in Fort Boise with Mr. McKay's money in a week or so. That town runs on that man's business. The deputized common folks surprised us and held up their end as well as expected. We had a run-in with a few Blackfoot warriors, too. That didn't go too well for them, though."

"A few?" Kit asked. "I'd say there were more like fifty." He poured three fingers of corn liquor from the ceramic jug and knocked it back in one toss. They could see his eyes water from the harsh and bitter smell as it stung his nose.

"I tried but never got a good count 'cause they were too far away. They kept popping up from behind rocks."

"Not far enough, I'd say, Captain. You shot the war chief from over six hundred yards, and he was mounted. You winged the second in command, too. That's some fine shooting in my book."

"You should see Levi and Rusty. They wouldn't have just winged the second man," the captain said, as his neck turned red with embarrassment. He wasn't used to talking about himself and his exploits.

"Being modest all the time never made a man a penny, pard. If you work as a scout, your reputation is what you get paid for. Plus, I doubt it mattered that much," Kit replied. "With that buffalo gun winged or hit, you're still dead."

"I've got a surprise waiting in the kitchen. It should be ready within the hour. But don't mind me. Go ahead and tell us all the details. I can hear y'all just fine from the stove as long as you don't whisper."

Angus wiped his hands back and forth on his apron as he grinned, his eyes full of expectation. Unlike Levi, Angus loved praise when he made a good meal. Today, he had a special treat and was excited just thinking about it.

"You go ahead and tell the story, Levi. Sometimes, I like to listen and not have to talk."

Carson sat at the table with a scrap of paper in his hand. He wetted the tip of the yellow pencil with his tongue and looked at his old and new friends curiously.

"Would you mind if I put some of your exploits on paper and have them published back east? All the things that happen on this mountain could fill a journal. How would you like to have your names known coast to coast?"

Strangely enough, nobody answered right away. It appeared they were all shocked by the proposition and had to consider its pluses and negatives.

"All right, it's fine with me. I'd love to be portrayed in a newspaper as a skilled mountain man," Money said, breaking the tension. "Money Penny. I can just see it in the headlines." He grinned like a possum.

Suddenly, Kit burst out laughing until he got a stitch, and soon, they were all giggling, chuckling, or laughing out loud. It was both a happy laugh of relief and an escape from all the built-up tension from the last days.

Kit noticed the bullet hole in the marshal's shirt. He arched his brow, bunching his lips as he weighed the seriousness and asked, "How'd it happen? Are you all right?"

Marshal Walker chuckled and said, "The bullet went through my shirt and was stopped by my diary and a stack of old wanted posters." He pulled it out and showed Carson.

"So, you're a journal man, are you? Just like me. Mine has never saved my life, but has made me a living."

"I'm a marshal and have to keep track of who's wanted and who's been caught. At least, I used to have to. Now I run around the mountains with this bunch."

Originally, Money expected Mr. Carson to be big like Levi, even larger than life, but he was quite the opposite and didn't appear to be the dangerous man the papers depicted. Despite the buckskins, he didn't look much like an Indian fighter. Then again, Money wasn't quite sure what one looked like.

They could all see the hope and excitement in Money's eyes. The previous year, he had heard his dad read all about Mr. Carson from a dime novel as they sat around the dinner table in their old ranch. The cheap newspaper was tattered and dog-eared from being read so often. At the time, the boy had difficulty imagining such a famous man, but now that he met him, he was both excited and a little disappointed, simultaneously.

"Don't be surprised by Money's size. Inside, he's as smart and as big as me. It's in here where it counts." Levi thumbed his chest. "Stick around for a spell, and you'll see. I was pleasantly surprised myself, especially after he asked me to be his mentor."

"I've known Rusty since 1837." Kit grinned. "We met at the Rendezvous, didn't we? He beat me at the shooting contest, but I doubt he could do it again." He looked at Levi and winked.

An orange glowing window and double lamps under the porch's roof illuminated the wide compound clearing. The yellow glow of kerosene lanterns reflected in the slightly steamed glass and spilled onto the ground in squares.

Money sat there staring blankly into the crackling fire like he had forgotten where he was. He was daydreaming about him doing all the things he heard that night at the table.

"How about you sit beside me, Money? I bet you have a story or two to tell yourself. I can see it in your face." When Carson smiled, he showed a row of corncob teeth.

Money pressed his lips into a tight smile as his heart rate flew off the charts because Kit remembered his name.

"Maybe—er, sure, Mr. Carson." Money shrugged so hard that his shoulders touched his ears. "I don't know what stories I could tell *you*, sir."

"We don't use mister or sir with me, young man. You can call me Kit from here on out. You got that Money?"

Money nodded so hard that his head looked like his neck was tied to a spring.

SURROUNDED

AT FIRST, THEY HEARD ONLY A FEW WOLVES, BUT THEY continued to howl half the night. Then came the choir of coyotes, which seemed much closer than usual. The large moon flung long, silvery shadows across the countryside. As the wind continued to blow, they appeared to move. Suddenly, a large pack of wild dogs jumped over the fence and raced across the yard like they were running from a mountain lion. They tore through the compound, only looking for their possible escape. They cleared the south fence as one. There were more than twenty feral canines.

Dog sat up beside the fire, threw his head back, and began to howl. The sound pierced the silence and woke everyone up in Rusty's place, even those in the second cabin and pair of teepees. In seconds, half-dressed men with guns in their hands walked out into the cold. Snowflakes as big as rabbits' ears slowly floated to the ground as the wind suddenly stopped. Noise traveled easily through the crisp night air.

"Get the girls out of those teepees and into the

cabins," Marshall Walker whispered. "That will render arrows useless." He drew his pistols and followed them across the night outside the brick-and-rail fence. Nickers and ninnies came from the corral. Everybody was on edge and expected something to happen.

"I think we better all head for Rusty's cabin, just in case," Levi said. "I'm getting a bad gut feeling. Something ain't right."

Even though they were whispering, the sound traveled beyond the fence. Every sound was as clear as a bell. Suddenly, bushes moved near the tree line. They had chopped down the trees and removed foliage and anywhere else to hide from the corral to the trees over two hundred yards out. They had a clear field of fire when attacked. Over the years, they slowly adapted to the times and the threat, primarily hostile Indians, since so few White men lived in these parts. They stood out to any passing Indian of the seven tribes that populated the area.

"What in the world is all that ruckus?" Carson grumbled. "Is your dog always waking people up in the middle of the night?" His arms hung limp, his revolvers in his fists.

"If he does go off like that, it ain't for nothing," Rusty replied when he walked out the cabin door, slipping his suspenders over his shoulders. He wore Colt Pattersons in cross-draw holsters.

Angus crawled out of his bunk in his faded red long johns, grabbing his new rifle from the gun rack over the fire. The bolt-action was loud when he levered the heavy forty-five-gram round home.

Betty, Bar-Chee, and Pine Needle all ran for shelter. Someone slammed the door, and the shutter closed with a bang as rifles poked through all three gun slats. Dahteste disregarded the danger and stood ready by her husband with a quiver of arrows strapped across her back and a bow in her hands. She was almost as dangerous as any man there. That was why she had been selected to be the war chief of the Crow stronghold if and when they waged war on another tribe.

The adumbrations of the horses' legs were like black elongated sticks in the flickering light as Virgil and the captain herded them all into the safety of the stables. It wouldn't do to let their horses be stolen. The compound members were as close to their mounts as they were to their friends. Birds chattered in the trees from across the clearing outside the fence.

"Thems Blackfoot talking to each other. I can't tell what they say, but I've heard them make bird calls. Make no mistake about it, those aren't night birds." Rusty cocked his ear and continued to listen. "Get all the guns into the main cabin. I'm not sure, but we may be surrounded."

"Surrounded?" Kit asked. "That's a pretty big statement. Don't you think you're overreacting? If there are Blackfoot warriors out there, I'm game. Of all the Indians, I hate them the most. They've killed too many of my friends to forget."

The metal clicks of over a dozen hammers seemed to sound at once. Now, they could all see the bushes rustle near the trees.

"I wonder what they want," Joseph said.

"Our scalps," Kit replied. "I doubt they're here for a friendly visit."

"And how can you be so sure?" Levi asked. "Maybe they're here to ask a favor. If not, why haven't they attacked yet? Usually, Indians hit at the crack of dawn. They aren't ones to linger when they have a job to do."

"I sure do hope you're right because I believe there're too many to count," Kit said, smiling alarmingly.

The women all saw it, but the men didn't notice. They were all preparing themselves to go to that place they went to for times of violence when they had to do their jobs flawlessly or suffer the consequences. Especially with so many enemy Blackfoot so close.

After hours of nothing, they saw the first hint of light on the world's rim. During the night, they had seen silhouettes appear for seconds only to dive back into the security of the deep shadows. The outlines weren't visible for long enough to take a bead. They felt that when a fiery disk rose with the color of steel, then the attack would come.

It snowed again that night. With the return of the breeze, fallen leaves lay like golden paper on the damp, snow-white surface of the compound. The only tracks in the yard were to and from the two outhouses on the edge of the fence.

Their shadows grew long as the sun appeared on the horizon, but now it wasn't only outlines they could see. Now, they occasionally got a glimpse of a Blackfoot warrior. Men's images would appear for a second or two all the way around the compound.

When they saw them, the churlish-looking Blackfoot warriors sucked their teeth and looked around with crazy eyes. Arrows sat strung in bows, ready to fire.

First, the sound, then their shapes finally became visible in the wavering rays of the sun. There were warriors posted in a circle every thirty feet, completely around the compound. There were far more hostiles than they could deal with.

The war chief was assembled with six warriors on a triple backdrop of the eastern horizon, like black images of marionettes with the sun rising at their backs. His headdress and modern weapons set him apart from the rest. Little birds chattered as the wind returned, and vultures rose from the ground, finishing their meal with bony wings: whoop, whoop, whooping like marionettes on a string.

"I don't see any white flags, do you, Rusty?" Levi asked. "It sure does look like a hard nut to crack if they want to have a go at us."

"Nope, I'm afraid not. But I don't see anybody pointing their bows and arrows toward us yet. Whatever you do, nobody shoots. We don't want to be the ones who start this. We may have bitten off more than we could chew."

"I don't speak much Blackfoot, but I know enough to be polite. Maybe I should walk out there and ask them what they want. None of y'all thought of that, did ya?"

"None of us are that crazy, Levi," Kit replied, but the unusual smile was still on his face. For all appearances, he didn't have a fearful bone in his body. He was as calm as a millpond early in the morning. "I speak a little Blackfoot. I've shot, killed, and captured too many not to have picked up some. Maybe between us, we can at least find out why they're ticked off."

"It wasn't that long ago you scamped that Blackfoot warrior. I hope they aren't here for that."

"Should we leave our weapons and carry a white flag?" Kit asked. It wasn't clear if he was in jest or serious.

"I want my guns on me where I can get to 'em, if I need 'em. The rest of you get into the cabin. If you see something's going down, start shootin'. You can watch us through your spyglasses to make sure. This looks like it might be hit-and-miss, but I can't think of anything else."

"I should go instead of you, Levi. You might think you run things around here, but I'm still the boss." Rusty moved his chew to his other jaw and spat.

"You don't speak half as much Blackfoot as I do. I don't wanna be the boss of anybody. All I wanna do is convince those fellas circling us to leave us be."

"Ya ready?" Kit smiled. He looked like he was headed to have breakfast with his Indian enemies. "Now that we've decided what to do, it'll be best if we go and get it over before they call for a full-scale attack. Then it will be too late, and there won't be any more choices to be made."

A tooth-clenched curse followed the marshal as he turned and headed for the cabin. "You two are crazier than cockroaches when the lights go on."

"Save the sun, a person could lie there and hide past the tree line and never be discovered," Levi whispered, "but there ain't nobody hidin' anymore."

This is gonna be the longest two hundred yards we've ever walked.

It was true that as soon as they stepped off the porch and into the snow, heading for the fence, time seemed to slow down to nearly a stop. They both felt themselves exposed to a well-placed arrow or bullet. They had to forcibly push the thoughts out of their minds and focus on walking. They didn't think about what they would say because they still didn't know.

"Any ideas, Levi?" Carson shot him a look from the corner of his eye. The smile remained cemented on his face. Levi wondered if it was a façade or if it was real.

"I reckon we'll ask 'em what they want, then I guess we'll go from there."

Their eyes hid in the shade of their hats as they kicked fresh snowflakes into the air. The Indians were so still that they almost seemed unreal. The only thing that moved was their eyes as they minutely studied their progress. The vein on Levi's forehead pulsated like a fuse as his heart hammered between his ears. He felt the palms of his hands go sweaty as a cold chill raced up his spine.

Fifty yards away, their feet felt like they weighed a hundred pounds, leaving drag marks in the snow. Now, they were close enough to see the wrinkles in their faces.

"*Oki, tsanitapi? Tsa kitsiska`sim?*"

"I got the hello, how ya doin', but what did you ask next?"

"I ask him his name," Kit answered with a voice that would calm a crying baby.

"*Tsima kitomahtotopa?*" the war chief asked. "*Tsa kitsiska'sim?*"

"*Nitsiska'sim* Kit Carson." He patted Beaver on the shoulder and said, "Levi Johnson. *Tsima Kitomahtotopa* Richmond, Kentucky."

"*Nitsiska'sim* Black Bear. So, you must speak English too," the war chief said as he carefully said the foreign words. "I am impressed with your knowledge of Blackfoot. Does your friend here, Levi Johnson, speak Blackfoot, too? We already know he speaks fluent Crow."

"I thought I spoke a bit, but it seems my friend here, Kit, speaks a lot more."

"If you only knew what an exaggeration that was." Kit laughed. "I sure am glad you speak English."

"So, you are the famous Kit Carson, explorer, soldier, and Indian fighter? I have heard many stories about you and your battles with my people."

"Yes, sir, but the latter only works when pressed." The same smile remained on Kit's face, but now it appeared genuine. "I don't deny who I am. So, while we're being honest with each other, why don't you tell us why you're here? You didn't just wander on this compound by chance, of that much, I'm sure."

"Why, I thought you would know why we are here."

"I reckon you're here to fight, ain't cha?"

"If we were here to fight you, we would have attacked at first light with the advantage of our backs to the sun and in your eyes. You are often sung of in our elders' songs as a great warrior, and I wanted to know who my enemy is. Keep your friends close but your adversaries closer."

"How come you speak such good English?" Levi scratched his beard to try to hide his confusion.

"I studied from a White man in Fort Boise. I dressed like those poor Indians who live outside the fort and beg for scraps. There was an old soldier there who had a picture book, and we began there. Then, he taught me my numbers and letters. In turn, I taught him how to make a bow and arrows and taught him some of my Blackfoot language, too. I guess I am a quick learner. Maybe that is why I am a war chief." Black Bear chuckled at his last remark.

"Well, I reckon the only thing we can do then is

invite you to eat," Levi said. "I'm afraid we can't feed you all since you're so many, but we can invite you and a few of your men for coffee and a bowl of black beans."

"This is good, Levi Johnson. You know how to respect your enemies when you meet them. Do you know that the Blackfoot people call you Beaver?"

"Why, back home, everybody calls me Beaver. Especially my friends and the Crow do too."

"Don't be confused by my gesture, Beaver. We will only be friends today. If we meet again, it will not be on these terms. We will be enemies again."

"If you didn't come here to attack us, why did you bring so many warriors with ya?" Levi asked.

"This is Crow country. We had to show enough force so no one would attack us if we didn't attack them."

"And you're willing to risk a fight with the Crow just to meet little old me?" Now, it was Kit's turn to laugh.

"Of course. I have spent my life preparing to fight and kill you, but that will come another day when all the stars line up, and the moon is right. Today is peaceful, and there will be no violence unless you or your people start it. Then, *we* will finish it."

"How about calling your warriors off so my people can enjoy our meal with you, Black Bear? I must admit my folks are a little jittery with fifty warriors or more circling them. We have our women we've gotta remember. We don't wanna upset them now, do we?"

Black Bear nodded with hooded eyes and gave an order in no more than a whisper. His men instantly jumped into action without a word.

Two of his six personal guards ran off and ordered everyone to stand down. They all made camp inside the clearing near the tree line in case they had to seek cover.

They immediately started fires and began making food. It was clear that this war party worked like a fine Swiss watch. The White men realized how fortunate they had been, but kept a note in the back of their minds to remember their discipline.

"Four of my personal guards will be joining me to eat. I always heard that White men ate enough for breakfast to last them all day. This is something that I am curious to see."

"Well, I reckon you heard right. Angus puts on a mighty fine breakfast." Beaver's stomach started to grumble as soon as they thought about food.

"I've been witness to that. He makes the best breakfast I've eaten west of Kentucky, and that's going some."

As strange as it all seemed, having a meal with the enemy proved to be an enjoyable one and even began to sway Kit Carson's belief that all Blackfeet were evil. Of course they remained enemies, but now he saw that deep inside, some of the warriors he fought against weren't all that different than himself.

HAPPY COUPLE

NOW THAT ALL THE CONFUSION ABOUT WHAT WANATA wanted with Levi and Potak seemed to be resolved, at least for the time being, Silvia felt safe enough to go for their last ride with Rusty before the winter weather arrived, making it too uncomfortable to enjoy the great outdoors. They decided to take advantage of an open space free of work to take a ride and enjoy each other alone. They had gotten a taste of being only two during their visit to the secret canyon, which turned out to be such a memorable occasion that it was all they could think about after the trouble was over: another escape.

Sure, the first snows had begun, but normally, the dangerous weather would come later in the year, although in the Rockies, nothing was written in stone except the mountains themselves. Occasionally, early fall suddenly became winter, albeit for just a while. When the real cold came, it was easy to tell the difference: it got too cold to snow, and everything was covered in ice.

Rusty dropped his reins and spread his opened

hands expansively as they rode single file through the canyon's hidden entrance. Silvia's eyes grew wider as her broad grin showed a line of white teeth. She had seen the canyon on their previous visit, but it was never covered in snow. She gasped at the beauty when she passed the end of the crack in the rock that made the entrance. The pines were covered in crystal white powder, as was the lush grass they had seen on their previous visit. The pond under the spring and all the creeks that ran from it had thick ice on the tops, although water continued to flow underneath. The thin stream of water that filled the pond was frozen solid. An icicle six feet long extended from the water source as though suspended in midair.

Their previous visit was a hypnotizing time for them both, and they wanted to repeat it, although they knew they couldn't get caught out by the weather. At this time of year, it changed like the shades of a chameleon. Whenever you ventured into the wilderness, you had to prepare for all that nature had to throw at you. Soon, the cold would arrive in earnest, and little by little, their activities would encompass less and less land around the compound until all they went out for was to trap and to the outhouses: one for the men and one for the ladies.

When the dead of winter set in, they couldn't even do that because they would be confined inside for two months or more. That was when they spent the captive weeks kneading buffalo skins and various hides to sell in McKay's Trading Post, hardware store, bar, and restaurant. Everybody who came to Fort Boise passed by to sell their furs and trade for their general needs. It was the heartbeat of that part of the wilderness, and without it, traveling along the Oregon Trail would be much more difficult. Fort Hall, three hundred miles away, was the closest semblance of civilization.

Silvia's face said she was of Mexican blood and had a certain mysterious beauty under her sun-darkened skin. She giggled again, and the frown eased off Rusty's gruff face. When he traveled, he was always prepared if trouble awaited them just around the corner. A reckless traveler in the wilderness could become a dead one in the blink of an eye.

She was healthy-looking, full of life, and even a little bosomier than the other women, something Rusty secretly liked but would never say. Although he loved his wife dearly, he wasn't that kind of man. There wasn't anything about her that he didn't like, and luckily, she got along with all his friends.

When Rusty saw Silvia's smile, his face and eyes always softened. She made him feel like no other did. When he was with her, it made him want to be a better man, and it was all for her. The Lord had blessed them when he crossed their paths.

Rusty picked Silvia up in his arms like a little child and carried her out of the freezing cold air as snow flurries swirled around them.

Silvia's hair was pulled into a ponytail, and her dark skin matched her brown eyes. When the freezing air went up her riding dress, she shuddered like a feather in a windstorm. Her mouth brushed against Rusty's. For an instant, they clung together like koala bears.

For Rusty, it wasn't her pretty face, flowing black hair, and well-formed figure that made her so beautiful to him. There was something in her voice that told him what was in her soul.

"It will be too cold to stay out here and watch the stars like planned. From the looks of the sky, the temperatures are gonna drop tonight. We'll be warmer inside."

They lie around the fire in a yellow, flickering circle of light. Rusty leaned with his back to his saddle and his hands behind his head as he stared at the flames. Silvia lay her head on his chest, closed her eyes, and listened to his heartbeat and the night birds chattering in the dark. From the outside, the teepee glowed orange like a lampshade in the night.

"You no longer have to court me, Mr. Steel."

He pulled her into his arms again and kissed her. Rusty grinned. "I've been waitin' for that all day." It seemed like forever before they broke their embrace.

When she caught him, Rusty's face went hot with embarrassment. Silvia smiled. "Don't worry, Rusty. I don't mind you staring at me because I know you love me."

———

WHEN THEY AWOKE the following morning, they could hear the wind howling. The buffalo-skin walls of the teepee fluttered in the stiff breeze. When Rusty untied the door flap and pushed it aside, he saw the color of the sky. He stopped like his blood froze as he stared into the distance. The snow appeared to be blue—a sure-fire sign of a blizzard.

"We'd best grab our things, darlin'. A blizzard is on its way and is maybe too close to head back. I don't know whether we should try to beat it home or wait it out in our teepee. It's quick enough to take down and store for the winter, but we're a good way from the compound. If we stay here, we don't have enough firewood to keep from freezing, and I don't know how much we can scare up with nearly a foot of snow." Rusty looked at his wife with worried eyes, making her gasp. "The only thing we can't fight here in the Rocky Mountains is Mother Nature. All we can do is try to survive her."

Close to her cheek, he whispered over the howling wind, "Don't worry, I'll take care of you."

"Are you going to save my life again?" She continued to stare at her husband with loving eyes, but he didn't know what to say. "I want to be with you forever."

"If that's what I've gotta do, I will. You stay here and stoke the fire while I gather some stones."

"What do you want rocks for, Rusty?" But he was already out the flap and had disappeared as Silvia sat looking perplexed.

When he came back, he had arms full of fist-sized stones. He dropped them into the fire and began to dig a recess in the hard dirt. When the rocks were hot, he used Silvia's and his Bowie knives to remove them and lay them in the depression. Then he covered it with dirt, laid the buffalo blankets on top of it, then they covered themselves with bear blankets. He looked at her and nodded, and she knew that everything was going to be all right.

"Don't you ever scare from the danger, you know, worry about losing your life during one of your encounters with violence?" Silvia asked as her ears filled with the sound of the roaring wind.

"I've never thought much about danger, now that you mention it. Believe it or not, I reckon nobody's had the gumption to ask. It doesn't seem like such a big deal if you don't ponder on it much. It's just another day in a mountain man's life."

Silvia started with another round of questions, but Rusty knew she was just trying to hide her fear, and with one look, she stopped. Right then, he had to think about what was to come and what more he could do.

"I'll be right back," he said, and he was out the door again as the wind made the flap flutter.

Silvia could hear her husband chopping on something, but she wasn't quite sure what it was. Then, just as suddenly as he had left, he returned with two chunks of ice.

"Give me the bean pot and the kettle so I can fill them with ice. It'll melt by the fire, so we won't go thirsty and have water for coffee to keep us warm. We've got plenty of hardtack to snack on, and I brought two cans of pears." "I reckon God's blessed us despite the storm," they said simultaneously, and both broke out laughing because it was the second time it had happened.

Rusty took her pretty face into his hands and kissed her on the forehead. Goose bumps instantly sprouted on her arms. That was the last thing they remembered before falling asleep beneath the snow cloud and howling wind.

"I can feel the warm rocks under us," Silvia whispered in Rusty's ear. "It's like a little oven. Maybe this storm isn't such a bad idea after all. Here, we're all alone, and nobody can bother us."

Instants before sleep took over, they both thought different things. Silvia thought about how lucky she had been to find a man when she was already middle-aged. Rusty was hoping that it was a flash blizzard coming and wouldn't last long, or this nice little warm teepee wouldn't do them much good before a massive winter storm. Still, he assured himself that it was too early in the season to be too concerned. Yet, now he knew that he had much more to lose than he had for the recklessly lived last ten years.

That night, while Silvia slept, Rusty feigned sleep, barely getting a wink. He knew what to do in extremely bad weather, but to be honest, despite knowing better, he believed he might have been caught out unprepared. Maybe that was something negative love gave him. He had more difficulty keeping his eye on the target. He snuck outside thrice in the roaring wind to ensure the teepee's ground stakes were secure and weren't about to pull loose. Then their shelter would fly away with the wind, and they could freeze.

At the height of the blizzard, the buffalo-skin walls shuddered, so much that they thought the stitching might tear. Despite being in a canyon, the wind still nearly swept Rusty off his feet every time he had to go outside. When he walked into the wind, he had to lean forward or topple over.

Amazingly, Silvia didn't wake up all night. Perhaps it was the fear that had worn her out and spared her a fearful night. Still, the stones under the dirt and her two thick, warm blankets left her cozy and warm. Rusty pulled the bison hide over her head to help block the sound.

Lucky for them, when they awoke, the blizzard had quickly worn itself out and turned into steady, thick snow. The wind had stopped howling and had dropped to a few knots. Until the sun rose in the sky, they stayed snuggled up within the circle of campfire light in the center of the teepee, cuddling to keep warm.

When Steel saw the sun shine through the teepee walls, he knew it was time to check things out. He undid the door flap and pulled it aside. To his surprise, the snowdrift was five feet high. He could barely see over the top.

"Give me the bucket and let me dig us out of here."

Both husband and wife labored, one with a frying pan and the other with a pot. Soon, they had removed the snowdrift and could see outside.

"I should have thought about bringing snowshoes, just in case. The horses can push through this, but our legs are too short. I'm gonna have to make some provisional snow shows, and we'll have to hike it home. At least we're alive."

GRIZZLY BEARS

THE MEN HAD TO LOOSEN THEIR BELTS AS THEY SAT around the table after their wild turkey dinner, with biscuits drowned in gravy, a pot of mush, and cornbread heaped with raspberry preserves. Several cans of peaches made the dessert.

"You know what I'd like to do before I get back to Fort Boise and get stuck there by the weather. Mind you, I can think of worse places to hang out. I want a set of those grizzly bear claws that Levi, Rusty, and Will wear. Now I know those bears didn't give them to you, so I want to do what you did to get 'em. It's one of the things on my list to do before I die."

"You keep a list of things you ought to do before you die?" Money asked, puzzled. "What's that supposed to mean, Kit?"

"It's a list of things that I wanna do someday but haven't got to it yet—before I kick the bucket. You might want to start one now while you're still young. I started mine when I was nine. I can't remember exactly when I added a grizzly bear to the items, but it's been a long time. It seems like I've always been too busy, but maybe now I'll have the chance."

The three with the claw necklaces laughed nervously. "You don't know what we had to go through to get these claws, Kit," Rusty said ominously.

"That's right. You don't wanna acquire them the same way we did," the captain replied. "I can guarantee you that."

"We nearly gave our lives for these. They weren't from the bears we shot." Beaver grinned, fingering his necklace. "We haven't even counted the ones we had to kill over the years. It's easy enough to run across a female in the birthing season, and they'll stand and fight. Be forewarned, if you run, they'll chase you down. Rusty and Angus have been killing bears for over fifteen years, and Mountain Dennis, before them, God rest his soul. No, sir, these were from bears that nearly killed us. I had two pairs, but I gave one to my apprentice. One day, he'll have to earn a set, too. Just like you, if you want to do it how we did, which I can assure you, you don't."

"There'll still be some of the big males around. They're the last bears to hibernate, but the mothers will be in caves with their cubs in this weather. The big boys are the last ones to head for their winter cave. Now that the salmon season has passed and there're no berries left on the vines, they'll eat just about anything before they bed down for the winter.

"Where's the place with the most bears, then?" Kit asked. "Or are they too territorial, so they live far apart? I've read enough about them, but I don't have any first-hand knowledge."

"From what the Indians say in the gossip, the Black Forest is the place with the most game, and the bears will follow the food," the marshal replied. "If I never run into a grizzly bear, it'll be fine by me. I find it a fool's notion to take such unnecessary risks."

Everyone gave him an angry look, especially the Indian women. For them, it was a place full of evil spirits. Even Rusty didn't like to hunt there. Then again, he was almost as superstitious as the Indian tribes. Everybody knew that there was so much game in the Black Forest because most hunters were too afraid to go there.

"How did you kill them in the end?" Now that he knew how risky it was, Kit was more interested than ever. Men like him chased danger around like wolves chased rabbits. "I'm like you boys. I live for this kind of stuff. It gets my blood roaring through my veins. The medical books call it adrenaline, which gives us a boost of energy. You almost feel like you're superhuman and can do anything."

"If it's a bear that you want, I'll find you a good and feisty one, but not in the Black Forest. We've only been there once, and all kinds of bad things happened. You know what the name for a person who makes the same wrong choice over and over again, don't ya? Crazy is what they are, and I'm not loco." Rusty chuckled as he looked down his nose.

"No offense, Rusty, but to be honest, I thought it would be Levi that took me grizzly bear hunting. I know you have a new wife to take care of. Plus, you just got back, and I've been sitting around the table talking for days. It's time we did something before it's too late and the serious snows set in. This might be my last chance for a while."

"You boys go without me. I better stay here with my

wife, Betty. I've been running off a lot lately. You and I have had our bit of fun, Kit."

"You have to pay attention to your wife occasionally, Will. Life can't be all fun and games," Betty said, fluttering her eyes. "Don't worry, I'll make it worth your while."

"We can go anywhere you want, but we had better go on foot, so we'll need to use snowshoes. Horses spook as soon as they get a whiff of a grizzly bear, and if we get caught out, they won't be able to defend themselves.

"Can ya blame 'em?" the marshal asked. "But Money stays here with us. I don't believe he's the right age for such a challenge."

"He'll go over my dead body!" Bar-Chee retorted.

She grabbed Money, stormed out the door, and headed for their cabin as she mumbled something in Crow. Money shot sad eyes back at the men at the table but remained silent and did as his mother said. He wasn't quite sure if he was ready for another encounter with danger for a while.

"You wouldn't have taken the boy, would you have, Levi?" Angus asked.

"Why, I guess I hadn't thought it through. Sometimes, I don't see him as a boy anymore. But you're right. This ain't something for anybody but the most experienced. If we want to sneak up on a grizz, it'll be best if it's just the two of us. Are you sure this is what you want, Kit? Once we locate one of those monsters, there'll be no turning back."

"You're danged right it is. Kit Carson don't shy away from any animal, including a grizzly ten feet tall."

"If you can say the same thing when you get back,

I'll eat my hat." Angus laughed. "Plus, they're only eight feet tall but weigh eight hundred pounds. If you get swatted by one's paw, you'll think you've been hit by a train."

"The only enemy the grizzly bear has is man," Rusty huffed. "And as far as who wins the day is a toss of the dice, even with a gun. But I doubt anything I say will sway your mind, Kit. I reckon there're a few of us here with the same tendencies. It's like a tall mountain. If it's there, somebody is gonna wanna climb it no matter what the risks."

Levi pulled off his gun belt and hung it on a peg in the wall. Rather than reaching for his high-powered rifle, he grabbed his bow, quiver of steel-headed arrows, a steel-bladed hatchet, and his Bowie knife. He eyed the Indian lances standing in the corner.

"What are you doing now, Levi?"

"You said you wanted to do it like I did, didn't you, Kit?" Beaver grinned, then chuckled. "Help yourself. There are plenty of Indian weapons to go around, too. But if you wanna do this right, no guns. Just like those savage Blackfoot Indians, you seem to hate so much. That's how they do it. Sure, they might send a few more hunters to aid them, but they don't have the bullets to waste on bears and such. They save their ammunition for their various enemies like us."

Kit stopped and looked at Levi for a moment, like maybe he was putting him on. When he saw he was serious, he smiled. "When in Rome, do as the Romans do."

"Where's Rome, and what's a Roman?" Dahteste asked.

"They were from the time of Christ in the Middle

East across the Atlantic Ocean," Virgil said. "It's briefly mentioned in the New Testament of the Bible."

"If it's in the Bible, Lovejoy is the one who will know all about it." The captain smiled as he brushed his blond mustache with his knuckles. "Even if we don't want to hear about it, still, it sort of keeps us in line when we begin to waver off our intentional paths. I reckon sometimes Lovejoy saves us from being ourselves."

"This time of year, we don't have the time to wait, so if you wanna go, we'll leave in the morning at first light. Maybe Virgil will do us a favor and put some food together for the trip. If we get one, it's yours to bring back. I hope you're ready to tote up to a hundred pounds. Don't worry, I can carry the claws and fangs for ya." Levi laughed loudly and hardy.

"First, let's find a grizzly, and if we manage to kill it, then we can talk about how we bring the fur coat back. I find it a bad policy to plan on something like what to do with the fur before we've killed the bear. We'd be tempting fate."

"As long as you're up to the challenge, I'll find a grizzly for you, Kit. It will be an interesting hunt with the two of us."

"I'll bring your snowshoes from the barn, too," Virgil added. "You won't get far without them after last night's snowfall."

"While we're at it, bring two of those long Crow lances. Better yet, make it four. We can strap the bows and arrows across our backs and carry a spear in each hand. It'll take everything we have to put a grizzly bear down without a firearm."

"What do we want a lance for if we have arrows?" Now it was Kit's turn to look puzzled.

"The bows are for Indians. You'll just tick a bear off with arrows. We're gonna go after him like the Crow does, face-to-face with lances. Usually, they go in groups of more than two, but I reckon with your grit, we'll get by. Whatcha say now, Mr. Carson? Are you up to the job?"

"I've never said no to a challenge yet, and I figure now's not the time to start. Of course, I'm with you. I could use the sport after fighting thieves and Indians. It's not so personal."

———

THE FOLLOWING MORNING, when they stepped outside, their breath disappeared inches from their mouths. Ice cycles hung from the edges of the porch. Their cheeks and noses instantly turned red. Both wore heavy bear skin coats and raccoon hats with flaps that hung over their ears if it got too cold. For now, they were tied with strings across the tops of their heads until they needed them.

"The Black Forest is farther up the mountain, so it will be colder there than here and more open to the wind. Still, if there's plenty of small game for a bear to kill, it won't take us long to locate a grizz. As I said before, they'll be eating everything they can find before they head for the winter den to hibernate. If they get a chance, they might even try to eat us." Levi grinned like a Cheshire Cat.

As the morning winds blew, snow flew from the tops of the ponderosa pines and through the air. As far as the eye could see, everything was white. They sat on the edge of the porch, fastened their snowshoes to their feet, using their lances as snow poles, and trudged off toward the north entrance.

As Dahteste and Rusty watched, they quickly became black dots in the distance and disappeared into the snow. They trekked all through the day, but before they made it to the Black Forest, they had some miles to cover. So, for the time being, their focus was on Blackfeet Indians and not wild animals—at least not yet.

Later that night, they made a roaring fire with the wood they had gathered during the long day. It was twice the work using snowshoes, but both men were fit and accustomed to such environments and were up to the challenge. Carson was ready to go. Levi believed that maybe he was even too anxious, which was dangerous when taking on the most vicious animal in all the mountains.

As they sat around the fire watching falling stars, Kit finished his whiskey-laced coffee and poured another. "What did you and the captain do before you were mountain men, Levi? Sure, I know you were a captain from West Point, but how did a man with such a stringent education abandon it all and end up here living at the end of the world?"

"We fought Comanche and a few Kiowa back in the Territories. The captain was hired to find new places to build forts west of Fort Scott. We were attached to an expedition of scientists, and Will and I were supposed to guide them and keep them safe. When we were overwhelmed by Comanche, that plan was shot all to hell. We even lost our famous scientist, Professor Jay Peabody. All but four of our men perished, and they decided they were better off trying to make it back home rather than continuing to ride with us. I'm afraid they made the wrong choice.

"By then, the captain believed his career was destroyed and didn't want to go back and face the music with his family as he was drummed out of the cavalry. Mind you, years later, the army discovered what happened, and all was forgiven. Will was even asked to come back, but since he moved here to the Rockies, he left all that in the past. Mind you now, we still scout for the cavalry out of Fort Boise when they have the need. The brass there pays us mighty well, and we can use the money since the beaver is gone."

"Mark my words, soon the buffalo will be gone too, partly due to that Sharps fella who made those rifles he so kindly gave you and your friends to test. It was Captain Forrester who shot a war chief from six hundred yards away. Will claimed that he saw you make shots twice that far."

"Yeah, but I was shooting at a massive two-thousand-pound beast that was standing still. But I reckon I could hit one even farther away if there was no wind. Up here, the air is rarely still."

"What did you think about the Comanche compared to the Blackfoot Indians?" Kit looked at Beaver from the corner of his eye, where mischief lay.

"I've fought them both, but I found it pretty much a toss-up between the two. But I did find the Comanche more determined. You said how those Blackfoot ran off when their war chief was killed. That wouldn't happen with the Comanche. They're so mean that they would probably stand and fight to the last man. To be honest, I've never seen the likes."

"I'll never forget them whooping their war cries and firing their rifles and bows like demons from the apocalypse on my first encounter," Kit huffed. "I still have the occasional nightmare from those days and weeks until we got away."

"We ran from the Comanche in the Territories all the way to Yellowstone Valley and the last Rendezvous. That was where we met Rusty Steel. For some reason, Will and I impressed him, and he took us on as apprentices."

Despite the violent nature of his tales, his eyes came alive with excitement, remembering the obvious terror they must have suffered. As old memories were rekindled, the fire in their eyes glowed like golden coals. Kit could see Levi's muscles tense. Then came the flinty look in his eyes. Carson decided it was time to change the subject. It wasn't any fun dredging up old bad memories. He had enough himself to know better than to prod any more than he had already done.

Levi pulled up his buckskin shirt, showing several terrible scars. Muscles rippled across his arms and chest. He pointed to twin cynipid-like tissue on his chest. "That's where the grizzly who owned these claws slashed me." He jingled the collar on his neck. "His claws were as sharp as that steel hatchet I brought."

Kit pulled up his buckskin pants leg and showed his scars. "That was from a Blackfoot knife. He nearly cut my leg off. If it weren't for a military surgeon, I'd have lost the leg. He got the other one, too, but not quite as bad. That knife fight laid me up for weeks. Unfortunately, I can't say the same for the warrior. I cut his throat with his own blade."

"I used to fantasize about doing everything that

you've done, Kit, you being a little older than me. I read about your exploits back in Fort Scott some five years back. I still feel strange going hunting with you. Mind you, I don't really know what being famous is like or even what it's all about. I wouldn't know what it was if it slapped me in the face."

"It's not all that it's made up to be when you're back east, where there's so many people everywhere you go. Men and women you don't even know walk right up to you and talk like you're old friends. I never have gotten used to that part of it. There are good sides to it, too, you know. I get lots of free meals. I also get paid better than just about any scout I know, including Jim Bridges. You get the best jobs and top dollar when you have a little fame around your name. Lucky for me, I'm hard to kill." Kit smiled.

"Are you any good with a bow and arrows? If you're rusty, you might wanna practice up before we have to use 'em. We can stop for a couple of hours before we camp and have a go. It's best if we have a go with the lances, too. I doubt we'll run into many Indians up there, but bears will be another story. Most of the tribes are afraid of the Black Forest, so once we get there, we won't have to be so careful. At least for Indians, but there're more wild animals up there than you can shake a stick at."

"I'd prefer pistols and a good rifle, but I learned how to use a bow as well as most Indians. I've just never chosen them out of preference. I fancy myself as a crack shot."

"It's a much bigger challenge when not using modern weapons. There is a special honor in it. You learn this when you live with the Indians. If you ever get the chance, don't miss out. Most of my mountain man education came from my mentor, Rusty Steel, but I got my deep studies of the wilderness and nature from the Crow, both hunters and warriors alike. I've even learned a bit from that old medicine man, Potak. The tribes have been in these parts for ten thousand years, so who will know more about these mountains and the valley below?"

HUNTER OR HUNTED

ALL DAY LONG, THE WIND MOANED LIKE A LONESOME beast. Lucky for them, it was a headwind that would hide their scent if there were any bears on the trail before them. All they had to do was find places where small animals could be located. That would be where they would find the tracks they were looking for. At this time of year, the bears ate anything they got their hands on to prepare themselves for their long winter sleep.

Days later, as they entered the Black Forest, ancient paintings with bright colors from hundreds of years before covered the cliff's walls. It gave them the feeling that they had just walked into some unknown part of the past from thousands of years before. Hackles stood on their necks as the penetrated the forbidden forest.

"Just have a look at the size of that footprint. That must be a mighty big bear."

"Is it a grizzly?" Kit squatted and ran his fingers around the deep indentation in the powdered snow. "I've never seen a black bear paw that big."

"No doubt about it It's a grizz all right but it's a

female. Now all we've gotta do is make sure we stay downwind, so he doesn't know we're here. Bears have the best sense of smell in all the wilderness, bar none. If he gets a whiff of us, we'll be the ones hunted."

Levi looked at his new friend as they traveled through the forest. "Would you mind if I asked you a personal question?"

"Of course, I reckon we're good enough friends by now."

"Do you feel anything when you shoot people? I just had to ask because of the way you talk about the Blackfoot Indians. I intend no offense. I just wondered if you felt differently than I do when I have to take somebody's life."

"Of course I feel somethin'. Now that you've asked, I feel a couple of things, actually. First, I feel elation because I've survived. Then I feel remorse for what I killed, be it man or animal. That hits me last and sticks longer, but eventually, you get used to it. I have no choice because I know I'll probably be called on to do it again, and it wouldn't do to hesitate. I push it into the back of my mind. Maybe when I'm old, I'll look back on it all, but I probably won't like what I see. Is that honest enough for you?"

"So, we're more alike than I thought," Levi said, with relief in his voice. He was becoming quite fond of Kit and didn't want to discover anything that would ruin the new friendship.

When they finally found a set of sizable grizzly bear's tracks, they were some of the biggest Levi had ever seen. From the depth of the print, he believed it to be all of eight hundred pounds.

"Lookee there, pard. There are more tracks. It's not

the same bear either. This place is full of 'em. Isn't that what you were looking for? There you go, just what you wanted. This one is much bigger than the first tacks we saw."

Carson let out a breath that he felt like he'd been holding for hours. He squatted and used his fingers to measure the width of the paw. He looked up at his friend with wide eyes.

Levi nodded in affirmation, tight-lipped. He whispered, "That's him all right."

Carson froze, not knowing what to do next. Pushing hair out of his eyes, he frowned. They carefully continued to follow the bear paw tracks as his eyes grew more and more concerned. How big was an animal with a footprint that large?

Completely without warning, all Levi's nerves in his body went dead, and he froze. He drew in a sudden, deep breath as his eyes spread. From the tracks, he knew a grizzly was in front of them upwind. What he abruptly realized was that something was downwind, too, following them as its prey. With the unexpected appearance of another predator, he saw his plans had gone to blazes in a handbasket.

Levi shot a look over his shoulder and sniffed the air again. "It must be a panther this time of year. Nothing else would have the grit to follow a hungry grizzly bear. My gut feeling tells me whatever it is, it's not far away." He took another deep breath and nodded. "It's a cat, all right." He turned, lifting his nose, and sniffed for the bear. "They're both too close for comfort."

Carson stopped and turned his head, puzzled. "Did you say a panther is hunting us while we're hunting the grizzly bear? Are you sure your sense of smell is that good?" As soon as he said it, he realized how stupid a question it was. If Levi said he could smell both a panther and a bear, then there was no doubt they were there. "Sorry, Beaver. Of course, you can."

The mountain lion's growls behind them came like daggers in Levi's ears, and his heart started to pound. They had been successfully tracking the large grizzly bear and hadn't noticed the monster cat following them. One dinner was chasing another.

Before he knew it, it leaped for Levi. He hurled his lance with all his might, but it glanced off his skull, leaving a deep gash. It didn't even slow, but it did veer off. Beaver reeled from the narrow escape, and then his heart went nuts when the cat turned and prepared to lunge again. How Beaver wished he had his rifle right then, but all he had was one lance left with his bow and arrows.

The panther was eight feet long, weighed over two hundred pounds, and was twice as fast as the bear. He could feel and smell the grizz step onto the trail, but he didn't dare take his eyes off the panther. Saliva dripped from his massive canines as its eyes hinted it was ready to devour its next meal.

As it sailed through the air again, narrowly missing Johnson, it waved its paws in the air like kitchen knives ready to slice and dice his dinner. Beaver groaned when the cat's pad made contact with the side of his head, sinking the tips of its claws into his scalp. Levi dropped to the ground, trying to clear his mind before the next pass as dizziness threatened to overwhelm him.

———

AT THE SAME TIME, Kit came face-to-face with the grizzly bear that he wanted so badly. Right then, he wished he had never put it on his bucket list. The bear was just above him on the narrow trail of the ancient Native American Indian paintings, thirty feet tall. The four-foot-wide path fell off a steep cliff into the distant valley below. When Kit's eyes locked with the bear, something unfamiliar ran through his very being. He suddenly realized it was raw fear.

Kit's heart was pumping when he watched what was happening. Beads of sweat popped onto his brow. He swallowed hard, trying to catch his breath. Suddenly, he couldn't wait any longer, so he charged the grizzly bear on his own. He saw Levi lying on the ground, bleeding from the head as red contrasting with his black hair and the white snow.

The strength seemed to rise from somewhere deep inside Carson, like liquid heat from the earth's core. With his heart racing, Kit hit the ground in a full run. He threw the spear, embedding it in the bear's neck, but he was surprised when the animal roared and pulled at his spear and flayed his paws. As Beaver had said, all it had done was piss him off and make him all the angrier. As he wheeled around, trying to pull the shaft from its neck, it neared the abyss.

The big male grizzly bear suddenly lost its footing, slipped, and pitched off the rocks into the emptiness below. The mountain man watched him fall into the calamitous void. Kit's grizzly bear coat went toppling into space. Now, he turned to the panther. The fight wasn't over yet.

Little did the giant cat know it had melded with a

serious fighter this time. Carson forgot about the bow and arrow because he knew he would only have time for one shot. He hefted the lance in his right hand, ready to let it fly. In his left hand was Levi's shiny steel hatchet with a razor-sharp blade as his blood sped into overdrive, even though it was full of dread. Kit had a one-in-a-million shot, and he knew it, but his new friend's life depended on it, and probably his life, too.

Carson squeezed his fists, feeling his blood come to a stop in his veins as his fingernails dug into his palms, breaking the skin while white-knuckled fists held his weapons tight. Right then, his stomach fell off a cliff. His eyes stretched wide as he whispered, "God help me."

Kit suddenly lurched forward as the panther crouched for the last lunge and the kill. Then suddenly, the massive cat was in the air, closing the distance between it and its prey at lightning speed. Carson grunted when he launched the spear with every ounce of strength he had. It hit the cat's chest, piercing its heart. It continued to fly into the air, but even though it was already dead, it landed on his chest, knocking the wind out of him. When he stood, he saw that one of his arms was twisted at an impossible angle. It was obvious it was broken top and bottom.

He made his way to his friend, Levi, just as he started to moan. For a moment, he had thought he was dead, but then he blinked his eyes open to see the whites contrasting with the red claret. Three puncture marks were visible on one side of his skull and one on the other. Lucky for him, it didn't tear his head off.

"Are you alive, Levi? Are your wounds bad?"

Beaver delicately touched the puncture holes and

said, "They're only surface wounds. Nothing that I won't survive. What happened to your grizzly bear?" He looked around, but all he saw was the big dead cat.

"I buried the lance in his neck, but like you said, it only made him angry. He pulled it out like it was a toothpick. But I got lucky when he tried to pull it free to ease the pain and fell off that cliff. I looked, but there's no way we can go down and get it in the shape we're in."

"Once the scavengers get to it, they tear it to pieces anyway. At least you have that wildcat's hide, and I must say that one's a beauty."

The panther's long, light-brown body with its white underbelly lay still as though it was asleep. "I better retrieve the lance. I reckon we lost the other one."

"Home is that way," Levi huffed as drops of blood turned the snow red. Sheets of winter fog lay across the valley below lay like pools of primal blood.

When they saw a spiral of smoke rising obliquely from somewhere just over the rise, they knew that they were finally home. Levi struggled with their snowshoes through the deepening snow, but the panther hide was packed, safe and sound, on Kit's back.

When Dog barked, Rusty roweled Flossy forward, coming out of the trees. His horse was as avid as his hound. There in front of him were the two friends he was just about to go and find, despite the Black Forest and all his superstitions. His worry overrode all his fears.

"Well, ain't you two a sight for sore eyes. I reckon I don't have to go and fetch you after all. It looks like that cat got the best of you boys."

Blood streaked their hands and faces but it only took one look to see they were alright, by their crooked grins. Despite their obvious hardships they had found their prey and had won the day. Still, it was obvious that it cost them. Every time a man wandered into the unknown wilderness they never know if they would return.

LAID UP FOR WINTER

DAHTESTE WRAPPED HER ARMS AROUND BEAVER LIKE SHE would never let go. Then he embraced her, too. She would never admit it, but she had thought she would never see her husband again, but like the war chief she was, she never showed a hint of concern, only her relief upon his return. Dahteste forced a tight smile, not feeling much like laughing yet still relieved.

After Virgil patched both Levi and Kit up, he shook his head and said, "Levi, you won't be moving for a few weeks, and Kit, I'm afraid you'll be laid up for six weeks to two months. You have multiple fractures, but you won't have any problem if you let them heal right. I'm good at setting broken bones because I've done it a hundred times. But if you push it, your arm will never be the same, so mind what I say now. We've got to make sure those wounds don't get infected and your broken arm heals right. Now that you look back on it, was it worth all that trouble for a single wild cat skin?"

"Every minute of it," they replied simultaneously. They both laughed, but there was a certain nervousness

in their voices, too. On their last hunt, just about everything that could have gone wrong went wrong, and they
had injuries to prove it. But they had a fine mountain
lion skin too.

Both mountain men laughed as they winced from
the pain. They were just happy to be alive, not alone,
returning with beautiful skin, a set of wild cat claws,
and two canine teeth. Kit had all he needed to make his
necklace, even if it wasn't from a grizzly bear. Maybe
they would have better luck next time.

"That's gonna make you a nice coat for the spring.
Maybe when the thaw comes, before you leave, we can
have another go at a grizzly bear. Or have you learned
your lesson? I've had a few bad run-ins with grizzlies,
and for some reason, they only make me want to go and
hunt them again."

"I'm not much at learning lessons." Kit chuckled.
"My boss, John C. Freemont, isn't going to be so happy,
though. Then again, I reckon, with a broken arm, he'll
just have to wait. I won't be much use to him like this.
It'll be best if all this information didn't get to him, but
it'll be too juicy not to publish in my journal." Kit
grinned despite the throbbing arm. "Maybe the captain
can help me get used to working with one hand for a
spell."

Strangely enough, the captain hadn't talked to Kit
about his disabled arm once since he returned. Perhaps
it would bother him bringin up his loss again. Nobody
ever saw him slouch on the job, and he always pulled
his own weight and then some. Will never let his
missing limb interfere with his duties, whether they be
foraging for food or fighting his enemies. If anything,
the loss had made him more deadly and determined.

But just the same he had never talked about it and nobody was bold enough to bring it up: even his wife, Betty Forrester Crockett.

Money Penny came busting into the second cabin. He suddenly stopped, realizing he had rudely barged in, stepped out the door again, and knocked. All three men laughed. This only added insult to injury, causing his face to turn red with embarrassment.

"What's your hurry, Money?" Levi asked. "You came in here like a herd of buffalo. What's the rush?"

"I just wanted to make sure you were both all right. I heard that you had a run-in with a grizzly bear *and* a mountain lion, and I wanted to be the first to hear all about it. Did you get the bear? From the looks of things, I think the bear must have gotten you."

Dahteste sat patiently in the corner of the cabin, near the table where Virgil was sewing up Levi's scalp with catgut and a shiny, curved needle, which he used to patch clothing. It was the best he had, but it did the trick. His Crow wife wasn't worried, though. She was a war chief, and her people suffered small injuries every season hunting, but not in the Black Forrest. Most of the Crow warriors that went there never came back. She knew everything would be all right once she heard they were home and alive.

Of course, she didn't like him going to such places. She didn't even like saying the name out loud, fearing that the Indian spirits might hear. All Crow knew it was a dangerous place and was to be avoided at all costs. Still, her husband was a well-known warrior despite being white, and she would never try to tell him what to do, nor would he force her to do something she didn't feel was right.

Dahteste sat patiently in the corner of the cabin near the table where Virgil was sewing up the holes in Levi's scalp with catgut and a shiny, curved needle he used to patch cloth clothing. It was the best he had, but it did the trick. His Crow wife wasn't worried, though. She was a war chief, and her people took such risks every season hunting, but not in the Black Forest. She knew everything would be all right once she heard they were home and alive. Of course, she didn't like him going to such a place. She didn't even like saying the name out loud for fear that the spirits heard her.

"Does that mean you're gonna spend the winter here with us, Kit?" Money asked as his eyes twinkling like little stars. "Maybe I can watch you write a story. That'd be great. You can bunk in our place if you want to. I'm sure my pa won't mind."

"You can't expect me to travel a couple of hundred miles with a busted arm, can ya. And by the time it's healed, it'll be too cold to try to make it home and not freeze to death. Don't worry, by the time spring comes and it's time for me to leave, you'll be tired of my stories. But it will give me time to write a small dime novel about my weeks and months spent here with my new family in Rusty's compound. That, itself, will be whopper of a tale, and I'm sure that the folks back east will gobble it up. Whatcha think about that, young man?"

"Are you really gonna write about us, Kit? Are you gonna put me in the dime novel, too? Imagine seeing my name written down on proper paper in real print. That'll be somethin'."

"Just make sure you don't tell them where we are because if we get famous like you, I don't want strangers

walking up to me and acting like they're my friends."
Levi chuckled. "We're doin' just fine on our own, lost
here deep in the forest. We don't want strange folks
walkin' all around near our homes. As it is, we're lucky,
and few people know exactly where the compound is,
even though we've been in a newspaper or two. Sure,
the small write ups about us are nothing like what I've
read about you. You must be the most famous mountain
man alive."

Money said, "Angus said if you're too late for lunch,
you'll go without. He claims it's not as good if we let it
get cold. I reckon I like his cookin' no matter how he
serves it—especially his peach pie. I could eat a whole
one right now."

"Well, we can't have that, can we?" Levi grinned,
turning too quickly, making his head spin as he winged
from the pain. He took a sip of coffee, waiting until his
mind settled. "I know that a meal will do me a world of
good."

"You might wanna eat slower today, Levi." Virgil
laughed. "That'll leave a little more food for us."

"Too bad we couldn't have butchered the wildcat
and brought back the meat." Kit said. "As it is, it's a
miracle I could carry it back. Lucky for me, it only
weighed twenty pounds."

"If we'd have killed the bear too, we would have to
lug back as much as sixty pounds more of fur with the
size of that critter." Beaver rolled his cheroot across his
lips from one side to the other. He slowly took a draw
and blew smoke rings.

"Wildcat meat's mighty tasty, but you have to know
how to properly cook it. But Angus's baby elk ribs
cooked in honey will beat a stringy cat any day. You boys

are good to go, but you'd better let me have a look at those wounds every day for the first week. Kit, you have to wear that sling and don't remove the splints, or it'll heal crooked, and you'll be lame for the rest of your days. Don't be foolish and do as I say."

The aging Black man was the best-natured of the bunch and handy with a scalpel and a stitch. So far, he had patched up every injury they had, including the odd gunshot wound. He was also the one who read the Scriptures to them and obliged the lazy to say grace whenever they ate at the same table. Lovejoy had been one of the lucky slaves. His old master, Englishman Fitzgerald Worstshire III, took him into his home and gave him a proper education. Virgil was always at his side until the day he gave him his freedom.

At six feet tall, with his hair cropped close to his head, and with a scraggly beard, whiskers on his chin, and the shadow of a mustache, he went from his owner to being a free man, but he knew he couldn't stay in the South. It would be too easy for him to be retaken as a slave despite having his freedom papers in order. Some Southerners disregarded the written law and took matters into their own hands. When Virgil left, he rode West into the wilderness and became a buffalo hunter. That was where he met Levi on a strange journey from his past. Of the compound family, he was the man with the most apathy for his fellow man, and understandably so. Fitzgerald had taught him well.

———

THAT NIGHT, thirteen people sat at the lone table in the main cabin. Since Kit got Money's chair and the boy didn't like sitting on the marshal's lap like a little child, Angus had brought him a tall stool from the kitchen, leaving him a full head above them all, which, from the look on his face, he loved. Penny had accepted his adoption into the clan like bees to honey without a single regret. Of course, he missed his pa and wondered what finally happened to his ma, but despite his former bad luck, things couldn't have worked out better.

"Come on, Kit, tell the story again. I might have missed something the first time." Money had hardly touched his food, he was so nervous about his heroes' return. Now he had two men to look up to. Levi, his mentor, and his new friend, Mister Carson. One of the most famous men in the country.

"We can tell it again tomorrow night, but this time, Levi should give us his interpretation. Every man sees things in a different way. Or even better, how about you let me write it down first, and then we can have Virgil read it out loud? Then it'll be just like they'll print it in the dime novel back east." I reckon he has the best reading voice of all of us."

"Can you imagine that? My name, Money Penny, in a dime novel with the likes of Kit Carson, Levi Johnson, and Rusty Steel? Who would have ever thought?"

"Well, I'll see that your name's on the cover if ya want, Son. We have all winter to write the story. Do you wanna help, Money? Maybe I'll make you into as good a storyteller as I am. Up here we won't be lacking good tales, that's for sure."

Money's eyes swelled at the extravagant notion. "I can't imagine somethin' like that happening to me.

"If you get famous, you won't have to worry too much about it, living way up here," Kit laughed. "Bein' known does have its perks, though. Sometimes I get invited to a meal, and if I'm in the storytelling mood, I get free drinks all night. It's not all a bed of roses, though. Sometimes, when I was back East, I had folks pester me constantly. People, I've never even spoken to came to my hotel room, and had the gall to knock on my door. Everybody wanted a trinket or for me to write them a short story. Why, in the end, I had no privacy at all. Then again, folks are in wonder of mountain men and what we represent. Anyway, I lit out of there like my hair was on fire."

"You sure do like to talk, don't ya?" Angus grumbled. He had always fancied himself as a good storyteller, and now nobody wanted to hear his tales.

"I beg for your forgiveness," Kit smiled. "I must admit, I've been told that too many times to count. It seems that I can't help myself from telling stories about the experiences I've had along the way and sometimes, even those of others. Why, I know for a fact that every man and woman here have a mountain of stories locked up inside. All they need is to be let out. How could you live in such a place and not have interesting events to relate. I figure Rusty and Angus could keep us up for days with all they've lived up here on Bear Tooth Mountain. I still haven't heard about Will and Levi during their crossing the Comanche territory to get to the Rockies."

SURPRISE VISIT

KIT LEANED BACK, STRETCHED ONE OF HIS SUSPENDERS with his thumb as he swept his eyes across the room. The other arm hung bandaged from a sling around his neck. He watched how the captain managed with one arm. He knew Will had lost his appendage in a hand-to-hand battle with a Blackfoot warrior, and he almost died. Carson found it a nuisance and wondered how he moved with such ease when he could hardly button up his britches.

He also knew he had been in many battles since and had survived. Kit wondered if he would have sufficient willpower and determination if the same thing happened to him. He often liked to think and put himself in the shoes of others. Now he realized how lucky he was when he and Levi encountered the grizzly bear and wildcat.

As the winter dragged on, he had gotten to know all those who lived in the compound and marveled at their success. Each one was different in their own way, and some he would even consider noteworthy, especially

Levi Johnson, who was doing for Money what Rusty Steel had done for him.

The cabins, barn, stables, corral, and chicken coop were all surrounded by a brick-and-rail fence with openings at the south trail down the mountain and the north trail a half day's ride from the massive Crow stronghold high on Bear Tooth Mountain. During the summer months, the occasional frontiersmen or buffalo hunters encountered their homes by accident.

Still, in the cold depths of winter, you could go the entire season without seeing anything more than the occasional Crow warrior who rode down to check on the compound. The leader of the stronghold always kept an eye on the only white men living on Bear Tooth Mountain. What was once a given, now living on Crow land was more tedious than ever.

Carson wondered if breaking his arm dredged up old memories for the ex-Calvary officer. He noticed how closely he watched him, with curious eyes. Of course, he couldn't compare a busted arm to a missing limb, but now he could imagine how difficult it must have been to adjust.

Angus crooked his fingers around a half dozen tin cups, then he brought a gallon kettle of coffee from the cookstove to the dinner table. A single pained glass window spilled squares of light onto the floor and illuminated the room along with the massive roaring fire. It snapped and popped as the green wood puffed steam, as the flames cast dancing shadows on their faces, while orange coals reflected in their eyes. Everyone's attention was on their important visitor, Kit Carson.

Brown bubbles popped from the spout, filling the room with the aroma of freshly perked java. Cheroot and hand-built cigarette smoke floated near the ceiling before the draft of the fire whisked it away. Angus came from the kitchen, located at the rear of the cabin, where a cast-iron cookstove radiated waves of heat.

The round metal smokestack disappeared into the ceiling, through the sod roof and snow, poking out behind the chimney, puffing dual streams of smoke. That was the only visible trace that white men lived nearby. That and the outhouses, which the Indians found ugly and smelly. Still, Pine Needle, Dahteste, and Bar-Chee all adjusted to ways of their white husbands.

"Who wants a dash of corn liquor?" Angus didn't wait but went ahead and filled their cups with hot coffee, then added a dash of whiskey to give it bite.

From the walls hung hides and skins in different stages of curing. Smoked legs of elk swung from the rafters. Around the main table sat the captain, Levi, Rusty, Kit, and Money as they idly picked at dried fruit.

Soon, Virgil would come to get Money. Although his dead mother had taught him and his brother to read and write, Lovejoy continued to perfect his skills. Now that Kit Carson had come to pass the winter, talking about the journals he had written, it made the little nine-year-old want to perfect his writing skills, hoping one day he too would write dime novels for the public back East.

Most of the days, they spent kneading the pelts, hides, and furs until they were soft and supple to the touch. That and the never-ending job of repairing everything from snowshoes to tack and saddles for the horses, and Virgil's and Rusty's mules. They cleaned and oiled their rifles regularly, even when they weren't in use, during the coldest winter months. At that time, they only went out of the cabin to feed and water the livestock and to go to the outhouse. In the worst part of winter, a man could freeze to death in minutes, and with the heavy snowfall came the whiteouts, which made moving from building to building perilous.

———

AFTER WEEKS of being forced to stay inside, time lost its meaning, and because it stood still, it dragged hope with it. Especially for little Money, who was too young to be locked up night and day. Finally, the snow had fallen in earnest, making it increasingly difficult to go outside. A core of wood logs stood neatly stacked by the front door for easy access. Six sets of snowshoes hung on the wall under the porch roof. Smoke squiggled out of the stone chimney as sparks ascended into the air, disappearing just above the tall pine trees surrounding the compound.

Half of the roof was visible, but the other half was buried into the hillside, insulating the main building from the plummeting temperatures and winter storms. It was also the safest building when hostile tribes attacked. When threatened, they all stayed in the main cabin with Rusty and Angus. With wooden shutters two inches thick and gun slats in the only door, it was a nearly impenetrable fortress in the middle of the wilderness. The protection it provided had saved them many times in the past.

Ropes on wooden posts ran from cabin to cabin so they wouldn't get lost during the blizzards. Another rope ran the length from the cabins to the outhouses at the edge of the property—one for the ladies and one for the men. Betty Crockett, Will's wife, had insisted, and as she was initially the only white woman in the compound, and she had gotten her way.

Of course, they didn't own the land they had spent nearly two decades on, from the time Mountain Dennis initially arrived. They lived there with the permission of Chief Wanata, the leader of the Crow camp, six hours' ride away. The old chief, Hachta, had been Rusty Steel's blood brother, so during his reign, there was never trouble due to the Easterners' presence. However, with the new chief, things were no longer the same. Lucky for them, Joseph's wife, Bar-Chee, was the chief's sister. Still, he wasn't half the man the old chief was and had always been jealous of the mountain men.

Everybody froze and their blood chilled when they heard a light scratching sound at the door. Who would be out in this weather, far below freezing? At ten thousand feet, the temperature was in the teens. Suddenly, everybody put their cups down and their hands neared the ever-present belted pistols. On Bear Tooth Mountain, they were armed night and day. Rusty was out of his chair, heading for the door with his gun in his hand. He opened it, spilling light onto the floor.

"Who is that out there?" Rusty growled with a ring of suspicion in his words as white-knuckled fists clutched his pistol's grips. The click of a hammer rang loud in the closed room. The sound repeated itself five times.

To their surprise, a Blackfoot Indian stepped into the doorway. He had streaks of ochre paint down his face, from top to bottom, making him stand out against the snow-covered background. They could see how he shivered as he stood frozen in the doorway, not knowing whether to bolt and run or stay. It was obviously an act of desperation. It looked like he had forgone the possibility of dying at the hands of white men and had taken a daring chance.

Captain Forrester felt the anger rise hot on his face, but he forced himself to calm down. Now wasn't the time to make rash decisions. Rusty talked softer, but there was still an edge to his voice. He didn't mind Indians coming for help, but not the Blackfeet Tribe—especially for Carson, who claimed they were his sworn enemies.

"Whatcha want?" Steel growled. "Where're your weapons?"

They saw the fear in the Indian's wide-open eyes, but he said nothing. They didn't even know if he understood. He had cuts, bruises, and contusions across his hands and face. They could hear his teeth chatter as they stood in the doorway. At first, a silence fell over the room. The last thing they had expected was to see an enemy warrior brave at their front door.

The Indian's head swiveled from one side to the other, taking in everything they saw. He had never been inside a white man's dwelling. Everyone was left speechless. Nobody knew what to say, nor could they even speak his language. He wore ragged, tattered, and ripped buckskins, as if he had run into a wildcat, and hadn't fared well.

Kit let breath pass his lips in a long sigh, fighting back the urge to spit. One of his lifetime enemies was standing in front of him, and there wasn't a thing he could do. Still, the will to kill him was there, and the warrior saw it in his eyes. When Carson realized he was baring his teeth, he shut his mouth, but his eyes continued to shoot darts at the Indian brave.

Rusty motioned with his head to come in, but he didn't put his guns down. He knew this man came from the most aggressive tribe in Yellowstone Valley and the surrounding mountains. The breeze caught the door and threatened to slam it shut. As soon as Steel turned, the smile faded. Suddenly, the amusement from his eyes was gone, and his mouth tightened.

When Virgil walked up behind the uninvited guest, the Indian startled, and his hand moved to his knife. Other than that, he didn't have any weapons, which was strange. Something had happened to the man's fur coat, bows, and arrows, not to mention the cuts and bruises he had sustained. Rivulets of blood ran down his arms and legs.

"Why, this man is half frozen," Virgil said as he instinctively took his arm and led him to the fire. "Here, have a seat and warm up," Lovejoy pointed, rubbing his hands together. "Whatcha just standin' there for, Angus. Get this man a hot cup of coffee and somethin' to eat."

"I usually don't mingle with the enemy," Angus retorted as he eyed the Indian cautiously. "Just because trouble comes a knockin' on our door, don't mean we have to offer it a place to sit."

"Enemy? What in the world are you talking about? Don't be foolish. When I find a man freezing to death, I don't notice what tribe he's from or whether he's white, red, or even black, like me. I never turn a man in need away."

Everyone was silent from then on, and no one asked any more questions. They already knew the answers— everything, but where he was going to sleep. None of them had ever lived under the same roof as a Blackfoot. No one seemed to know what to make of it except Virgil, who was a religious man and felt he always had to help those in need, regardless of who they were.

"How can we trust him not to try to take our scalps?" Kit whispered to Joseph, who shook his head.

"I ain't sleepin' under the same roof as this one, I can assure you that." The marshal's fingers wrapped around his pistol grip as his thumb neared the hammer.

"Don't think I didn't hear what you just said?" Virgil retorted. "Where is your Christian charity, now when it's needed?"

Kit felt the anger drain, leaving him feeling bewildered. He knew Virgil was right, but he thought he was right too. No matter what anyone said, he didn't know if he could sleep under the same roof as a man from a tribe he swore to kill on sight and who had tried to kill him every chance they got.

Silence crept over the gray gloom in the room as fear grasped the warrior like a vice, churning his stomach into a grinder. But he fought the feeling and jutted out his chin in defiance. He felt the hate radiate from several of the mountain men, but he also saw the kindness in Virgil's eyes. He had no choice anyway. It was, take a chance with the white men or freeze to death. Another hour and he knew he would be dead, so he had nothing to lose one way or another.

Levi still held his revolving pistol at his side. He was so surprised that he didn't remember it was there. The granite-faced Indian stared stonily at the white men. But Virgil clucked his tongue and wrapped his arm around him like he was an old friend. It left everyone speechless.

The warrior looked back and down the muzzle of Rusty's gun and froze where he sat before the fire. Both

Rusty and Levi saw he wasn't afraid, like most would be. His actions gave both men second thoughts as they wondered what would happen were it them rather than him.

"Put those guns away, this very minute," Virgil admonished his friends. Rusty was so shocked that he slammed the pistol into his belt. "He ain't gonna shoot us with a skinning knife, so why the fuss? Let the man warm up and have something hot to drink while we try to figure out what to do. I must admit, it is rather unusual for somebody from the Blackfoot tribe to come and visit."

A mist of uncertainty clouded Carson's face. His voice got louder as his raw-boned jaw tightened. "I ain't gonna sleep under the same roof with no Blackfoot Indian! I'm sorry Virgil, but I don't care what your Bible says. I'm not the kind of fella that turns the other cheek. My first instinct is to kill him before he kills me."

"Then he can sleep in my cabin with the marshal, Bar-Chee, and me," Virgil said gently, knowing that tensions were high. He didn't notice the look on the Jospeh and Bar-Chee's faces.

To the north, out the window, Levi saw that the sky was dismal, grey-green, and depressing. "It looks like we've got a doozy of a snowstorm comin'. We may well all have to stay in the main cabin tonight. It had the thickest walls and the biggest fireplace. All this sort of throws a wrench in the works, don't it? I reckon it's gonna make for an uncomfortable night."

The captain had the sort of face that needed the brim's shadows to soften his sharp, gaunt features and hard lines. If you didn't know him, you would think he was angry most of the time. Right then, it was impossible to decipher what he was thinking. His face was expressionless, but he was watching everything unfold as if he were listening to a detailed story. He watched how everyone reacted without reacting, himself. Will didn't seem to have an opinion and was simply watching the cards fall where they may, or maybe he was just being guarded. He did have his fingers wrapped around the handle of his calvary saber.

Angus grumbled as he begrudgingly headed for the kitchen to fetch some dried meat and fruit for the unwelcome visitor. So far, Virgil's will had overcome all their feelings and aggressions, at least for the moment.

Virgil smiled and took the food and a cup of coffee, then offered them to his guest. When he gave it to the warrior, Kit almost growled. The room was mixed with angry, noncommittal, and one friendly face: and then there was that of the apparently humbled warrior. It was an impossible mask to decipher.

It almost looked like the Blackfoot Indian was embarrassed. For a man like him, it must be hard to ask the enemy to save your life. Had they encountered him on the trail in normal circumstances, they would have all tried to kill one another.

That night, everyone in the compound was in the living room, sitting around the large dining table. Virgil served potato and egg omelets from his nest of hens in the chicken hut. He brought out pie pans full of steaming biscuits and several deep bowls of gravy. He ladled portions out onto everyone's plate, finally, taking their minds off the elephant in the room. Even the Blackfoot Indian was distracted when Virgil went to the kitchen and made him a serving too, despite Angus's refusal. His wife, Pine Needle was Crow, and if she saw him serving her tribe's mortal enemy, she would never forgive him.

In the winter, they lined the hen house walls with bales of dried alfalfa to keep the heat in and the cold out. When the temperatures plummeted, Angus piped in heat from an ancient cast-iron oven in the stables. The cold weather was brutal for both the animals and humans. Pine Needle wasn't a warrior like Dahteste, but she had family that had died by Blackfeet blades.

After dinner, Money tried to get Kit to tell another story, but he seemed to have his mind somewhere else and in another place. He was distant and moody and didn't want to talk. Marshal Walker was downright angry. When Virgil told him the warrior might be staying in their cabin, he said he would shoot him before he slept under the same roof. Eventually, the storm mandated that they all remain in the strongest and warmest shelter. When the blizzards arrived, the intense winter storms came with them, and it was best to share their body heat at night. Still, nobody wanted to sleep beside the Indian brave.

Bear skin furs covered the floor under bedrolls stretched side by side the length of the room. Virgil slept in the back beside his cookstove, because he was always the first to rise and prepare hot coffee and biscuits first thing. During these long winter months, when they caught up with their work, they had little else to do but wait for their first mild weather to arrive.

A stack of logs stood beside the roaring fire, ready to provide fuel all night. Virgil had his cookstove lit as well. Outside, smoke rolled out of both chimneys, contrasting with the white surroundings. Snow flew off the pine branches as a stiff breeze began to blow. That night, they expected gale-force winds. Still, one just never knew what Mother Nature would throw at you when she was angry, especially in the Rocky Mountains.

Even after they had turned in for the night and were all lying down, only Angus and Virgil snored deeply asleep. The others twisted and turned. Dahteste lay with her knife in her fist, hidden under her bearskin covers. Kit stared at the ceiling, grinding his teeth with his hand firmly on his pistol grip. If the Blackfoot Indian so much as sneezed, he planned to shoot him dead. He couldn't help himself. He had fought the enemy tribe all his adult life and couldn't help but feel hate for those who had taken the lives of friends. Most of the men in the room felt the same.

Still, despite their anger and nervous tension brought on by paranoia, everyone eventually fell asleep as they listened to the rhythmic sound of the howling wind. They knew that when morning came, there would be more than two meters of snow. Then they would have to find a moment of warmth and little wind to clear the deepening powder between the cabins and outhouses. For the moment, they all slept except Levi, who always kept one eye open when danger lurked.

Beaver suddenly shifted his eyes and yelled, "Kit, quick!" He felt his patience suddenly wear away.

When Carson felt the blow, the wind rushed through his ears, and a red flash seared across his brain, and he nearly blacked out. Levi looked up just in time to see the door slam after something furry slipped out.

"Everybody, wake up!" Beaver yelled. "Where did that Blackfoot Indian go? And where's my bearskin coat?"

There was a vacant perch on the wall. That was

when they saw the empty space over the fireplace where an old muzzle-loading musket had been. As a precaution, they had all slept with their rifles and pistols at their sides. Luckily, the warrior had only gotten away with one of the old long guns. Still, they were excellent shooting weapons and just as dangerous in an Indian's hands as a white man's.

"Why, he'll never survive out there," Virgi huffed, his voice full of concern. "I wonder why he took off like that."

"If he comes back here, he won't survive, for sure, now that he's shown his true colors," Rusty growled. "Are you happy with what you did, Virgil? You left a clear and present danger into our home when we were all against it. Being nice to men who don't deserve it doesn't work in the wilderness, no matter what your Good Book says."

"I did what any God-fearing man would do. I helped a fellow human being when he was threatened with his life. Would you do the same if you were in his situation? Let's see who casts the first stone."

"You owe me the price of my gun," Rusty retorted. "Sometimes you just can't go by what it says in the Bible. Not when you're dealin' with men who don't even know what a Bible is."

"And what about my bear skin coat?" Levi angrily asked. "You all know what price I had to pay for that fur. Hunting large bears is a risky business. Just ask Kit."

"You can hunt for two grizzly bears when they come out of hibernation," Money said, hoping that Kit and Virgil didn't get into a fight. Even Beaver and Rusty were all riled up. He had never seen them show such anger among themselves.

"That's not the point," Rusty spat. "We don't let the enemy sleep under our roofs. That's always been that way until now, and as you can see, your way was a mistake."

"I beg your pardon, Rusty, but savin' a man's life is never a mistake." Virgil clucked, his Bible in his hand. "Do good unto others as you would have them do unto you."

"In the Rocky Mountains, do good unto your enemy and he will kill you, dead," Dahteste said, as if it were a fact of life. "Things are different here in the wilderness. Sometimes your Bible lessons don't work so well. The Crow people don't have such forgiving natures. Indian spirits don't encourage us to share your pallets with our enemies."

WINTER'S END

WHEN THEY AWOKE, THE SUN SHONE THROUGH LEVI AND Dahteste's cabin window. Dust danced in the rays of light and felt warm on their faces. It was so bright they had to shade their eyes with their hands. This was the first time it had shone in weeks, but it felt like months. They uncurled from their embrace, curious as they wiggled their toes and batted their eyes. Levi used the heels of his hands to rub the sleep away. His Crow wife smiled, revealing a mouthful of white teeth, as she pushed her black hair out of her face as her dark eyes twinkled with mischief.

"Why rush?" Dahteste asked. "It's so warm and cozy here in bed."

"Don't you want to get a breath of fresh air? It's stuffy in here."

The yellow disk was perched on the end of the world, already crowding the sky with bright, white light. It flashed off the snow-covered ground, making their eyes sting as it refracted through the wavy glass. Long shadows grew on the western side of the buildings, trees, and mountains. The first signs of the end of winter and the beginning of spring had arrived.

That winter had been hard, cold, and boring, and everyone was looking forward to basking their faces in the sun again despite the deep snowfall on the ground. The long icicles hanging from the porch roof began to drip as they started melting under the glaring ball of heat. Levi threw the buffalo blankets off the bed and jumped up, stretching his hands over his head.

"Come on, Darlin'," Levi said as he turned for the door. "Let's go outside and get a breath of fresh air. This winter's been long and cold, and I'm ready for a change."

Dahteste climbed out from under the buffalo blankets, and they wiggled into their heavy buckskins, and both pulled on warm coats and hats. Despite the sunshine, they knew that the temperatures would still be low for a few more weeks, but it was the beginning of the end of winter in the Rocky Mountains. Everyone in the compound was ready for Spring.

They tiptoed through the cabin's main room, so they didn't wake Will and Betty from their deep sleep. Beaver's best friend and his wife snored softly. The wooden floor gently groaned underfoot.

Levi put his shoulder against the door, and when it didn't budge, he forced it slowly open. Snow had formed that night and drifts a yard deep stood against the front of the cabin wall. When they stepped outside, they found themselves thigh-deep in white powder. They turned toward the sun: it warmed their faces. The only sound was the rooster crowing his morning welcome of a new day from inside the chicken coop.

Levi stepped to the porch's edge with his back to the

snow and spread his arms out wide. Then he slowly let gravity take over, and he fell backward like a chopped-down tree. Beaver laughed when his six feet seven, two-hundred-pound body, almost disappeared in the snow, raising puffs of fine white powder.

"Help me up, Darlin'," Levi chuckled. He reached out his hand as Dahteste gave him hers, but to her surprise, he pulled her into the snow with him.

She fell backward and into the soft blanket of powder beside her husband. They both began laughing like small children who had just discovered a new game. The change in weather made them forget the deadly winter they had just survived. Although it had been extra cold and dark, the sunlight made them quickly forget the hardships. Will was the first to follow them onto the porch, his rugged face bearing a questioning expression. His empty sleeve was pinned at the elbow.

"What in the world are you two laughing about?" Will asked from the doorway. Betty saw his outline framed in a silhouette of white. "You know you woke us up."

"The end of winter's near," Dahteste smiled. "It's my favorite time of year."

Unconsciously, Beaver's eyes followed the fence around the compound and looked toward the stable and an empty corral. The only sign of life was the birds flittering through the trees. He let out a deep breath and smiled.

That was when Betty, the captain's wife, pushed him aside and dove headfirst into the snowdrift and in seconds was laughing just like their friends. The captain watched and chuckled but didn't offer to join in. He was too conservative. His reserve didn't allow him to take a chance of making a fool of himself. Sometimes it seemed as though the captain had forgotten how to have fun despite his young age.

A few minutes later, they saw Money step out of the entrance of the cabin next door, rubbing his eyes with balled-up fists, pushing away the sleep. Blinking, he took a second look at his mentor and friends. To his surprise, they were acting like little kids, making him want to join in instantly. But when he stepped off the porch and into the snow, his small body nearly disappeared. This brought laughter from them all.

"Money, are you all, right?" Will asked, his voice full of concern.

But Money immediately poked his head up and out of the snow, grinning like a possum. He struggled his way to his feet. Now the snow came up to his ribcage, but he pushed through the deep powder and to the other cabin to join in on the fun. A smile stretched across his face, from ear to ear.

Once he struggled out of the deep snow, he took a running dash across the porch and somersaulted, again burying himself in white powder. This time, when his head popped up, he was laughing so hard that tears streamed down his face.

Money dove in again, this time landing on his belly, face down, as his stiffening fingers clawed at the soft snow, and powder muffled his laughter. Seconds later, they were all playing like they were little children his age.

Whirlwinds stood like smoke in the distance as the last of the snow flurries swirled around, racing across the ground. They saw drifts of white powder across the compound. It stood the deepest against the outside fence.

"What in tarnation is goin' on out here?" Rusty growled when he stopped on the main cabin's porch with a hot cup of coffee in his hand. Steam rolled off the black surface, disappearing inches away. He looked up and saw the tall pines sway as clumps of snow dislodged from high above, landing with a plop onto the ground.

"It looks like we've got more kids living in the compound than just Money, don't it, Angus?" Rusty asked as his eyes sparkled in amusement.

McFarlin just laughed as he watched. He knew he was too old for such nonsense but enjoyed the fun just the same. As soon as Kit Carson appeared in the door, he set his cup of coffee down on the outside dinner table and ran across the snow-covered porch and joined his new friends. They jumped up and down like they were all children playing in a powder pond. Rusty and Angus continued to laugh as they puffed their pipes. The orange coals of the smoking bowls glowed in their twinkling eyes.

"Now I've seen everything. Levi doesn't surprise me, but Kit was the last man I expected to join in on young-sters' games."

"If I were a few years younger, I'd be there right beside them, and you would too, Rusty," Angus laughed. "There's nothing like the feeling of being young. Watching them I can remember what it was like. It looks like Money's ways are rubbing off on some of us. Good for him. The fresh breath of youth in the air to end a long, cold winter is good for the soul."

"Lucky for us, there's nobody around to see half the

compound making fools of themselves." Rusty took a second to trace his eyes around the brick-and-rail fence to make sure, but the only living things in sight were the mountain bluebirds and black-rosy finches. He saw no visible tracks on the ground.

"I reckon that's the end of that. Winters come early. It was long and hard, but early Spring is quite a surprise," Rusty said, sipping hot coffee to take the chill off.

The aging mountain man gazed out across the rolling hills and mountains, peppered with lodgepole and ponderosa pines. Everything was white as far as the eye could see and there wasn't a footprint in sight.

"In all the years we've been up here, I've never seen good weather come so early," Angus smiled. "Nor has it ever been so welcome."

In the cold air, the gunshot sounded dead, flat, and empty. A curl of smoke rose from the bushes outside the main fence. A lead slug slammed onto the porch post beside Kit Carson's head. For once in their lives, they had wandered outside without their weapons, and they all suddenly realized their mistake. All of them scrambled through the deep snow, keeping their heads down as the men bolted for their guns. Everyone waited for a second shot, but it didn't come.

"Money, stay down!" Levi yelled as he jumped up and made a mad dash for the cabin door.

But before they could make it to the porch, Marshal Walker ran out with a pistol in each fist, ready to protect his recently adopted son and family. Bar-Chee, his Crow wife, was right behind him with a bow and a quiver of arrows in her hands. She growled like a rabid dog protecting her son.

Joseph pressed himself stiff-backed against the log wall. His heart jerked in spasms, and his chest heaved for breath. When he saw the trail of gun smoke behind the outhouses, he shot off several rounds, hoping to hit the intruder or at least run him off. They all waited, listening, but nothing happened. By then, everyone was armed.

After several tension-filled minutes they heard the soft clopping of a horse's hooves approaching. Suddenly, they all turned toward the southern entrance. Levi sniffed and drew a breath. He instantly knew it was bear fat, which Indians used to rub on their skin to keep warm.

They saw a solitary silhouette of a rider walking his horse out of the rising sun. The covering of snow almost reached the pony's belly. It was impossible to miss the stolen rifle in his hands. It was the Blackfoot warrior that Virgil had welcomed into their house. Now he was back to take someone's life. The hostile Indian seemed to be a free-fall descent into malice and self-destruction. Now it looked like he wanted to take the entire compound on. The very same people who saved his life.

Kit's knee touched his long gun. He drew it in his mind. He wove his horse, Apache, out of the stables and through the corral then he pulled to a stop. Now he saw the man at the edge of the brick-and-rail fence had a rifle and it was pointing at him. Carson ducked, and the bullet cracked when it zipped by his ear. He quickly neck-reined the buckskin toward the threat and set his spurs. Everyone's eyes followed his charge. It was like the famous mountain man had almost expected the confrontation as they faced off. Carson's mind quickly went past fear, worry, and dread.

A stark silence came over them as two enemies on horses face off. Steam snorted from the Indian pony's nostrils as the Blackfoot's eyes became slits. Then the hostile Indian charged too. It appeared he wasn't interested in the rest of those in the compound. It was clear that he was there to challenge the famous mountain man and Indian fighter. He must have known who he was the whole time.

The warrior brave dropped the long gun, and it disappeared in the deep snow. He arched his back as he prepared to launch his lance. At the same time, Carson raised his rifle in response. This time, the blast was deafening, and the echo rang through the valley, bouncing off the surrounding mountains. His quick shot was slightly off. The bullet hit the man in the shoulder, spinning him off his pony. Blood stained the ground as the brave was thrown off his horse.

Although they didn't expect him to attack again, he was up in the blink of an eye with a Bowie knife in his hand. He drew it back to throw. Kit pulled his Colt Walker, drawing back the hammer, and he pulled the trigger at point-blank range. The bullet slammed into the Indian's chest with tooth-jolting impact as the shockwave roared through his body and showed in his eyes.

Kit kicked his leg over his horse's head and slipped off his horse bare back, the pistol still in his hands. When he walked over to the prone body of the man he shot, they locked eyes.

In broken English, the Indian said, "You kill my father. I come here to kill you... or die. Either way, revenge is mine." He smiled through red-stained teeth, and then died.

Levi cautiously walked up behind Kit. "It's me, buddy. Your friend, Levi. Take your finger off the trigger, Pal."

For a moment, Carson stood there like he was in another world. One full of death and violence. Then, little by little, he returned to his senses and his pistol dropped to his side.

Kit nodded his head and turned his eyes to his Beaver. "I knew that man was up to no good. He's spent the winter waiting for me to show. I should have shot him that first day when he came scratching at the door. I believe it was all a trick to confirm who I was. You heard he spoke some English. I knew it was a mistake, and I should have known better."

"I reckon he got his chance, but it didn't work out," Rusty said as he joined the men with his Sharps in his hands.

"I could have sworn he was a peaceful man," Virgil said in a whisper. "I would never have thought, after saving his life, he would try to kill one of us."

"That was all a ruse," Kit replied, angrily. "He was after me all along. I must admit I've killed my share of Blackfeet Indians. I reckon I killed his paw. In the end, what we did for him didn't mean a damned thing."

Strangely enough, it was Kit who was most angered by the turn of events. Virgil was the one who was in shock. He had offered another apparently needy human shelter and food, and he turned his back on him and tried to kill one of his friends. He clutched his Good Book in his hand, but his face was puzzled. When he looked down, this time, it was full of doubt.

Virgle had always believed in the way of the Bible, to turn his cheek and give all men another chance, but now he saw that in some cases it was indeed a mistake. An error in judgment that could have cost one of the compound members their lives if not more. Even the safety of little Money was jeopardized, who had slept on the floor not five feet from the hostile warrior brave.

"How long have you lived in the wilderness, Virgil?" Kit asked. "You'd have thought you'd have learned your lesson by now."

Virgil nodded and replied, "I reckon I just did. When in such wide country, I guess that sometimes there's no room for compassion. Maybe I've led myself astray all these years."

"Don't take it like that, Virgil," Rusty said in almost a whisper. "You're kindness to our fellow man is what binds us all together. If it weren't for you, some of us would fall into the spiraling of violence and would never find our way back. You and your Good Book made us toe the line, so I reckon you were both right in a way. It's just that some men are Hell-bent on violence and revenge. I reckon God made us that way, too, didn't he? If the world was like you, Mister Lovejoy, we'd have no more wars or conflicts. But most men ain't like you, my friend. There are others of the same version as this one out there in the wild country that you can never trust."

"He's right, you know, Virgil," Kit said. "Without you, we might all be wicked men. I must say you do bring the best out in me, and I'm a hard act to follow."

"Still, for the safety of our young friend, Money, I should have known better than to take such a chance. I could have gotten one or more of us killed."

"No, I reckon he was only after me," Carson said. "Maybe I've worn out my welcome." When he looked back and saw Money there staring in shock, it made him feel bad. They locked eyes, and Kit nodded. "You follow Levi's lessons and don't try to grow up and be a man like me, Money. You're made of better stock than that. And keep studying that Bible with Virgil. One day maybe you'll learn enough to write your own journal."

SAD GOODBYES

DESPITE THE FINE WEATHER, MONEY LOOKED LIKE HE HAD just lost his best friend. Still, he was confused by how aggressive Kit became when threatened. Of course, he realized he wasn't the only one in danger. The Blackfoot Indian had placed them all at risk. Young Penny had seen enough violence in his life to understand the world was full of wicked men.

But he never considered that one of his friends would be capable of the same aggressions as their enemies. It was almost like the famous mountain man had changed into another person, albeit for only a fleeting moment, but Money had seen it in his eyes and knew the story.

"I hope you won't think the worst of me, Son. One day, you'll understand why this country does the things it does to me. I reckon it makes some of us harder than others, kind of like your one-armed uncle, Will. I reckon he's even a harder man than me. I struggled, living like him with only one hand, and I only had a broken arm.

As you grow older, you'll understand. Why, I'm still learnin' things a about the world an even myself."

"He'll learn," Captain Forrester said. "I agree: I doubt that you're any angrier than I am. Some things life dishes out make us into something different from what we were or even thought we would ever be. I reckon that Kit and I are both products of our environment. You put a Comanche warrior in front of me, and I'd be the same as him. We all have our lifelong enemies. Some men can't become friends no matter what Virgil and the Bible says."

Three days had passed since the incident, but ever since it happened, Kit had become restless and fiddle-footed, and soon, he was saying it was time he got back to work. He had lazed about the whole winter. Still, no one believed him. They all knew he was uncomfortable. He felt he had brought danger to their abode and didn't want it to happen again. It was true that fame was like a magnet, and it did more than provide free drinks and friendly faces. For the enemy, it made targets, especially of men whose fame often came from the enemies they had killed.

"I hope I didn't cause you any..." Virgil said, then he got stuck on how to express his feelings and chocked up for a moment. "I realize that sometimes I'm a pest and go on and on about the Bible. But the Good Book is what got me through times in my life I never thought I'd survive. Sure, in the end, I had an owner willing to forego the narrative with white men and black and gave me my freedom at a time when such things weren't done. Maybe that's why I dwell on it so much, but I'm afraid that's how I am, and at my age, I don't see any changes in the future. I apologize if I've caused any misunderstandings or hard feelings."

"Don't be silly, Virgil," Kit forced a smile. "I only wish I were a better man. Maybe even as good as you, but for me, it wasn't meant to be. I'm a warrior before a scout, hunter, trapper, and guide. I have a calling to help settle the West, and I reckon that's just what I'm gonna do until the day I die. Still, you taught me a lesson or two, my friend. People like y'all make me wanna be a better man."

Kit climbed astride Apache and tipped his hat without another word and clicked his tongue. His horse carried him out of the south gate and onto the trail that curled down the mountain and into Yellowstone Valley. He said he wanted to see it one more time before leaving the Rocky Mountains. He had no idea where he would be off to next. It would be wherever his boss, John C. Frémont, decided where they were needed. He had a sneaking suspicion it would be California, Oregon, and the Great Basin. Despite the situation, he smiled when he thought about seeing new country.

As the famous mountain turned to leave, Money waved until he disappeared far below as the trail snaked out of sight. A tear cut a streak down his face, and he rubbed it away with the heel of his hand. Then he smiled at how many stories he had to retell to whoever would listen.

A Look at: Alone & Afraid
Levi Johnson Mountain Man Scout
Book 31

Some are taken for profit. Others, for power. All must fight to survive.

By 1845, the Yellowstone Valley was no stranger to violence. But when slavers cross into sacred lands, they stir a fury they can't outrun. Money Penny is gone—snatched alongside a young Crow girl. The compound reels, but no one takes it harder than Marshal Walker and his Crow wife, Bar-Chee. The boy they adopted is headed for Fort Boise, bound in chains with three wagons full of valley Indians—sold off to fight in a war not their own.

Levi Johnson rides west with Captain Will Forrester, chasing a trail cold with danger. But time is running out, and Marshal Walker refuses to wait any longer. He rides out, heartsick and angry, toward a reckoning no father should ever have to face.

Inside the prison wagons, Money and the girl know what's coming—and what must be done. In the shadow of a brutal fate, they hatch a desperate plan. One chance. No guarantees. But freedom is worth the risk.

In the wilds of the West, there are no promises—only the strength to fight and the will to escape.

AVAILABLE DECEMBER 2025

ABOUT THE AUTHOR

Ash Lingam was born and raised in Southern Ohio, not far from the mighty Ohio River. He had somewhat of an isolated upbringing on a family farm with his sisters. His best friends were his horse, Sugar, and his grandfather.

Born in 1886, the family patriarch grew crops, raised cattle, and doted on the young boy. At his grandfather's side, Ash learned about livestock and firearms at an early age. His grandad carried an old Colt with him at all times. It helped spawn a young boy's dreams of yesteryear.

Ash was only eight years old when his grandad taught him how to trap muskrats to prevent them from draining the farm's ponds. He gave him a double-barreled shotgun at twelve and taught him how to hunt to put food on the table.

It wasn't long before Ash was breaking horses. His spirited Tennessee Walker never allowed any other rider on her back. Together, they searched through the plowed fields in the spring, looking for Miami Indian arrowheads to add to his grandfather's ample collection.

Ash's family was among the early settlers in pre-

Revolutionary America. He has traced his lineage back to around 1746 when his ancestors immigrated from Europe to the aspiring American Colonies.

A retired marketing executive, Ash devotes his spare time to training police dogs and writing novels. He has found his niche in the Western, historical fiction, and adventure genres. With his vast vault of experience, he never runs out of sources for new stories. He has lived in eleven different countries and worked in a total of forty-six to date, Ash has written approximately 130 novels, short stories, and poems. More than one hundred of his eclectic titles help the American frontier come alive for his readers.

https://www.ashlingam.com/
Join the Lawless Waters Western Readers & Writers
Facebook Group